The Last Cop Out

MICKEY SPILLANE

The Last Cop Out

E. P. DUTTON & CO., Inc. / NEW YORK / 1973

Published simultaneously in Canada by
Clarke, Irwin & Company Limited, Toronto and Vancouver

SBN: 0-525-14353-x
Library of Congress Catalog Card Number: 72-97714

For the critics, reviewers and unbelievers, I suggest a slow perusal of your newspaper files . . . and special attention to a certain police file coded 3D-SSR-02

To the Big Man . . . thanks.

M.

The Last Cop Out

1

He reached the newsstand at exactly three minutes to eleven, picked up the early edition of tomorrow's paper, a copy of *TV Guide*, then waited another minute scanning the headlines in the light of the booth before crossing to the other side of the street. The dachshund on the end of the leash clambered over the curb, looked back quizzically, then turned right on command and led the way east on the deserted sidewalk.

It was precisely one minute to eleven. He was totally punctual because the other one was fetishly punctual too and when the dark sedan passed the man and the dog, slipping into the open parking space in front of the old brownstone, it was as if watches had been synchronized hours earlier for this one brief meeting of their hands at the ultimate moment of destiny.

The driver of the car cut the engine, switched off the lights and put the gear lever into park. He locked the right side doors, the left rear one and was feeling for the window handle beside him when he automatically looked up at the pedestrian walking his dog home, the innocuous one he had seen seconds before buying his paper and dismissed because people in New York still walked dogs, bought papers and went home, which an enemy would never do, and almost smiled back when the stranger smiled at him.

Then he felt the ice in his stomach and a horrible dryness in his throat because he knew the face and recognized the curiously strange smile and knew that forty-six years of life were about to come to an end on a dismal little street on the West Side where he had no place being at all. There would be no more luxury penthouse in one of Manhattan's towers, no more chubby wife nagging at him in broken English, no more backtalk from too-wise teenage kids, no more relishing his life or death power in the far-flung organization. And all because of a stupid blond cunt in a cold water flat who knew how to assuage his sex problems and bring him to that white glow he thought had disappeared forever.

He saw the newspaper in the hand come up and tried to snatch his own gun from his pocket but he was much too late. Victor Petrocinni achieved one final orgasm when a heavy caliber bullet tapped a hole in his forehead and blew his brains all over the front of the car.

The dachshund barely glanced back at the silenced *whup* of the discharge.

Neither the man nor the dog had broken their leisurely stride in their walk to the end of the street.

A month ago twenty-one of them had sat around the long table in the conference room of Boyer-Reston, Inc. This time only seventeen conservatively dressed men of various ages occupied the dark oaken captain chairs. Legal-sized pads and pencils were in front of each, coffee was available from an ornate urn against the wall, but the cups were empty and the pads were blank.

At the head of the table Mark Shelby, whose original name had been Marcus Aurilieus Fabius Shelvan, silently fingered the gold Phi Beta Kappa key that ornamented his watch chain and let his eyes touch each one of the persons lining the table before him, remembering twenty years back when he had first sat at a meeting like this one.

They had been old country faces then, with accented voices, and the garlicky smell still hung over them from the dinner that Peppy had served. Empty wine bottles had doubled as ash trays and he alone did the note keeping because he alone had the skill to transpose two languages into a coherent English to be referred to later. Only a few weeks before he had made his bones, a double kill of Herm and Sal Perigino, the attempted killers of Papa Fats . . . a little late in life to be put to the test, but then, he had been preselected to obtain the university education to benefit the organization and the murder assignment was more a formality, more a fraternal initiation than anything else.

That other table had been a handmade plank affair in the back room of Peppy's tavern and he had sat at it many times, working his way ever closer to the head. Now it was he who occupied the big chair and commanded the attention of the various corporate heads who fronted for the new, modern organization, the other society whose fortunes were made from the ills and vices of the Manhattan sector of New York City.

Shelby's voice and choice of words had a classic courtroom aura but there was no doubting the steel behind each syllable. Since the Perigino affair he had ordered the elimination of some thirty-odd persons whose actions he had found intolerable to organizational activities, personally attending to four of them as a constant reminder that he was still totally capable and as determinedly ruthless as any of his predecessors and worthy of the title he legally enjoyed as well as the *sub rosa* one employed behind his back. They called him *Primus Gladatori*, the First Gladiator, not because of his true given name, but for the way he dispatched his opponents— quickly and with pleasure.

"Last night," Mark Shelby said, "Vic Petrocinni was killed." He shuffled the papers in front of him, found the one he wanted and held it down with a forefinger. "For six weeks, on Mondays and Fridays, he went to the same address at the same time for the same purpose. His excuses were all different and he thought he had everybody fooled but he walked right into an ambush because there was somebody he didn't fool at all. That makes four of our people in one month." He paused and looked up, his face as frigid as his eyes. "The question now is . . . why?"

Leon Bray ran the computer section that serviced the organization's long list of activities. At fifty, he looked a decade older, his face seamed from years of intense detail work, eyes owlishly large behind thick-lensed glasses. He tapped the table top with his pencil and waited for the soft murmuring to cease.

"None of our people showed any unbalanced books," he said. "I've triple-checked everything and the accounts were right, down to the last penny. Joe Morse and Baggert had upped their figures over twenty percent from last year and both Rose and Vic were doing great with their new territories. No complaints anywhere."

Shelby digested the information and nodded, then looked to his right. "Kevin?"

Arthur "Slick" Kevin rolled his unlit cigar in his fingers and looked back at the chairman. He was nervous, and he didn't like to be nervous, but what was happening had all the earmarks of something just beginning and promising to get bigger and bigger. His eyes narrowed and he shook his head.

"I checked with all the other offices and nobody's trying to move in or take over. Chicago and St. Louis want to lend us some of their men who might be able to spot any new faces around in case it's a push by some of those wise punks from Miami or Philly, or even K.C.

They ran into some trouble like that last year, but cleared it up in a hurry. I told them we'd wait a while to see how things developed."

"How about Al Harris? He's been out of Atlanta a year now."

Kevin waved the suggestion off. "That was all big talk and his day is past. Al's got that place in Baja California and hasn't left it since he got there. The Mex authorities keep an eye on him all the time and let him blow his loot in that little town where he lives and the old boy seems happy about it. On top of everything, he's got T.B. So even if Big Al Harris has the contacts and the loot to finance a return he's got too much sense to try it."

"You sure?"

"Positive."

"How about you, Remy?" Shelby asked.

All the little guy did was shrug, but that single gesture implied an intense investigation utilizing some two hundred trained men whose reports were analyzed down to the last detail. Finally he said, "Vic and Baggert both handled narcotics, but their territories didn't overlap. Morse had the books and Rose was handling the shylocking. Nothing connects at all. None of them even had the same friends. I cross-checked them in every possible direction and couldn't come up with a single connection except that Rose's and Vic's kids went to the same elementary school together."

Almost a minute passed before Shelby let his eyes come up from the papers again. He studied each face in turn, then seemed to take them all in at once. At that moment he looked more like one of those stern faces of past jurists whose portraits in oils hang in the courtroom than the chairman of the underworld's most affluent board of directors. "No one," he told them softly, "kills four of our head people without having a reason."

At the far end of the table the one they called Little Richard because of his huge bulk said, "We can't be sure there's just one." Richard Case was the organization's liaison man to the political spiderweb of the city. Ostensibly, he headed a mammoth real estate concern, was public-spirited and politically active, but like everything else, it was only a front, a cover for his true business.

"Go on, Richard."

Three hundred pounds shifted in the chair, making it squeak under his weight. "No two guns were alike. Vic and Morse got it with thirty-eights, Baggert with a forty-five and Rose with a nine-millimeter job. The only thing the same was that each was a one-shot deal expertly placed."

"We have hit men like that," Shelby reminded him.

"No," Case disagreed. "They would have made sure and placed a couple more in there. Besides, our guys wouldn't have picked the time and places like that. These were all top ambush jobs and it looks like they were done with silenced rods. So far the cops can't find anybody who heard a damn thing and whoever pulled off the hits must be either an expert at disguise or different guys altogether. The pattern's the same, all right, but what witnesses were around can't remember seeing anybody on one kill who matches up with anybody on another. If it is one guy he's a damn top pro and there's got to be heavy money behind him. That kind of talent costs."

Case scraped his chair back, his face still thoughtful. "But one thing with a pro like that . . . he'll know we're alerted now and he won't feel like exposing himself any further. He'll take his money and go cool off somewhere and let them shop for another gun somewhere else. He sure as hell is good and although he knows the territory he can't be local and my bet is that right now he's long gone from here."

"Let's suppose it's more than one guy," Shelby offered.

"In that case it'll be all the easier to find out what the hell is going on. Somebody's going to make a bad move or a wrong one and we'll know where it's coming from. All we need to know is *why* and we can take it from there."

"It's a raid," Kevin stated flatly.

Across the table Leon Bray squinted at him through the thick glasses. "I'm not so sure. None of the properties have been touched. There hasn't been a squeal any place. There's still a chance that this can be a personal vendetta."

"Vendettas went out with the old regime," Kevin told him.

"Perhaps," Bray agreed, "but with girls and greed, they can always be reinstituted."

Remy looked a little annoyed at both of them and slammed the table top with his palm. "I've already told you that there wasn't any connection between them. That was the first angle we looked into and there's absolutely no match at all. The only thing they had in common was this group right here and I don't think I have to go any further than that."

"Relax, Remy," Shelby said. His mind had been sorting out the information and the possibilities and when he was satisfied he sat back and reached for a cigar. Everybody else except the three who didn't smoke did the same. "There's only one conclusion," he said. "It's a raid, all right."

"So what do we do?" Slick Kevin asked him.

"Simple," Shelby answered. "We wait. They eliminated our people to shake up our control. Now they try to move into the loose areas and try to take hold. All we do is wait and see who is stupid enough to match their manpower against ours. Meanwhile, we restructure our table of organization and the operations will continue as usual. I don't think our opponent will be trying any further hits."

But Mark Shelby was wrong. That night a hollow-tipped .22 went into the left earhole of Dennis Ravenal and the sub-chieftain of East Side prostitution died on silken sheets in a high rise apartment building whose door he thought was absolutely pick-proof.

Nobody heard a shot. Nobody saw an intruder.

At the offices of Manhattan's Homicide Assault Squad Captain William Long sipped from a paper coffee cup and grinned at the commissioner. "Why break up a nice war like that?" he asked.

"Because it looks like the police department is pretty damned inept," the commissioner glared.

"Oh, we're ept, all right," the captain told him. "It's

just that you can be more useful being useless sometimes. So far there aren't any innocent bystanders."

"That won't last long. The other side hasn't turned on
their hoses yet."

"Seems to me they don't know where to look," Long
said.

"I suppose you have a few ideas?"

Long nodded, still smiling. It was nice to get under
the commissioner's skin. In two weeks he was retiring
out and he couldn't think of a better situation to mark
the end of his career. "A few," he admitted. "Nothing
concrete, but after twenty-five years you sort of get an
instinct for these sort of things."

"I don't suppose you'd care to explain them," the commissioner said caustically.

Long finished his coffee, crumpled the cup and tossed
it into the waste basket. "There're only two possibilities,
business or personal. Frankly, I can't picture anybody
dumb enough to go after the organization's top men
from a personal sense of vengeance. Ergo . . . it has to
be business. Somebody wants in and they have to move
somebody else out first. They have to be tremendously
big since this is a move—not against a part—but against
the entire network of the syndicate. They wouldn't dare
allow a chunk like that being bitten off without jeopardizing their entire situation. This new force moving in is
playing the old cute game of removing the top men to
rattle the rest enough to let them get a toehold in the
game or an attempt to soften the operation so they can
leech in themselves."

"That's a pretty dangerous play."

"Nevertheless," Long told him, "it's been tried before and it's worked before. Sometimes the big guys see the value of assimilating the new ones instead of fighting them. They're absorbed, making their overall power even greater. There's always new blood coming along."

"And that, captain, makes it even worse. For a while there we've been able to push them back and with another year or two might even break them wide open, but if they start working from strength again everything we've done will be shot to hell."

"Not if this war keeps on the way it's going."

"You know better than that."

"Yeah. It's just too good to last. They're five down and I think the lesson is about over. By now they ought to be ready to expose their hand and call their shots."

But Captain William Long was wrong too. At two-fifteen the next afternoon a taxicab was stolen from in front of a diner on Eighth Avenue. At two forty-eight the same cab was spotted, seemingly abandoned on a Greenwich Village side street, by a driver from the same fleet company. In the back seat Anthony Broderick, the former dockworker who was the enforcer for the organization's shylocking racket, was slumped in the corner, a bullet from a .357 Magnum in his heart.

Gillian Burke sat in the balcony section of the Automat forking up beans and meat pie, washing it down with milk. In all the years he had been on the force nobody had ever referred to him by his first name. Always, it had been Gill, and even *The* Gill. Now here was another quarter-page editorial bringing up the past, the departmental trial, his suspension from the force because he was too much cop for the politicians to live with and spelling his name correctly and in three places. The writer reviewed his career in brief, commenting much too late that more men like him were needed, not fewer, even if a few official ears were scorched and perhaps innocent if unsavory hides were scratched.

Gill looked up when he saw Bill Long come over with his tray and pushed his paper aside to make room at the table. There was no doubt about the profession of either of them. The marks were there, inbred and refined to such a point that any aware citizen could recognize them after a minute's scrutiny, and anyone outside the law could spot them immediately and at a hundred paces. Years of law enforcement, crime prevention-detection and association with the raw nerves and open hostility that fought against the normal society were a mold whose grain was indelible, even to the penetrating depth of a casual glance from eyes that saw more than other eyes could see.

There was one uneasy dissimilarity though. Bill Long was still there and it showed. Gill was outside the periphery of it all now and there was something in his demeanor like the ebbing of the tide on a low, sandy beach, a sadness, growing deeper with each receding wave. Yet the high-tide mark was still there and you knew that the water would be back again, and sometimes even higher when the storms come.

"Why didn't you wait?" the captain asked.

"I was hungry, buddy." He pushed the chair out with his foot. "Besides, I'm ready for seconds."

Long sat down, took the dishes from his tray and arranged them in their usual order, putting the tray on an empty chair. Gill left, was back in five minutes with another meat pie and a wedge of cake balanced on top of a fresh glass of milk. The captain grinned and cut into his meat loaf. "I would have taken you up on going to 21, but I don't want to get exposed to any of that rich living."

"Balls."

"How's the new job going?"

"Profitably, pal. Not everybody bought that crap about me."

Long spooned sugar into his coffee and stirred it with a clatter. "Forget it, Gill. You lucked right in. So you dumped a pension because you were disgusted with the system and wouldn't fight it, but a fifty grand a year job beats it all to hell. Besides, it's the same kind of work."

"Not really."

"You know how many retired inspectors would like to be head security officer at Compat?"

"Tell me."

"All of 'em. And you were just a sergeant. I just hope something like that turns up for me."

Gill looked up from his cake and smiled. It wasn't a smile that had humor in it. It was simply one that had to be understood. "Not you, Bill. You always were the idealist. That's why you bought that farm eight years ago. You're all cop and a good one, but it's something you can turn off and stop being when the time comes."

"But not you?"

"No, not me, Bill. It's one of those things I hid from the psycho team all these years."

The captain made a wry face, went back to his meal again, then paused with his fork halfway to his mouth. "You seem to have made the transition to civilian pretty smoothly."

"The job has its compensations. Nobody is on my back for one."

"I wish I could say the same."

"Problems?"

"Just this big splash with the syndicate. Nobody knows what's going on. Six on the slab and so far not one farting lead."

"Yeah," Gill said, "but at least the papers have a cheering section going for you."

"When some poor slob gets caught in the crossfire the mood will change fast, my friend. And it's going to happen. Right now we have word that all the shooters are on the street covering the bosses and just hoping for some action. The big meeting in Chicago last night laid one thing on the line . . . since the Manhattan end couldn't clear things up themselves, get out where you can be a target and make the opposition show themselves. That order's got the big boys working on their own personal shit hemorrhages. Anyone under the red line in the chain of command has to play this new version of Russian roulette or answer to the big board."

"And now the department is doing bodyguard duty too."

"That's about it," Long agreed.

"A new twist, covering those punks."

Long twisted his mouth in a disgusted grimace before he looked up at Gill again. "The only redeeming feature is that you're not involved any more. Right now it's distasteful, but at least it's temporary. If you ever were assigned to that detail we'd all be picking bone splinters out of our eyes and busting our asses to keep it under cover."

"I wasn't all that bad, captain."

"No, but blood never was a deterrent to working out things your own way."

"How many times was I wrong?"

"A few times."

"Never on the big ones."

"No, not then. You never left much room for discussion, either."

"There are ways and ways of doing things," Gill said.

"Like the right way, the wrong way and your way."

Gill nodded slowly. "That's the way the other side played the game too."

"Sure." The captain got up, wiped his mouth and stuck out his hand. "You take care. I have to run. See you over the weekend."

"Right."

At a quarter to six Gill Burke turned the key in his apartment door lock, walked inside and latched it behind him. He caught the news on TV, then opened a mock-secret door in the leg of the old rolltop desk. Three guns of various makes hung there. He inspected them once, nodded silently and went back to watching TV again.

At eight o'clock he switched off the set and went to bed.

2

Until the present meeting, no one except Mark Shelby had met the Frenchman. Francois Verdun was the special envoy from the head office of the organization, a troubleshooter answerable to nobody save the top three men who controlled the vast machinery of the third government and whose very presence left a pall of fear that was almost a tangible thing. In every respect, he was seemingly medium, a nonentity in a crowd, a pleasant sort of person who enjoyed being called Frank by everyone.

Frank Verdun's kill record made that of Mark Shelby insignificant by comparison. Administering death was a pleasure he had long ago learned to appreciate, whether done with his own hand during those periods when he decided to polish his expertise, or upon his command when the results were relished through reading the newspapers or watching the report on television. When he was fifteen he had killed his own brother; at twenty his best friend went down under his blade when the organization demanded it; at twenty-five he had personally arranged for a West Coast family of sixteen persons, who had grown too demanding, to be extinguished in a single bomb blast. At thirty he had reassembled a broken European narcotics ring, delivered it intact to his bosses, who, out of sheer admiration for his work and devotion to their cause, had installed him in an enviable position of supreme importance where death became a matter of simple routine to be accomplished quickly and untraceably . . . with great material recompense to the Frenchman whose tastes were extraordinarily bizarre and extremely expensive.

And now the organization, at a hurried summit meeting, decided to take matters out of the hands of the New York chapter and expedite the solution. Frank Verdun was assigned to locate and kill any and all persons connected with the disruption of the organization's business. Everyone was instructed to cooperate. They were ordered to obey any order Frank Verdun decided to issue.

In Chicago, alone in his penthouse office, Teddy Shu, second underboss of the Great Lakes sector, made a final call to the red phone on the desk of Papa Menes who was vacationing in his place in Miami, told him that Frank Verdun had arrived in New York, set the wheels in motion and they should be seeing some action within a few days. Papa Menes was pleased, but more than a few days would make him very displeased and Teddy Shu would be the first to feel his displeasure.

Teddy hung up, wiped the sweat from his upper lip and told the delivery boy he had called for coffee to come on in. When he looked up the delivery boy had an all too familiar face and before Teddy could get the name on his lips he had no mouth at all because the .45 had taken away most of his face.

Papa Menes was seventy-two years old, a short, chunky man with a ring of gray hair that circled his head like a wreath. Both his oversize hands seemed warped by age and arthritis, but actually they were twisted because they had been broken that way, one in a street fight and the other by Charlie Argropolis who was trying to make him talk. He would have talked, too, but Charlie made a mistake by always carrying that ice pick in a sheath on his belt and before he could finish the torture treatment, Little Menes had snatched it out and drove it up to the hilt in Charlie's eyeball. Little Menes had been twelve years old then. Now, at seventy-two, he was the presiding dictator of that gigantic clan whose empire of fear extracted taxes from people of every nation of the world.

On the street he could pass for the friendly neighborhood grocer. Behind a pushcart he'd seem perfectly normal. In his suite overlooking the whole of Miami Beach and the Atlantic Ocean he was out of time and place. But he was comfortable and one of the prerogatives of his age and position was to set his own schedule and one of the items on that agenda was that nobody could disturb him before ten o'clock in the morning.

Outside in the hall George Spacer squirmed in the divan next to the elevator, worried because his partner, Carl Ames, didn't want to wait another half hour.

"Will you sit down and relax," he snapped.

Carl Ames fiddled with the zipper on his golfing jacket and stabbed his cigarette into the sand-filled ash tray by the wall. "Damn it, George, the old man's going to eat us out for not letting him know. You know what he did to Morrie last month."

"He was only taking a nap then. You know his orders."

"Look . . ."

"Teddy Shu is dead." He glanced at his watch. "He'll still be dead in another twenty minutes."

"Chicago's been trying to get the old man since they found out!"

"Chicago should have its head examined. At least the switchboard's smarter."

"Okay, watch, we'll be back hustling broads in Jersey."

George Spacer gave his partner a dirty smile. Two weeks before an Air Force private had kicked one of his balls loose from its moorings and Carl had been hurting ever since. "At least you'll be able to get more ass than you getting here," he said.

"Fuck you," Carl told him.

At five minutes after ten they followed the waiter into the suite of their boss, allowing him time to be far enough into his breakfast to take the edge off his usual restless night, and stood at attention beside the glass-topped table by the window.

Papa Menes dunked his toast, popped it into his mouth and said, "So?"

"Teddy Shu got bumped last night."

"I heard," the boss told him. He turned his paper over and tapped the headline of the article that carried the story. "A real fancy job. Who called you?"

"Bennie."

"Any details?"

"Just that nobody can figure it." The old man didn't seem too upset and Carl's stomach started to quiet down. "Teddy was alone, but there were a dozen people in the outside offices. Nobody came in or went out that they didn't know."

"Somebody figured it," Papa Menes said softly. His eyes were like little black buttons roaming over the pair in front of him.

George Spacer looked puzzled. "Who?"

"The one who did it." The old man took a sip of his coffee and pointed to the phone. "Call Bennie back. Maybe by now he'll know."

Spacer picked up the phone, got the outside line and dialed the number in Chicago. He got Bennie at the re-write desk of the newspaper, listened for a full three minutes and then hung up.

"Well?"

"The last one they remember going in was the delivery guy from the delicatessen. He brought some stuff for a couple of the others besides. Teddy didn't want to be disturbed and he was on the phone when everybody left, so they just locked up and went home."

"Now maybe you can figure it too," Papa Menes told them. When neither of them answered those black eyes told them how stupid they were. "That delivery guy worked for the deli like a week or two, enough so everybody got to know him. He waits until the time is right and makes the hit. On the way out he lifts the phone off the hook so it'll sound busy in the outside office. Everybody thinks Teddy is still there, everybody goes home. Very simple, very neat. Call that deli. See if the guy still works there."

It took Carl fifteen minutes to locate the deli and ask his question.

Their delivery man hadn't shown up for work that morning. The owner gave him the address of the place where he lived.

"You want me to send somebody over to the place?" Carl asked.

"Don't be an idiot," the old man said. "He won't be there either. Start packing my stuff and get the sedan ready. Not the limo . . . the sedan."

"You want us to . . ."

"All I want is for you to keep your fucking heads closed. Nobody knows nothing. I'm going on a trip and nobody knows where or why or how or when. You two are going to stay in this room and answer that phone and say what you're supposed to say and nothing else. Understand?"

"Sure, Papa," Carl said.

When it was done an hour later George Spacer sat drinking a scotch and water, looking down at the people on the sundeck beside the pool. Until they were told otherwise, they had all the privileges of a king with the inconvenience of a prisoner. "I wonder where the old man took off to?"

Carl built his own drink and sat down gingerly, favoring his sore ball. "Who knows, but at least this beats hustling broads in Jersey."

Neither one fully realized just how smart the old man really was.

Ordinarily, Bill Long wasn't given to frustrated anger. He had lived with rules, regulations, politicians, public indignation and apathy, citizens' committees and crime commissions so long he had learned how to accept and deal with them without having the hairs on the back of his neck stand up out of sheer rage.

Now, when the assistant district attorney finished his little bit of business and sat back with his fingers pressed together waiting for an answer, Long felt his chest straining against his coat and the muscles in his legs knotting up. "Mind telling me whose idea this is?"

"Let's say it comes from higher up," Lederer said.

"Then higher up is a nest of nitheads. What makes them think Gill will come crawling back here after all the shit they dropped on him? Hell, he's got a good job, makes a bundle and would like nothing better than to splash every one of those fat-assed creeps who booted him out."

"You're his friend, aren't you?"

"And a good enough one not to throw that kind of garbage at him. How the hell do they get the nerve to ask something like that?"

Lederer stretched his tall frame in the chair and scowled. "His dismissal wasn't entirely unjustified, even by you, Captain."

"You're no cop. How the hell would you know?"

"Because you're cop enough to know that rules are rules. The police department is a public service governed by specific regulations."

"Sometimes those regulations aren't enough to serve the public, either."

"Nevertheless. Gillian Burke was a specialist and he kept files in his head he should have committed to the department. Somehow he made contacts and had sources of information the entire department can't duplicate."

"Now you're admitting he was a good cop."

"In that area . . . yes. Nobody ever denied it. His attitude and actions about other things were far from being above reproach. In fact, they were almost criminal."

"He wasn't dealing with solid citizens, Mr. Lederer. Whether you like it or not, he got results."

"And the department got the blame, don't forget that."

"No, I don't forget it. I know how money can buy enough heat to get anybody bounced out and nobody asks where that money comes from. It takes money to buy picket crowds in front of the mayor's office and get people to write letters and the TV bunch to slant the newscasts.

"Do you really know how close he was to busting up the whole fucking syndicate? Did you know that he had gotten on to something so damn big it would have blown the top right off their operation and guaranteed you guys a hundred lifetimes in jail?" Long paused, turned his lip up disgustedly and continued. "No, *you* didn't know . . . but *they* sure as hell knew something was going to pop and beat Gill to the punch by delivering the heat in your direction. They made you guys pull the cork and take the teeth out of the tiger and even when it was over he would have given me what he knew, except I didn't have the guts to ask him to. A week later when he had time to think it over he wouldn't have given anybody the sweat off his balls. You made him look like a slob, but when you take a close look at the picture, you sure as hell can see who the real slobs are."

"You're getting out of line, Captain."

"Let's say I almost did. I was about to tell you more."

"Don't jeopardize yourself on his account, Captain. You know he deliberately withheld evidence on the Berkowitz and Manute murders."

"Why would he cover for two dead guys who made dirty movies? You could see better stuff in any Times Square sex joint than those stags they were turning out. We confiscated the whole lot and identified every last man and woman who did the bits and there wasn't a one worth messing with. We couldn't even stick a charge on them."

"Sergeant Burke could have spoken in his own defense."

"Certainly, and have you guys blow everything he was working on."

"Police work isn't a solo operation, Captain, or have you forgotten?"

"Like hell it's not, and I don't forget that either. There are some cops who can get things done their own way and you leave them alone to do it. They never hear of time off or vacations because they're damn well dedicated to the job and when you take that type out of play you leave one hell of a hole in the line you couldn't fill with a hundred pencil pushers."

"Perhaps we'd better get back to the proposal."

"Gill is going to tell you to piss up a stick." Before Lederer could answer Long held up his hand. "No, it's not a metaphor. He'll just look at you and say to go piss up a stick. In fact, he might even get a little more diagrammatic. Remember what he said at the hearing? Remember what he told all those slobs face to face afterwards? Now he's had more time to think of better things to say."

"Still . . ."

The big cop stopped him with a twist of his mouth. It was an odd smile that worked its way up to his eyes and he sat back in his chair and let all the tension ease out of his body. "You know, Mr. Lederer, I think I *will* put your proposal to him. "I'll tell him every damn detail of it . . . how the D.A.'s office wants him to cooperate as an agent of their department, giving of all his time, energy and experience . . . and knowledge . . . out of the goodness of his heart and love of police work and abject desire to be taken back in the good graces of a batch of ingrates, without salary or recognition. Then I want to put down his verbatim answer and deliver it on an inter-office memo where everybody from the desk clerk to the mayor's office can see it." He paused and grinned at the uncomfortable expression on Lederer's face. "All I can say is whoever runs your think tank must do it in a pointed cap."

When he got done, Bill Long sat back and waited. He watched Gill finish the sandwich, then down half his beer and finally blurted out, "Well, say it."

"Say what?"

"For them to piss up a stick."

"For a police officer, your language is atrocious, Captain."

"Oh, shit. Say anything then."

"What took them so long to ask?"

The cigarette almost fell out of the captain's mouth. His eyebrows arched up into his hairline and a look of bewilderment made Gill's lips crack in a smile. "What the hell's going through your head, Gill?"

"Just remembering."

"You *like* the idea?"

Burke shrugged and finished the rest of his beer. "Part of it."

"Why?"

"Let's call it a sense of ego."

"You're not going to do it, are you?"

"Tell them I'll think about it."

"Look, stupid, you can fall right into a trap again. They're caught right in the middle of some kind of crazy mob war they can't do a thing about and wouldn't they just love to have a fall guy handy. No matter which way it goes you'll get screwed. Come up with an answer and they take the credit . . . mess things up and you're the patsy. You're no cop any more and if you stir up those stinking hardcases you're dead. There's no way of winning and every way of losing."

"Maybe."

"Screw maybe. You know the score as well as I do. Besides, there's something more."

"You mean about the Frenchman being in town?"

Long looked at him a few seconds before he asked, "How the hell would you know that?"

"Some people I know don't care if I'm a cop or not any more. They still pay back favors."

"Frank Verdun would like nothing better than to see you hit."

"Wrong, buddy. So I shot him. He lived and beat the rap. It was all part of the game and in the past now. The Frenchman is too much of a pro to bother tapping out an old adversary."

"You know why he's here?"

"Certainly."

"I suppose you got an idea of what's going on."

Burke's shoulders made a gentle shrug. "There are several possibilities."

"Name one."

"Somebody doesn't like somebody else," Gill said.

Frank Verdun listened to the reports impassively. He didn't appear to be deep in thought, but every fact was registering in his mind, falling into categories and probabilities. There were new faces in the conference room of Boyer-Reston, Inc., this time that Mark Shelby didn't like but didn't dare disapprove of because they were faces that belonged to the Frenchman's private squad, the kind of faces that might have followed Attila the Hun. Six of them had investigated every detail of the killings, buying, forcing and smelling out every bit of information that was available. Bits and pieces had cropped up that not even the police were aware of and now it was all laid out to be studied.

When the discussion was over the Frenchman said, "No two descriptions match. No guns match. The methods all taste the same and the target is just us. You're split down the middle about it being one man or different men. That's no answer."

For two weeks Mark Shelby had been thinking the same thing. He tapped his pencil against the table top until he had their attention. "It could be a team trained by one man."

"Sounds reasonable," the Frenchman agreed, "but that makes it an organized operation with a higher chain of command. If that were so, by now there would have been a secondary stage going. So far nobody's moving in at all. You don't pull off all those hits and let it go at that. Somebody wants something big and something bad."

"What does Papa Menes say about it?"

Verdun's voice was quietly deadly. "You like it where you are, Mark?"

Shelby took the push, but not all the way. "I'm fine," he said.

"Good. Then stay fine. I'm speaking for Papa Menes. Remember it." He paused and looked the room over again. "We're up against an organization. That's one. They're damn smart and damn good. That's two. There's one hell of a showdown coming up. That's three."

When he stopped, Arthur Kevin said, "Who do we look for, Frank?"

"The hit men. They won't be contract boys, you can bet on that. They're right inside the organization itself. That's their weakness. All we need to do is get on top of one of them and he'll scream his head off. We can backtrack him to the day he was born and no matter who's pulling this crap, we'll find them and it'll be the last time it ever gets tried again."

Nobody spoke at all.

Frank's eyes had a reptilian glitter and he smiled. "Everybody scared to ask how?"

There was a general scuffling in the seats and a subdued murmur of disavowal.

"Maybe you don't get the picture all the way," the Frenchman said. "They're picking us off from the top down until they can get to where they can handle us. Believe me, it'll never happen. So like Papa Menes wants, you stay on the streets and in the open and take your chances on getting hit. You don't have to make it easy, but you don't run either. We got the soldiers out covering everybody and even if we lose a few more, we're going to get somebody sooner or later. That's it. Meeting's over."

That night they lost two more. They weren't gunned down. They simply took advantage of an option they had prepared for long ago, an unobtrusive exit with a suitcase full of money to a strange little country where the food was lousy, the water worse, but where there was safety in a new identity and total disassociation from a world that meant sudden death if they dared return. In view of the circumstances, it was assumed that they had fallen to the enemy who had added another dimension to its method of operation.

The other meeting three miles farther downtown was reminiscent of kids who were kept after school waiting to be lectured to by the principal. There was a sense of uneasiness you could almost feel and the seven persons waiting for Gillian Burke and Bill Long to arrive were still trying to develop statements that wouldn't make them look like complete fools.

When they finally walked in everybody nodded politely, took their seats at the table with Gill at the far end opposite the district attorney. Gill gave Bill Long a wry smile and took them off the hook. "Let's start off without any bullshit," he said.

That got their attention right away. Lederer stifled a

cough and the man from the mayor's office dropped his pen.

"You got yourselves a hot chestnut and nobody knows how to handle it. The computers all came out zero and now you need all that beautiful inside stuff that used to be available for the asking. You guys'll sure do anything when it gets warm, but I don't blame you a bit. I'd do the same thing myself."

"Mr. Burke . . ." the district attorney started to say.

"Can it, I'm talking," Gill told him.

The D.A. said nothing.

"Don't tell me you give a damn about the people who got bumped off. Each one down is one more you can close the files on, but when a bite comes out of their organization and they close ranks enough to lean on the right people, you start sweating. So now you want me back in again. Okay, that's what you want and I'll come back."

All the eyes were on him now.

"Conditionally, that is," Gill continued. "I haven't told you what I want yet."

"There weren't any conditions stipulated, Mr. Burke," Lederer said.

"Naturally. You're trying to get everything for nothing. Just don't forget . . . you're the ones doing the asking, so I lay down the ground rules or go home. Take it or leave it."

"State your conditions," the district attorney said.

Gill nodded, looked at each one in turn, his face an angular mask of hard competence. "An official position, access to all police files and materials, guaranteed cooperation of any department I choose and no interference from any political faction."

"Are you sure you don't want a salary?" Lederer asked insolently.

"Being public-spirited, a dollar a year will do."

"You expect to take a year to find out who's behind these murders?"

"Mr. Lederer," Burke said, "those weren't murders."

"Oh?"

"They were killings."

"What's the difference?"

Burke's lips pulled tight across his teeth. "If you don't know, telling you won't make you understand at all. Now, you got one minute to give me a yes or no."

Actually, they had no choice.

Over coffee at the diner in the next block Bill Long threw Gill a begrudging laugh and shook his head. "Pal you didn't say it, but you sure made them do it."

"Do what?"

"Piss up a stick," he said.

3

The pair in the anteroom made him the minute he pushed the door open and the big guy tried reaching for his throat while he scrambled for his rod and had his nose smashed wide and flat in a crimson splash so fast he never knew what happened. The other wasn't so lucky because his gun was showing and Gill Burke broke his arm before almost splitting him open with a single, terrible kick up between the legs. The only sound was their twisted bodies thumping to the floor and the heavy breathing of the beautiful brunette behind the desk. It was all too quick for her to absorb, or to remember to scream and she watched wide-eyed while he picked the guns off the floor and let them dangle with one finger through the trigger guards.

He said, "The man inside?"

The brunette nodded, her breath held so deeply in her chest that her breasts almost burst through the sheer fabric of her dress.

"Push the button," he told her.

There was so much weight in his tone that she couldn't help herself. One finger found the button, held it down, and while the automatic lock was clicking he went through the door and shut it behind him.

The Frenchman looked up from the papers on his desk, almost frowned, then relaxed with a smile. "Hello, Mr. Burke." His eyes went down to the guns in Gill's hands. "Are you planning to shoot me again?"

Gill dropped the guns on his desk, pulled a chair over with the toe of his shoe and sat down. "Not today, Frank. Later maybe."

Frank Verdun fingered the guns, turning them around so they both pointed at Gill. "My boys aren't very good, are they?"

"Not hardly."

He slipped the clips out of the two automatics, checked the loads, making sure there was a cartridge in each chamber, and put them down again in the same position. "They'll have to get a refresher course, I guess."

"Teach them better manners. They'll live longer."

Verdun's face took on an amused expression. "You

have a lot of nerve, Mr. Burke. I thought you were smarter, but you sure have nerve. Now, to what do I owe the pleasure of this visit?"

"Curiosity, Frank. I heard you were having a lot of trouble."

"Nothing we can't take care of."

"You haven't been doing so good this far."

"A group like ours always has a few minor problems. It's to be expected."

"Horseshit. You've lost your key men right here and now it's spreading out."

"That shouldn't make any difference to you. By the way, how did you feel being busted to a private citizen . . . and marked lousy at that?"

"Part of the game, Frank. It wasn't entirely unexpected, so call it a minor annoyance."

"Now it's my turn to say horseshit."

The two of them smiled at each other like a pair of male cats about to cut loose over territorial rights. The claws and teeth were sharp and ready and all that was needed was the slightest move on either's part to unleash a deadly slash. There was mutual respect, but no fear at all.

"You didn't say what you wanted, Mr. Burke."

"Just to let you know I'm still around."

Frank Verdun nodded sagely, his eyes half-lidded. "Are you trying to tell me you're looking for a job on our side?"

"Hell no, Frank. I just wanted you to know I'll bust you guys wide open any chance I get and right now there's a great big chink in your armor plate. Whenever Papa Menes sends in his biggest gun he's running scared and I'm going to be climbing his ass all the way."

The Frenchman didn't bother to glance down at the pair of automatics. His hand hovered over the nearest one and he was almost ready to do what he was about to say. "I could kill you right now, Burke. I have the perfect excuse. All it would cost me would be a day in court."

"Not quite," Gill said. He lifted the hat off his lap and the .45 in his fist was pointing directly at the bridge of the Frenchman's nose.

Verdun chuckled and sat back, lacing his fingers behind his head. "I didn't figure you being that sneaky, not being a cop any more. You know what would happen if you knocked me off?"

"That's your second mistake, Frankie boy." He reached in his pocket and flipped open the wallet so the Frenchman could see the badge. "Times change."

The snakelike eyes half closed again. "Don't try to sucker me, Burke."

"It's for real, Frankie," Gill told him. "I wanted you to know so you can think about what's going to happen." He put the wallet back, lowered the hammer on the .45, stood up and walked to the door. "Just like the good old days, Frank, only now the stakes are higher."

The two hoods on the floor in the outer office had messed up the rug with their own blood and vomit and were making forced mewing noises as the pain tingled their minds back to consciousness. The brunette stood over the one with the broken arm, her lower lip clenched between her teeth, trying to keep from retching.

She was taller than he expected, touched with a light tan, a body made to tease or please, yet carrying an aura of class that was just a little out of place around Frank Verdun. The Frenchman had his own peculiar tastes, he remembered, and she wasn't the type at all. He looked at her again, frowning, then took her raincoat and hat from the rack, put his hand through her arm and led her outside.

There was no resistance. She followed him blankly until they reached the ladies' room, then she said, "Please . . ." and he let her go in and waited. Five minutes later she was back, her eyes moist and reddened, a taut look around the corners of her mouth.

"Let's get some fresh air," Gill told her.

She nodded, slipped into her coat and they stepped into the elevator. He walked her down four blocks, then turned into a grill just off the corner of Sixth Avenue and led her to a booth in the rear. "Iced tea for the lady and a beer for me," he told the waiter.

"Iced tea?"

"It's easy to make." He smiled funny and the waiter nodded and hurried away. When he came back he laid the two drinks down and took the pair of singles Gill held out.

When she finished half the iced tea she took a deep

47

breath and leaned against the back of the booth with her eyes closed. "That was terrible back there," she said with a husky voice.

Gill said, "I've seen it a lot rougher, Helen."

Her eyes came open slowly. "How do you know me?"

"I was in court when you were a witness for the defense in Scobi's trial. If you hadn't testified, that stinking little creep would have wound up on death row. Why'd you do it, kid?"

She gave him a tired little smile. "Because it was true. He *was* with me."

"Lennie Scobi was a punk hit man for the mob."

"And that night he barged into my room totally drunk and passed out on my bed."

"Nobody believed it, but they had to take your word for it."

"That's right, and I never worked again after that, did I? No more night clubs, no more Broadway. Just a receptionist-typist-hostess in a big, impersonal office building."

"You know who you work for?"

"Of course. At least they showed a little gratitude."

"Your father was a cop, Helen. Joe Scanlon was a great cop."

"My father is a dead cop."

"You know how he died?"

"I know how they *say* he died," she told him bitterly. "You know how much gratitude the public showed afterward."

"He knew the odds."

48

"But he didn't have to live with them afterward."

"Nobody has it easy."

Helen Scanlon shook her head slightly, then looked into his eyes. "And you . . . who are you?"

"Gill Burke."

She let the name pass through her mind, then her face tightened. "Aren't you the one . . ."

Gill didn't let her finish. "The same."

"Then what you did up there was, was . . ."

"All in the line of duty, Helen. It seems like I'm needed again and when the need hits certain people they don't care what they have to do to fulfill it, even to swallowing their own pride."

"You just left them lying there!"

"They're lucky I didn't kill them. I was feeling generous today. Your Mr. Verdun will clean up the mess, give them a few rough lessons on how to bodyguard his precious person and forget about it. We had a nice long talk, and if he isn't sore about it, don't you be."

Her face was expressionless, but the tendons in her neck were taut against her flesh. "Thank you for the iced tea," she said and stood up. Gill went to rise, but she shook her head. "Don't bother. I'd rather go back alone." She hesitated a moment, then looked back at him again. "I'm glad I don't have to know you, Mr. Burke. There's something indecent about people who don't care which side of the fence they're on as long as they can hurt other people. As a policeman, even one disowned by his own kind, you might have had something I could admire, but for a turncoat, you're as repulsive as a skinless rat."

He reached out and grabbed her wrist. "Turncoat?"

"You heard me." She drew her hand away, her eyes still hot with anger.

Gill Burke let out a quiet, sardonic laugh and picked up his beer. "Hardly likely, baby," he said.

On the way back to the office she kept remembering his laugh and the straight line of his teeth. There had been something funny about his eyes, too, something hot behind the icy veil that filmed them, and she could still feel the way his fingers had circled her wrist. A shudder ran down her spine and she took a deep breath, idly wondering whether or not somebody would have cleaned up the public relations office annex of Boyer-Reston, Incorporated.

At the post office in Homestead, Florida, Artie Meeker picked up the single letter addressed to Mr. John Brill, care of general delivery, got in the two-year-old blue Ford sedan and drove back to the small cottage on the south end of Plantation Key. He parked, carried in the carton of groceries, handed Papa Menes the letter and went back to the kitchen to make a lunch for the two of them.

In the shade of the porch the old man stopped watching the sports fishermen in the gulf pulling in the thrashing dolphin and ran his finger under the flap of the envelope.

Ordinarily, the Frenchman would take care of details himself, but this one he wanted Papa to know about. That former cop who had raised so much hell had been poking around. Somehow he had come up with a badge and it was a good guess that despite his past record, somebody needed an old-time heavy hand and talked him into the job. In a way, it could be a good thing to have the public authorities pushing the hunt for whoever was pulling the raid, but if Papa didn't like the smell of this particular authority because he was close to breaking them the last time, it could be taken care of on order.

Papa Menes didn't like the smell of it at all. Even less, he didn't like the smell of having to take care of anybody carrying a badge. Cops were funny people, loyal to their own. That crazy man Burke hadn't been a bad cop. He had been too damn good a cop and had to be squeezed out. Maybe the public thought he was a rotten apple, but all the other cops knew better and even on the outside Burke would be one of their kind. But with a badge again it was different . . . he was one of *them*.

Maybe the Frenchman was right, he thought. If his assignment was to nail the hit men and whoever was behind the mess, let him do his snooping. Little Richard would know everything that went on and if Burke wound up with something the organization could always beat him to it or take it away before he could use it.

He looked out at the glassy green water again where they were still boating the dolphin. A warm breeze sifted through the screen and he could smell the salt and sun-drenched air. It should have smelled nice, but it didn't. The other smell was too powerful and he knew what it was because he had smelled it before, several times, and the strange smell of fear you never forget.

Silently, he nodded to himself, then wrote out a telegram for Artie Meeker to send to the Frenchman. They'd lay off Gill Burke until he became a threat to the organization again and this time there wouldn't be any smear campaign . . . just a nice, quiet permanent disappearance that would completely eliminate the source of annoyance once and for all.

He called Artie in, gave him the coded message and instructions, then leaned back in his chair. He should have been satisfied, but he wasn't, and frowned. That damned smell was still there.

The stiff drink didn't do a thing to steady Mark Shelby's nerves. His stomach was acting up again and his throat was dry no matter how much scotch he poured down it. Helga, the busty Swedish blond he kept in the apartment on the East Side, sat cross-legged on the sofa, naked under the sun lamp, hoping he wouldn't get drunk and start to slap her around again.

Not that she minded. He always used his open hand and it was a small price to pay for what he had given her. Most of the money was safe in the bank or tied up in securities, her charge accounts were paid promptly, the clothes and furs in the closet were all new, all expensive and all hers. Once or twice a week Mark Shelby would come up for a couple of hours of sex, be teased into arousal with the erotic love games she was so practiced in, then with five minutes of oralistic activity he would be reduced to limp impotency until the next time. He always called before he arrived, giving Nils a chance to leave and get a little stoned at having his own sex life interrupted.

Mark stood at the bar, stripped to his shorts and poured himself another drink. Helga looked at the clock, then switched off the sun lamp. She was good and tan, with no strap marks showing. She ran her fingers through the natural blond silk of her hair, then softly stroked her pubic area that was almost the same color.

"Mark, dear," she said.

"Shut up."

She didn't know if he was mad at himself because even the love games couldn't get him erect, or if it was his business again. The past two weeks he had been unusually irritable and she wondered why anybody in the wholesale grocery business should be so upset. The way prices were, one would think he'd be overjoyed. Men were funny, she thought, even a solid citizen from Trenton, New Jersey, who had a frigid wife who liked to play bridge every day rather than take care of husbandly needs. She smiled inwardly. When she and Nils were married it wouldn't be like that at all. He would never need another woman. Before he left for work she would weaken him with an orgasm, and when he walked in the door at night she would be standing there naked so that he would throw her on the couch right in front of the cleaning woman who would gasp with embarrassment and run off, only to peek at them from behind the curtains. At night they would make wild sounds and laugh at the creaking and wrenching of the bed boards and one day have the whole thing collapse on the floor as a result of their outlandish exertions.

It was either the way she was sitting, a little glisten-
ing of wet reflecting the shaft of sunlight, or the scotch
that was getting to him, but Mark Shelby felt the fingers
of arousal touching his groin. He put the glass down,
took one moment to study the ornate candle in the jade
holder that was the centerpiece ornament arranged on
the back bar, then he slipped his shorts down, let them
fall to his feet and walked across the room to where she
was sitting. He stood in front of her and she looked up
at him and smiled, knowing what he wanted.

When her mouth touched him he groaned and shuddered. Gill Burke, the incessant funerals, the awesome
thing he had accomplished, the terror of Papa Menes' almost unlimited power . . . they all swept away in
pounding hardness and the sudden gush of manhood,
leaving him soft and vulnerable once more. Before he
sank to his knees in fatigue, his head resting on her
bare, warm thigh, all he could think of was a small, flick-
ering flame that could scorch whether it was lit or
burned out.

The photo of Mark Shelby that Gill Burke studied
was twenty-eight months old and showed him coming
out of a fashionable midtown bistro, smiling at someone
cropped out of the picture. It had been taken privately
with a telephoto lens from the building opposite the restaurant. Since Mark Shelby had no record, there was no
official police front and profile shot of him and Shelby
was notoriously camera shy.

Bill Long said, "The case is closed, Gill."

"Yeah, I know," Burke told him. "You got the gun, the

motive and the man all at one time, except the man was a corpse."

"A police officer shot him during the course of a holdup. He was wearing Berkowitz's gold watch and when we checked his room out we found Manute's wallet along with a lot of other stolen items."

"How often do chintzy holdup men keep souvenirs. They aren't *that* stupid."

"They are if they're stupid enough to pull a robbery."

Burke glanced over another of the sheets, reading it to the end. "No track record at all on this guy. He even held down a job."

"Part time," the captain said.

"That's more time than any crooks work."

"Not always. It makes a good cover. The guy was a loner, had a drinking problem and wasn't too bright. Check his income. He couldn't support a drinking problem on that and eat too. He had to supplement his income. Hell, Gill, you know it's an old story."

"Berkowitz and Manute were processing film they had shot. There wasn't any dough in the joint and none of their equipment could be fenced very easily. It wasn't the kind of place a holdup artist would hit."

"Gill . . . they were in a partially deserted area, alone, and that guy . . . what's his name . . . Ted Proctor just saw an easy target. As far as we could determine, Berkowitz had over a hundred bucks on him and Manute was probably good for fifty. Enough to justify a holdup, anyway."

"And Mark Shelby was in the area about the same time."

"The supposed witness retracted his statement. He

was parking lot attendant and had only seen Shelby once before when he dropped off his car."

"Balls."

"That's what he swore to."

"A parking lot beside a mob-owned restaurant. He had seen plenty of Shelby."

"You're pushing, Gill."

"Maybe, but it was the pushing I did before that got me laid out like a squashed bug."

"You were after Papa Menes, friend."

"A rung at a time and you reach the top man, Bill. Somehow I was just about to shake the apples out of the tree when they cut the branch out from under me."

"Forget it, will you?"

The side of Burke's mouth curled in a smile. "Would you?"

"No."

Burke laid the papers down on the desk and stretched in his chair. For a minute or so he stared at the ceiling, then leaned forward and stared at his friend. "How'd they work it on me, Bill?"

"You've been a maverick a long time, Gill. That citizens' committee instituted the probe."

"Their two lawyers had mob connections."

"No way of proving that."

"Why didn't somebody try to cover for me?"

"Because we all have ourselves to protect, Gill, you know that. They gave only what facts that were drawn out the hard way. Nobody volunteered a damn thing."

"The papers had a field day. The TV boys pulled me apart."

"You always made sensational news. When you shot those three guys in that subway it gave them something to chew on."

"Bill, those guys all had guns. Some of those bastards in the crowd grabbed them and ran when I dropped them."

"You almost started a race riot."

"Don't believe it. There were plenty of cool heads there."

"Why didn't they speak up then?"

"And get labeled Uncle Tom? Get the boot by their own people? Maybe if my life was on the line they would have, but I was just another cop getting the squeeze and squeezes aren't new to them. Those guys were all carrying the loot they lifted from that heist and the shooting would have been justified even if I *thought* they had a gun."

"So what are you going to do?"

"Begin where I left off."

"Here we go again," Long said resignedly. "Just keep in mind what they wanted you back for. There's one hell of a gang war brewing and they're hoping you might be able to add that one touch that could stop it." The captain paused, watching Gill's face. It was the kind of face you couldn't read at all. "Do you think you can, Gill?"

"It's a possibility," he said, "but I don't suppose they'd mind a few fringe benefits on the side."

"Like what?"

"Like putting a crimp in the whole fucking syndicate."

"You've been away too long, Gill. They're too big. It can't be done."

"In the pig's ass it can't," Gill told him. "Somebody's doing it to them now."

When the eleven o'clock news was over, Gill Burke switched off the TV and poured the rest of his beer into his glass. It had been a long day and tomorrow would be even longer and he was looking forward to getting to bed early.

The sudden rasp of the door buzzer made him snap his head around wondering who the hell it could be at that hour. Any friends he had would have called first and anybody else he didn't want to see. He put the glass down and picked up the .45 from the table, then stood to one side of the door and yanked it open.

She was in a short sweater and skirt combination with a white raincoat thrown loosely over her shoulders, and her hair was a dark frame for startled, wide brown eyes and a rich, full ruby mouth.

Helen Scanlon said, "Are you going to shoot me, Mr. Burke?"

Burke smiled with his lips, but his eyes remained impassive. With a casual movement he put the gun inside his waistband. "Not tonight."

"Aren't you going to ask me in?"

"These are hardly visiting hours."

"Make an exception."

"Come on in then." He made a deprecating motion with his head toward the apartment. "Don't mind the mess. I wasn't expecting company."

"Apparently not since you've lived here. You aren't very neat, Mr. Burke."

"Who gives a shit," he told her. "Can I make you a drink?"

"No, thank you."

"Then get to it."

"Don't be so abrupt. May I sit down?"

Gill waved toward a chair and eased himself down in the worn recliner. Something, he thought, was very, very screwy.

"I've come to apologize," she said.

"For what?"

"My remark about you being a turncoat."

"How about being as repulsive as a skinless rat?"

"Did that really get to you?"

Burke shrugged and sipped his beer. "That's nothing compared to some of the things I've been called."

"But it got to you."

"Just the repulsive part."

"I'm sorry," she said. The sincerity in her tone was real.

"Why?"

"Because I overheard Mr. Verdun making a phone call. He said you were a policeman again and poking around. Apparently you are some sort of a threat to his . . . business."

"You're damn well told I am."

"Mr. Burke . . . things get very confusing sometimes."

"Don't believe everything you read in the papers. How old are you?"

"Thirty."

"You don't look it at all."

"How old are you?"

"A hundred and ten."

She smiled gently. "You don't look it either."

"It's all mental, kid."

"Why are you a threat to them?"

"Because I made a career out of trying to break them."

"You know it isn't possible, don't you?"

"That's what everybody seems to think, but they're wrong. What goes up can come down."

"My father thought that too."

"Joe Scanlon had just obtained the murder weapon used to gun down a key witness who could have testified against Papa Menes and six other top men in the syndicate. The fingerprints of the killer were on that gun and it would have brought the walls tumbling down around some important political figure. The mob had him run down by a stolen auto and they retrieved the gun. It was classified as a hit-and-run accident."

"There has never been any proof otherwise," she stated flatly.

"If a little old lady were still alive . . . the one who heard the last words he ever spoke, she'd tell you differently."

"What little old lady?"

"She died of a stroke two days later. Seeing that incident probably triggered it. She gave the information to Hanson, who was the local beat cop then. All he could do was report it, but as courtroom evidence it was out."

Helen Scanlon nibbled on the tip of her thumb and

tried to blink away the wetness that clouded her vision. She had come only to apologize, not resurrect the past. It was something she neither wished to discuss or even think about, but sitting opposite Gill Burke, seeing all the hardness reflected in his face and the way he carried himself and sensing the controlled violence that was an integral part of himself, the past kept forcing itself into the present.

"That thirty thousand dollars they found hidden in my father's home . . . he never could have saved that. Every cent he made went to pay medical bills for my mother. Everything I could afford I sent on too."

"It made a pretty picture for the headline hunters, though," Gill reminded her. "There you were starring in a mob-operated showplace, dating some of the top eche-lon hoods, glamorizing their social events . . ."

"Only part of the business. There were others who did it too. I told you, my mother . . ."

"People only look at what they want to see," Gill said. "When you testified for Scobi that tied the knot in the cat's tail."

"But he *was there!*"

Gill watched her a moment and nodded. "If you had cut loose from them after your father died he wouldn't have been there."

"Damn it, Mr. Burke, I needed the money, don't you understand that? Where else could I have gotten it? Mother died two weeks after my father and left medical bills that wiped everything out."

"Okay, I believe you." And he did.

Her clenched fist pressed into her thigh and her

breath seemed caught in her throat. When she regained her composure she said, "The night I heard them booing from the audience I knew it was over. So did my agent and the management. I took a month off and came back to New York, but it was the same here. Nobody except the scandal writers even wanted to speak to me. One day I ran into Roller . . ."

"Vic Petrocinni?"

"Yes. He was dice happy. They called him Roller out there. He introduced me to some people and I got the job at Boyer-Reston as a receptionist."

"Well paid?"

"Yes," she said softly. "They were mighty considerate of me."

"That outfit," Gill told her, "is one of the legitimate fronts for the syndicate operation."

"Boyer-Reston runs parking lots, a chain of funeral parlors, dry cleaning establishments and two major restaurants."

"That's what I said."

"What?"

"Nothing," Gill mused. "How well do you know Frank Verdun?"

"I met him once in Vegas. He's a public relations director."

"He's a first-class funeral director, baby. He makes his own clients, or didn't you know that?"

"Receptionists don't ask questions."

"But you've been around long enough to hear things and recognize faces. After a while facts and rumors start to make sense and you can ask yourself a question and answer it at the same time. You might not like what comes out of your mental computer and shrug it off, but don't tell me you don't *know* about it."

"I try not to think, Mr. Burke."

"You got emotional enough about it when you told me off."

"I said I was sorry."

"No need for an apology."

"Perhaps not," she said, "but I have a strange sense of moral values my father instilled in me."

"That's why you testified for Scobi," Gill stated.

"Yes. It was true."

"Tell me," Gill asked her, "do you like those people?"

"Nobody ever hurt me."

"I didn't ask that."

She made a noncommittal gesture with her eyes and spread her hands. "No."

"Why not?"

After a few seconds she met his eyes again. "Because, as you said, I've been around long enough to ask myself a few questions."

"Then why stay with them?"

Helen Scanlon got to her feet and tossed her raincoat over her shoulders. "Mr. Burke . . . there's no place else to go."

Gill's expression said that it wasn't so, but he didn't put it into words. He got up and walked to the door with her. The sound of her heels tapping on the hardwood floor and the faint fragrance of her perfume were things foreign to the place he had lived these past years and he felt a sudden loss of wasted time.

She held out her hand and he folded his fingers around hers. "Good-bye, Mr. Burke."

He tried to tell her good-bye, but the words wouldn't come. Those liquid brown eyes were sinking into his and he could feel the frown knit across his forehead. There was a lightness in his stomach, a little crawling sensation across his shoulders and another person that wasn't him at all drew her closer and closer until their bodies touched and her breasts were against his chest with the curve of her belly and thighs matching the outline of his own. Just before their mouths touched she closed her eyes slowly and made a little cat sound and he felt the tremor in her hand. It was a soft, languid kiss that only took a few seconds of time, but it was like water rushing through a breach in the dam that threatened to grow into turbulent violence.

He let his fingers slide away from hers and she let her breath out, deliberately controlling herself. She smiled, but there was a puzzle in her eyes. She had been kissed before, many times, but no kiss had ever made her react like that at all.

As she stood in the open doorway she turned, still smiling, and said, "You aren't at all repulsive, Mr. Burke."

Gill put the night latch on and stuck the Fox bar in place. He looked around his apartment, still aware of her perfume. "Someday I'm going to clean this dump up," he muttered.

4

Stanley Holland was feeling very pleased with himself. It was raining and even though he hated rain because it made his sinuses drain and his temples pound, he still felt pleased. Even the smog and the smell that hung over Cleveland, Ohio, couldn't make him feel otherwise. A year ago, when Papa Menes transferred him here from Los Angeles to put back together the narcotics operation the Cleveland police had broken, he was unhappy, but no longer. The new setup was structured so carefully and organized so efficiently that the roots of it would be imbedded too deeply into Ohio soil for anybody to dig out again.

And it had been all his doing. *He had given his life to his work,* he thought. *It should have been good.* Papa Menes would be grateful. The entire board would be grateful. There would be a better town now, a bigger town where his rewards could be well spent in the pleasures he enjoyed.

The organization was solidly entrenched, the new source of narcotics his own discovery and he was totally, absolutely unknown. He was a respected businessman who operated two hardtop movie houses and a drive-in, made a substantial profit with all and had a foolproof drop for his supplies.

One week ago today he had finally learned the identity of the informer instrumental in destroying the old layout and had personally taken care of him with a massive overdose of heroin on his own rooftop. Since he was a known addict, nothing was made of it. But the others in the trade got the message.

Two days later the pair of crooked cops from the neighboring city Holland had used to retrieve nine key code words from the book impounded in the police files had tried to shake down his contact man for a full grand a week apiece. The initial meet was arranged and both cops showed up in time to be dispatched quietly by his own hand via the drugged drink and garrote route, encased in a steamer trunk of cement and dropped in Lake Erie. It had been difficult, but it was done. Papa Menes and the board would have the details by now, the machinery of supply and demand could begin operating in the absolute security of secrecy he, Stanley Holland, had instituted and his star would rise another degree on the organization's horizon.

He pulled into the parking lot behind the middle-class office building he occupied, cut the ignition and reached for his briefcase. He was about to open the door when the jungle instinct beat through his self-satisfaction and he remembered that the car in the slot beside his was not the white Caddie that was supposed to be there, but an undistinguished black Chevy. He couldn't see the face of the person behind the wheel because a hand with a heavy caliber gun in it blocked the way.

All Stanley Holland could reflect on in that last tiny moment was that he had given his life to his work. Everything should have been perfect. But it just wasn't good enough.

When Bill Long met Gill for lunch he was still carrying the anger he should have left in his office. "What's with you?" Gill asked him.

"They found Stanley Holland's body in a parking lot in Cleveland."

"Who's he?"

"His right name was Enrico Scala." Long waved the waiter over and told him to bring a pastrami on rye and coffee. "Remember him now?"

Gill doubled the order and nodded. "I thought he died in a car smashup in L.A."

"Apparently that's what he wanted us to think. Identification was made from his personal effects. He had plastic surgery done on his face after he beat that narco rap out there and changed his base."

"You sure?"

"Well, most of his face was gone, but the tissue scars were there and his fingerprints matched. It was him, all right."

"When did it happen?"

"About nine-thirty this morning. The Cleveland police got an anonymous phone tip from somebody about a dead guy in a car behind an office building and checked it out."

"Who goes around looking into parked cars?"

"Somebody did. A couple of the guys who parked there said their cars had been rifled on occasion. Cigarettes gone, some change laid on the dashboard . . . things a kid might do."

"Then why are you sweating it? Cleveland's five hundred miles away. We don't have jurisdiction there."

"No, but we're on an interdepartmental cooperation basis and the commissioners are raising hell. It's all part of the same damn war and if it keeps up it's going to explode all over New York." He stopped, tossed a sharp glance at Burke and said, "I don't suppose you have anything to say?"

"Did I ever?"

"Not unless it was pertinent and provable."

"Let's keep it that way."

"That attitude might have gone in the old days, but you're working under a different department now. The district attorney isn't me."

"Fuck the district attorney."

"He can put you back on the street again."

"But he won't, old buddy. He just can't afford to. Now eat your lunch."

Halfway through the sandwich Bill Long said, "Papa Menes seems to have dropped out of sight."

"Oh?"

"Got any ideas?"

"Sure. He's got some sense."

"The old man could hole up in any one of a dozen of his places and it would take an army to get him out. He isn't in any of those places. He left Miami and simply disappeared."

"Permanently?"

"He isn't dead. Orders are still coming through. We'd know it in a hurry if anything had happened to him."

Gill grinned and bit into his sandwich. "You know, it's interesting to speculate on what would happen inside the syndicate if somebody nailed Papa. They'd cut each other to bits in the rush for the top."

"Like hell. They got everything worked out in advance."

"You used the wrong tense, pal."

"What do you mean?"

"They *used* to have it worked out. This year isn't last year or the year before and there's a new breed of cat running around. Things are changing just as fast inside their own world as it is everyplace else. Governments and businesses, legal or illegal, are like buildings. You can only make them so big or they'll crumble or be too unwieldy to be useful."

"Don't you believe it."

"No?" Gill said. "Look at them now, scared shitless because for a change they're the target and they got nobody to shoot back at. Guys who thought their power or protection made them invulnerable suddenly get dead and it's panic time. Papa Menes quietly detaches himself from the scene and will sit it out until it's over. A real dependable bunch of people to work for."

"Menes will show. A guy like that can't stay hidden."

"Balls. He's always had a few alternate caves to crawl into. He'll be packing a bundle in hard cash and won't have any crowd around him. He'll just disappear into the scenery somewhere with his own special means of communication to the organization and sit tight."

"Where, for instance?"

Gill blew on his coffee and grunted. "He had one place in New Paltz, New York. Don't bother checking it because I did and it's empty. The power's on and the phone is live. A maid cleans the place once a week, runs the pickup truck in the garage to keep the battery charged and gets paid by money order once a month. She's never seen the owner, although he's occupied the place several times. Anybody with the time to be an amateur pirate could hit that place when she wasn't there and with enough house wrecking or garden digging, pull up a small fortune in cash."

"How did you get that tidbit of information?"

"Using my spare time checking on visitors going into a certain spaghetti joint at a certain time on a certain day."

"When Papa Menes was there?"

"Very astute, pal. One of those visitors was an upstate real estate broker. The rest was sneaky, but easy."

"That doesn't give us Menes *now*."

"You couldn't charge him with anything anyway. Besides, there's better game to hunt."

"The game preserve is going to be pretty crowded," the captain said sarcastically. "The families got the orders out and all the shooters are going onto the streets. They're shifting all the soldiers around to the hot spots and most of them are coming here. Last night there was a job pulled at National Guard Armory in Jersey and twenty-two tommy guns with sixty thousand rounds of ammo were lifted. The same thing happened in a naval depot in Charleston, only there it was grenades. Gill . . . we're sitting right on the shady side of hell."

Burke finished his coffee and nodded.

"You could say something about it," Long prodded him.

"Sure," Gill said. "Want some dessert?"

The supper he had at Cissie's wasn't sitting too well with Mark Shelby. Ordinarily he would have enjoyed the speciality dishes she served the patrons who had originally financed her East Fifty-fifth Street retreat. The gourmet magazines played her up regularly and she had been on the local TV channel twice with her own brand of Mediterranean cooking.

He tried the wine again, an imported rosé that cost twenty-five bucks a bottle, but it went down like water without improving his digestion a bit. It had always been like that when he had to look at the Frenchman. He had made his bones and kept his hand in whenever it was necessary to prove a point, but essentially he was an organizer, a compiler of facts, a recorder and adviser.

Essentially the Frenchman was a killer.

Nothing else mattered.

The Frenchman was a homosexual killer and nobody could ever prove it because whoever he went down on suffered the same fate as a male black widow spider, except that there was never any drained corpse to identify. It was only rumored, of course, but nobody had the temerity to challenge the accusation because the Frenchman had an unusual penchant for killing people in lieu of sex, without regard for position or reputation, and as long as it didn't interfere with the machinations of the organization, his private life was his own.

Murder, to the Frenchman, was the same as an orgasm. He enjoyed it best when one followed the other, but he could take each separately if the need arose, but inevitably one would follow the other anyway.

If he had to take his choice, Frank Verdun would rather murder. The orgasm was much more intense then.

And at that moment, Mark Shelby didn't like the way the Frenchman was looking at him.

"Whoever hit Holland was on the inside," Mark said flatly. "Only two people could recognize his new face and they're both dead—the doctor and the nurse."

"The hit man knew," Verdun reminded him with a tight smile.

72

Shelby's irritation got the better of him and he leaned forward on the table. "Listen, Frank, there were no photos and no files. It was cash in advance and a guarantee of safety. The only ones on the outside who knew about his operation were Papa Menes, you, me and six members of the big board."

"We know Papa wouldn't talk, and the board wouldn't talk, so that just leaves you and me, doesn't it, Mark?"

The little .25 Mark Shelby always carried was aimed at Frank Verdun's gut under the table and his finger was almost ready to squeeze the trigger.

"Put it away," the Frenchman said through his curious smile. He lifted his glass in a silent toast and drained it, then refilled it from the bottle in the ice bucket.

"You think Papa hasn't figured that out already?" he told Shelby.

Mark's finger came off the trigger and he looked at his supper partner. Verdun's hand was under the table too and he wondered what he held in it. He was being stupid and knew it, said "shit" softly and stuck the little automatic back in its holster. "Somebody's getting to us, Frank," he said.

Both of the Frenchman's hands showed on the table and peace was declared. "Sure it's inside," he said. "It has to be inside. The only thing is, how far inside can you get? Who knew everything about Vic Petrocinni and Taggart and Holland . . . you know how many people we lost so far?"

"I'm the one who keeps the records, remember?"

"Yeah, so you know, but who's that *far* inside?"

"What are you getting at, Frank?"

"The big board's getting shook, Mark. They don't like what's happening. The first time out they figured they were fooling with some wise ass son of a bitch, then they saw a raid coming on and got all set for it, now they can't put it together at all unless some outfit is just lining us up for an all-out war and trying to take out the generals before they commit the soldiers."

"Don't be silly. That's impossible."

"There's another bit that they're considering."

Shelby studied his glass, tasted the wine and put it down again. "What's that?"

"The United States Government might have decided to take on an internal diversion for publicity purposes to cover up all the other crap that's going on."

"Frank, you're nuts. Who the hell they going to use . . . the CIA?"

"Consider it a possibility."

"They got the FBI. They're bad enough. Right now they use any excuse to go across state lines and their damn director doesn't even give a shit for constitutional rights. Only we have our people there too and there haven't been any directives out to nail us."

Frank Verdun swirled the wine in his glass and sniffed the edge. If Shelby didn't know better he would have thought he was a constant habitué of the more gracious Paris bistros.

Mark said, "Why should they? It's even better this way. Let somebody else pick us apart and go in after the pieces. No, Frank, it isn't the FBI and it isn't the CIA. I wish it were, because we'd know who we were dealing with and how to take care of it, but what's happening is pure insanity. Nobody's made a fucking move yet."

Verdun nodded, conceded the point. "They will, you know. They have to. You don't go through all the trouble they went through without finally making a move. Nobody does anything for nothing and so far it's been their game." He stopped twirling the wine around in his glass, finished it and slid the ornate crystal to one side. "It's really simple, you know."

"I don't know," Shelby said.

"What's the most important thing in the world?" the Frenchman asked. He was hunched over his arms and his eyes were a bright electric blue as they stared at Mark.

Shelby would have said something else, but he knew what the Frenchman wanted to hear and said, "Money."

The curl in his lip the Frenchman didn't ordinarily show appeared now. He had inherited his mouth from his mother, had a plastic surgeon take out the birth scar, but there were times when the defect was evident despite the operation. His mind was like a tumescent sore about to burst.

"Somebody is after our treasury," he said.

Mark Shelby wasn't about to lance his throbbing boil. "Reasonable," he agreed. "There's nothing as important as money." For a moment he thought he saw a flicker in the Frenchman's eyes about to dispute the point, but didn't press it.

Abruptly, Frank Verdun said, "What about this shithead Burke?"

"I heard he was back."

"You know he's working for the D.A.'s office?"

"I heard."

"So what about it?"

"You saw Papa's orders," Shelby told him. "Lay off the cops. What the hell could he do anyway? They got twenty-five thousand cops in this city. One more's going to matter?"

"He's a specialist."

"Screw him."

"He was after you, Mark."

Shelby let a smile touch his mouth that turned into a laugh. "So he got screwed and we can screw him again. Come on, Frank, you terrified of one stinking ex-blue-coat just because the D.A.'s office is grabbing at straws?"

"No," the Frenchman said, "I'm not." He sat back in his booth and waved the waitress in the black miniskirt over. "Are you?" he asked.

Papa Menes had sent his driver into Miami to get a big Rand McNally map of the United States. Artie Meeker had thumbtacked it on the wall as the old man directed and circled the areas he indicated. He leaned back against the wall thinking of the beautiful whore he had met and didn't have time to service and waited for Papa Menes to finish thinking.

The old man said, "Draw a dotted line toward Phoenix, Artie."

He had no idea where Phoenix was, but remembered Nicole telling him about the fly-in whorehouse she worked in and how she used to shop in Phoenix, and after locating the state, he stuck the pencil tip on the city of Phoenix and sketched a line between it and New York.

"What's in Phoenix, boss?" Artie asked.

"An idea," Papa Menes told him. "Now draw to Cleveland."

Artie Meeker knew where Cleveland was and drew a line up to it. "Okay?"

"Fine," Papa said. "Go to Seattle this time."

Artie did as he was told and found Seattle by accident.

"San Diego is in lower California. Draw a line to there."

Artie nodded and followed Route Five all the way down because it was the sure way not to make a mistake. He stepped back and looked at his handiwork. It was like when he was in his geography class at P.S. 19. He wished Miss Fischer were watching right now. He was always the dumbhead, but right now she'd be proud of him. Hell, once he couldn't even find Philadelphia, and just now he had drawn a line down to San Diego.

"Go to Dallas," Papa said.

Artie was like a little kid enjoying the game. He had seen enough weather men on TV and knew right where Dallas was because that was where they made those big circles with the L or the H in the middle and where Kennedy got killed and they just had a crazy cold front last week with a tornado in the north end. He always wanted to hear a tornado go past because everybody said it sounded like a train going by. He drew the line to Dallas.

"Very good," Papa said. He leaned back in his chair

and studied the map. He could have had Artie draw in some more lines, but they weren't really necessary. He could have put in numbers to indicate the continuity of killings, but they weren't really necessary. He knew their sequences and nothing made sense at all. "They're very mobile," he said.

Artie Meeker didn't know the meaning of the word so simply bobbed his head as though he did.

Papa Menes said, "Is that little whore you met in Miami coming down here tonight?"

A long time ago Artie had stopped questioning the old man's intuition or sources of information. He knew better than to lie and said, "Yeah, boss."

"How much?"

"A yard. Hundred bucks and she's happy."

"Anything?"

"Sure, boss."

"Tell her to bring a friend. Call the West Wind and we'll see them there. You sure she's three way?"

"Come on, boss, you know me."

"That's for sure," Papa Menes said.

The two cottages on the Gulf were separated from the others by fifty yards. Ordinarily they were used for the benefit of Harvey Bartel, the bartender who had learned how to bypass the locks, but when the *man* came down from the big city, the broker with enough money to buy or sell you, or get you booted out of your lovely sun-tanned job where the pussy was easy and the money substantial, or get you beaten up by those frigging

Miami toughs who didn't understand you just wanted some fun, you just closed your eyes and took your date to a movie twenty miles away and were glad nobody caught you with the skeleton key or screwing a local blonde whose husband was six inches taller and forty pounds heavier.

Sometimes Harvey Bartel wished he could see just who owned those cottages, but being a coward he was too scared to inquire and satisfied himself with a hand on the bare thigh of the fat girl from Summerland Key who had driven all the way up to see him. She wasn't much. She was all lard and excitement, but she had a nice, wet mouth and liked to use it. Her father owned a machine shop in Miami and four sport-fishing cruisers too.

The girl screamed because she thought the old man liked it that way. She got a belt across the head and Papa Menes said, "Shut it. I don't pay for noise."

Louise Belhander stopped screaming and twisted her head back so she could see the old man propped in position astride her legs. She laughed, made herself comfortable on her stomach and spread her legs as far apart as she could get them. "Okay, have fun, daddy," she said.

Fuck him, she thought, she liked it this way anyway. He wasn't all that big and she had plenty of baby oil going in the way of lubricant and if he wanted to lay out all that green for a real piece of ass, he was the customer and the customer was always right. She felt his fingers separating her buttocks and nestled her head in her arms. *Have fun, baby*, she whispered to herself. That slob who got himself drowned last week was even better. He was too long and too big, but he was too strong and too heavy to fight. He had damned near wrecked her little goodie hole and sent her to the clinic with an anus rapist story that made those damn fucking interns pass snide remarks until they saw the actual injury.

Papa Menes even felt good. Louise raised her behind so he could get a better advantage and smiled. *Like brushing your teeth,* she thought, *or shining your shoes.* Most women didn't know why guys had their shoes shined. They sat in a chair while somebody made their feet come with a brush and a rag and it was just like they had been laid. The cheapest screw in the world. You got your feet tingled, had a toe orgasm and went home never knowing where you had been.

Right now Louise Belhander was having her ass tickled and having all the experience of relaxation, all she was doing was enjoying it, thinking of where she was going to spend the money. If tiny cock up there was going to be a steady, she might even be able to afford the payments on that new convertible she wanted. Louise knew he was about to reach his climax and brought all her expertise into being. For her, a professional since high school, it was simple.

One half hour later Papa Menes was completely drained, his mind refreshed since his monthly requirements had been satiated and he could think again. He picked up the phone and dialed the next cottage.

Artie Meeker had had too much to drink and that wild orgasmic feeling escaped him completely. When the phone rang and the girl looked up from what she was doing to listen to him say, "Rightaway, boss," all she could think of was that she might have been better off getting married to that Tennessee catfish farmer who only took two years to accumulate a half a million bucks. Weird, but rich, but he sure could come a mouthful and that was her pleasure in life. This was a puff of dust and she bet Louise, in the next cottage, didn't do any better. Those Wall Street boys were all alike. All money. No cock. It was hell to be a whore when you really liked it, she thought. Someday she'd go back to Lessiland.

Papa Menes looked at the map again until he found that little town in Pennsylvania and remembered when he had met Sylvia whom he had married. She was a virgin, her father was a rabbi and he was a crazy wop who made the hospital workers strike as a cover for killing Rierdon after they put him in jail. He was young then and the ones on the board had approved. They let him marry the virgin, have his stupid kids who grew up threatened between two religions, and after he had wiped out everybody who stood in his way, they were very happy to let him control the uncontrollable. Papa Menes was the boss. His stupid Jewish wife was a slob he endured. His idiotic kids had long ago gone into Star-of-David graves because he couldn't tolerate them. The opposition thought they were his weak spot.

They were wrong, they died, he was justified in the records of the programmers and was counted as a man who could be expected to fulfill his obligations. When he was thirty-eight years old those obligations were filled and they began calling him Papa.

His wife still had a foible about letting him screw her

up the ass because she had an enema complex, but by then it didn't matter because Papa Menes had too many women around who didn't care about foibles when it clashed with a small sheaf of bills on a dresser top.

All Papa could think of was the chubby little broad he had married protecting her puckered little anus the second week after the ceremony. She had scratched his face, gotten one hell of a broken nose out of the process, and aside from the few times he had come in loaded and screwed her whether she liked it or not, that was the end of their physical relationship. The rabbi father-in-law was dead, her mother was beside him, and she was playing canasta down in Miami, making sure her diamonds flashed and her furs were the best.

Too bad she didn't like to get screwed up the ass, Papa thought. They might have had a damn good marriage, rabbi father or not. He even would have let her play around with that little schmuck Aaron whose father ran the dry cleaner's place on the corner. Aaron was all cock and no sense. Not at all like a wop or an Irisher. At least you knew what to expect from the Irisher or wop. The crazy kikes had their own ideas.

Papa Menes was scared of Jews. That's why he killed them every chance he got.

Maybe he shouldn't have listened to his cousin when they put Mark Shelby in. His grandfather on his mother's side was a Jew and that wasn't what they had in mind. The old man fell asleep remembering his cock up a young broad's ass and the way she squirmed and groaned. The only trouble was the dark shadow that kept hanging around the edge of his dream with a bony hand waiting to touch him with the mark of the dead. But the specter was blindfolded and couldn't find him and he was able to enjoy himself to the fullest.

Artie Meeker wasn't very bright, but he had a memory remarkable for its ability to take down a fifteen-minute conversation, repeat it verbatim and forget it before the sun rose the next day. He had paid off the two girls with tips to equal their fees, dropped them at a taxi stand in Homestead with an extra fifty to get them back to Miami, then took his bag of change and went into the pay phone booth on the corner while the car was being serviced and got the number in New York. He finished two cigarettes while he listened, dropping in quarters whenever the speaker went overtime, said a simple "Right," when it was done, paid for his gas and oil and got back on the highway.

Papa Menes was already up having coffee when he got to the house, standing on the porch watching the sun dance on the incoming tide. He asked "Well?" and began his briefing.

The Cleveland police had gotten a break. A girl who worked in the building opposite had noticed the car driven by Holland's killer because it was in a slot normally occupied by the manager in the neighboring office and the plates contained three consecutive zeroes. When they checked out every available combination, the only car whose make and color coincided was a rental job.

Crime paid off because the agency had been held up

four times the past year and had installed a hidden camera that photographed everyone at the counter and the person who had rented the car was now on film. He was tall, wore a blue raincoat over a dark suit, a gray hat, carried a small suitcase still tagged with an airline baggage check, had glasses, a thin mustache and cut marks on his chin from a hurried shave. The name on his driver's license was Charles Hall from Elizabeth, New Jersey. He had paid by credit card. The Cleveland police were interrogating all the airline personnel, looking for an identification. Copies of the photo were being sent to departments in all the other cities but not being released to the news media. Papa Menes would have his own copy in the mail tomorrow. The old man nodded and finished his coffee.

Gill Burke handed the photo back to Captain Long and said, "Mister Anybody. The glasses and mustache could be phony and who doesn't cut themselves shaving? The marks would be gone by now."

"Encouragement is great," Bill Long said. "Just what I need."

"How about the credit card and address?"

"Phony, what else? The address was a garage that never heard of the guy and the card was only used once. We're checking up on the reference he used when he applied for credit but not hoping for much luck."

"That took a lot of preparation, buddy."

"Nothing more than you'd expect from a pro, Gill."

"A little more," Burke said. "The usual contract

84

boys don't like any kind of paperwork, you know that."

"Yeah, so this smells a little more businesslike. Either a high-price deal or an organizational endeavor. At least we got a toehold now. Somebody's going to recognize that photo sooner or later and we'll get our first break. The lab's got their specialists working on that negative and if there's anything that can be brought out, they'll do it."

"Anything from the air terminal?"

"One big blank, that's what." He looked at Gill's face and scowled. "What's so damn funny?"

"The whole bit could be a decoy. He could have even known about that camera. If he was a good pro he could have switched clothes and slapped on a disguise in the men's room and taken it from there."

"Maybe, but that camera had only been there a week."

"Then you got your toehold."

"We have a better angle, or haven't you talked to the D.A. yet?"

"He doesn't offer me anything at all."

"Stanley Holland," Bill Long told him, "was a very well-kept secret. Now that we know who he was we're putting the picture together. His activities were known only to a few of the higher-ups in the syndicate and whatever bunch got inside their little plan had to be an extremely well-financed, well-informed group. The L.A. police are really hammering at it and we ought to be getting a break any time."

"Good luck," Gill said.

"Yeah," Long muttered. He put the picture back in

his pocket and held a match to his cigarette. "Now what have you got?"

"Nothing concrete yet. Maybe by Wednesday I'll toss something out at the meeting."

"You'd better. There's a little shit-assed columnist who's got a mad-on at everybody in uniform who smelled out your participation in this thing."

"Meyer Davis?"

"The same."

Gill chuckled in his throat. "He didn't like that boot in the tail I gave him for the job he did on Joyce Carroll. He nearly loused up my whole case."

"Well, he's sniffing around and he's got that whole pinko paper behind him."

"Another kick in the behind can straighten him out."

"You lay off that shit."

"Sure, boss."

"Quit that shit too."

"Yes, sir."

"Come on, Gill."

Burke laughed at him. "Okay. See you Wednesday."

5

Calling Willie Armstrong "Junior" was as diminutive as calling Mister Ruth "Babe." He was a span over six feet, weighed two hundred thirty pounds and could talk like the college graduate which he was or drop into the dialect of a Georgia cotton farmer which his father had been. His teeth were a dazzling white in the blackness of his face, framed in a huge smile as he greeted Gill Burke at the door of his apartment on Lenox Avenue in Harlem.

"You sure got your nerve coming up here, white boy," he said.

Gill gripped his hand and squeezed just as hard. "None of you cats ever give anybody trouble in the morning. You're all too happy."

"We're tigers, man."

"Only when the sun goes down. How's Cammie?"

"Great, man. She started making the grits and red-eye gravy soon as you called."

"I wanted sausages and pancakes, Junior."

"All on one plate, buddy. Just like the old days. Remember Looney Mooney, that cook we had in basic training?"

"Old take-care-of-the-troops Looney Mooney," Gill said.

"Right on, friend. Cammie's cakes makes his look sad, like sad."

"Then let's eat."

Over breakfast the three of them recounted the days from when they had seen so much hell together, through their occasional reunions to the present. Junior Armstrong had opened a neighborhood discount house, survived the economic trends and emerged as a powerful spokesman for the black community. His heavy hand and influential contacts had kept his area cool and not much went on he didn't know about.

When they finished, Cammie, his pretty little wife who had the only voice he actually feared, sent them into the living room to talk while she cleaned up, setting the coffeepot on the table between them.

Junior offered Gill a cigarette from his pack and

snapped the lighter on. "You been hurting since the bust?"

Burke blew a stream of smoke toward the ceiling. "Not really."

"Don't fake me out, buddy."

"So I hurt for a little while," Gill said. A touch of humor showed in his eyes and he added, "I'm back again."

Junior nodded, showing no surprise at all. He listened while Gill sketched in the details and nodded again. "You need some help?"

"A little."

"Say it, man."

"A young guy named Henry Campbell who'd be about twenty-five years old. His last place was a furnished room down on Bleeker Street, but he didn't leave any forwarding address."

"How long ago?"

"Couple of years."

"That's a lot of time."

"I know, but there aren't many places he can go, either."

"Yeah, I know. Being black means being *located*. You only got one ghetto or another to hole up in. Suppose he left the city?"

"Doubtful. He was born here. Parents dead, two brothers in the Post Office Department who haven't heard from him in years, but he's got to have friends."

"How far did you get?" Junior asked him.

"If he's working, he's not using his social security number. He isn't listed on welfare or unemployment books. He has no known skills, but likes to work around cars. The last time I spoke to him he parked cars in a lot owned by the syndicate."

Junior took a drag on his cigarette and tapped the ash off into the tray. "That would be the witness who finked out on you that time."

"Uh-huh."

"You going to lean on him?"

"Nope. I just want to know why he changed his story. Maybe somebody else leaned on him."

"He may not have a good memory."

"Not for me," Gill said. "For you it might be better."

"I'd hate to see his tail caught in a sling."

"So would I. It hurts."

"You can take it. He's got the odds going against him already."

"There are ways and ways of sweetening things up, Junior. He does me a favor and I guarantee him a big one back. What do you say?"

The big man sat there smoking a minute, then nodded. "Everybody needs help sooner or later. Let me see what I can do. How soon do you need it?"

"Yesterday."

"Settle for tomorrow?"

"Any choice?"

"None at all." Junior grinned, his teeth flashing in the light. When Gill got up he said, "You want an escort back to your end of town?"

"Don't be silly," Gill smiled back. "It's still happy time outside."

"Only for us cats," Junior told him. "We're still nature lovers."

Gill laughed at him and nodded toward the window. "Sure you are. Who waters your flower box, buddy?"

"Cammie does. She's the farmer 'round heah. I water hers."

"You're a nature lover all right, Junior."

The pudgy old lady who ran the rooming house on the West Side wouldn't go inside because she was too comfortable in her canvas chair with the sun warming her and made Gill talk to her on the platform of the sandstone stoop. A bunch of kids made a racket in the street and a pair of winos were sharing a bottle on the curb just a little bit away.

She remembered Ted Proctor, all right, mainly because he was killed the day before his room rent was due and she never did collect it. The few items he left behind she tossed on the garbage can and were picked up before the sanitation men ever arrived. She sold his suitcase for a dollar to a whore who was leaving and his broken watch she had kept for herself and still hadn't gotten repaired.

"He have any friends around here?"

"Maybe if he had some money, he'd have a friend," she told him. "You know how these stew bums are."

"Any visitors?"

She made a face through the folds of fat. "Sometimes Andy from next door if he thought Proctor had a bottle on him."

"Andy still around?"

"That idiot fell asleep in his doorway last January and died of pneumonia."

"How often you go into Proctor's room when he was here?"

She looked at him, her eyes a little wise. He held out the five dollar bill and watched it disappear into her dress pocket. "I changed the sheets and pillowcases every week."

"What did he keep in his closet?"

"A lot of dirty clothes is all. He didn't . . . say, you don't think I go nosing through a tenant's things, do you? You'd better know . . ."

"Just tell me, will you. I already paid."

Her fat shoulders hunched in a shrug. "Nothing, that's what he had. At least nothing that counted. A couple of old letters and cards, them stubs from a paycheck . . . he worked, you know."

"Part time."

"Still paid the rent on time."

"You know what the police found in his room."

"They didn't show me nothing. I only read about it in the papers."

"Ever pull his bottom drawer out all the way? Those wallets were lying there on the catch board."

"I didn't even know there was one."

"A couple of boxes in his closet had some other items besides."

"They only had dirty clothes when I looked. I told the cops the same thing."

"How long before he was killed did you look?"

She thought a moment, then: "He died the day before rent day and that's when I changed the linen. It had to be a week before."

"He have a gun?"

"Where would he get a gun?"

"I didn't ask that."

"He didn't have nothing I didn't know about and he didn't have any gun."

"Proctor had one when he held up that pawn shop. A brand new gun that sells for a hundred and ten bucks if you buy it legally and maybe twenty hot, but no less. It was a gun stolen from a sporting goods shop and would go for twenty any place on the street."

"Mister," the woman said, "if Proctor had twenty bucks in his hand, you could bet your sweet ass he wouldn't buy any gun with it. He'd be right down the corner slopping up booze in Barney's joint until he was too drunk to walk, then would come crawling back here to sleep it off. He was scared of his own shadow and if he even found a gun someplace he'd try to sell it before he'd use it."

"If a guy needed a drink he'd go pretty damn far to get one."

"Sell the gun, yes. Use it, no," she insisted. "He was nothing but a bum." She looked up at him again. "You want more talk and it'll cost more."

Gill shook his head. "Nope. You did pretty good. Thanks."

"The pleasure's all mine," she told him, patting her pocket.

"Sure I remember. He came in here barreled to his ears waving that gun around and telling me to put my money on the counter. That's what scared the hell out of me. I see these guys all the time and when they get like that you don't know what the hell they're going to do. Mister, I was scared. You know how many times I been held up? Fourteen times and the last one was only two weeks ago."

"You ought to be broke by now," Gill said.

"Look, I let them hit the register themselves. I only keep a certain amount in there anyway and they take it and run. It isn't like I was sitting on a bundle."

"Where do you keep the rest?"

"In a tight little box welded to the steel floor joists with a time lock on it and a bank deposit three times a week."

"You said you never saw this Ted Proctor before."

"Just that once when he tried to hold me up. If it wasn't for that beat cop seeing it happen that damn drunk could've killed me. Look, what the hell you cops going back two years for? Only last month . . ."

Gill shook his head at the pawnbroker, trying to keep the dislike out of his eyes. "I do what they tell me to, friend."

"They ought to get more beat cops up here."

"I'll tell the commissioner."

"Sure. What else do you want to know?"

"Nothing." Gill snapped his pad shut and stuck it in his pocket. "Thanks," he said and went outside. On the sidewalk he paused and stared up the street. Something was bothering him and he couldn't quite put his finger on it. Nothing big, just some detail he'd lost somewhere. Well, it would come back to him. It always did when he let it ferment long enough. He looked at his watch. It was almost one o'clock.

Mrs. Cynthia Berkowitz was still wearing her widowhood like a cape of royalty. Her indignation, anger and frustrations had been salved with grief, self-pity and the solicitations of neighbors who had borne the same burden and were only too happy to reminisce about the late Mr. Berkowitz who had been such a dear man, good provider and never ate anything except kosher nor missed attendance at the local synagogue no matter the weather or condition of his health. Not at all like Mr. Manute whom she classified as practically an infidel who had led her dear departed husband into photographic activities he actually knew nothing about, telling him they were processing art films when actually what they were working on was showing in the neighborhood theaters this very day. Had he known, he certainly would never have had anything to do with it at all.

Gill Burke drank his tea and agreed with her. "What happened to the business, Mrs. Berkowitz?"

"Sold. We got practically nothing. If it wasn't for the insurance . . ."

"Who bought it?"

She spread her hands and heaved her immense bosom. "Who remembers? Some things here, some things there. Myron, my cousin, he took care of things. He's a lawyer, Myron is. If you ever need a lawyer . . ."

"What about the files?"

"The papers?" Gill nodded. "Bah, papers. Bills they paid, bills they got. Some checks that bounced. Downstairs is a whole box of papers that should get thrown out. Myron, he's the lawyer, he says I should keep them in case they ask questions about taxes. He knows about taxes, Myron does. Tell me, Mister . . ."

"Burke."

"Yes, Mr. Burke. Why should the police want to know about Mr. Berkowitz after all this time? That little foreigner who got killed did it and we couldn't even sue. If it wasn't for the insurance . . ."

"Could I see those papers, Mrs. Berkowitz?"

"Maybe I should call Myron. He's my lawyer, you know."

"Call him," Gill suggested.

"So why should I bother Myron? You are a nice man with the badge and everything. Before everybody from the station house was very nice too. Downstairs in the cellar next to the furnace is the big box of papers. Look all you want, then come back and I'll have some more tea ready. You'd like some soup, maybe?"

"Just tea will be fine."

He crouched in the dim light of the dusty forty-watt bulb in the ceiling fixture squinting at the array of papers. Their equipment had been purchased all second hand, sixteen millimeter cameras, lights, development supplies and a lot of inexpensive accessories. It had been paid for in cash and receipted. After that their biggest cash outlay seemed to be for a bimonthly delivery of raw film ends from a large midtown supplier. Three months before their deaths, Manute had bought a used thirty-five-millimeter Nikon, a swivel chair and had double locks installed on their office door.

Myron, the lawyer, had left an inventory sheet on top of the pile along with a sales sheet from the auction. Everything had gone for the total price of a little more than two thousand dollars. The sheet was signed by Mrs. Cynthia Berkowitz and Mrs. Irma Manute. Myron's illegible signature was below theirs.

Gill Burke put everything back in the box, folded the cover into place and went upstairs for some more tea. He spent an hour probing for anything that might fit and something out of place, but all he got was bloated from the inexhaustible teapot.

He told Mrs. Berkowitz good-bye, promised to keep in touch and went downstairs to find a cab. It was almost six o'clock and he was going to see Helen Scanlon for supper. Why, he didn't know.

Maybe it was the way she kissed, he thought

They had the guy in a loft over the garage in Brooklyn. He was tied to a chair, his hands and feet numb from the loss of circulation, and all he could do was moan softly behind the tape that covered his mouth. What made it worse was that he couldn't see. The last thing he remembered was the sharp crack against the back of his head and then total darkness. The darkness was still there behind a cloth whose knot was biting into the wound on his scalp.

When Frank Verdun came in with Slick Kevin, Bingo Miles and Shatzi Heinkle stood up respectfully. The guy in the chair moaned and rolled his head.

"Who is he?" Frank asked.

"All his I.D. reads is William R. Hays. He's from East Orange, New Jersey." Bingo pointed to the open attaché case on the floor. "He was in Chicago and Cleveland on the right days. He sure looks like the picture, Mr. Verdun." ·

Frank pointed toward the case. "Check it," he told Slick. He walked over and stood in front of the man in the chair. "He wear glasses?"

Shatzi held out a broken frame and several pieces of the lens. "Same kind as in the picture. They broke when we took him."

"Clean snatch?"

"We used Bingo's cab. No problem at all. He wanted to go to the Hilton."

Kevin finished going through the papers and dropped them back in the case. "He's got a good cover, Frank. Fabric salesman to upholstery places."

"Check him out all the way, Slick." He glanced at Bingo and Shatzi. "You two keep him here and take care of him. I don't want anything to happen to this guy until we know all about him. He might have a lot to tell us." He took an ink pad and a white card from his pocket, went behind the chair, daubed the man's fingers on the black sponge and rolled his fingerprints onto the card. He only used one hand and two of the prints were messy, but they were enough. When he dried the card off he put it in an envelope and stuck it back in his pocket.

The guy moaned again and a wet stain darkened his trousers.

"Your call was a pleasant surprise," Helen Scanlon told him. "I really didn't think you'd want to see me again."

Gill told the waiter to bring more coffee and lit a cigarette. "My turn to apologize for being so rough on you. I could have been nicer in the office . . . or more hospitable at home."

"It wouldn't become you, Mr. Burke."

"Can't you call me Gill?"

"All right."

"Don't figure me for a social outcast, will you."

Helen Scanlon smiled gently, playing with a cube of sugar. "You remind me of my father, always the dedicated policeman. Nothing else mattered."

Gill reached out and laid his hand over hers. "In case you're interested, this isn't question and answer time. I felt like inviting you out to dinner because I had you on my mind all day."

"Why?"

"Not because you work in the Frenchman's office. They don't stop me from rousting them if I want to and if I need information I don't have to play any games to get it, either. I wished to hell I knew why I wanted to see you, but I don't. I just wanted to, that's all." He felt annoyed at himself for some reason.

"You really don't know much about women, do you?"

"Depends. Why?"

"Because you just gave me the best reason of all," she said.

"I did?" he said querulously.

She laughed again, turned her hand around and

squeezed his. "Do you know what would happen if some journalist saw us together and decided it would make a good story?"

"Limit that to just a couple of journalists, baby. The rest were all on my side and as for the other couple, I'd scratch them so fast it would make their eyes cross. Besides, we're both old news now anyway. Anything that could be said has already been said."

"Not with you, Gill. You still have a lot more to say." She took her hand away, glanced around her and reached into her handbag. She found the small oblong she wanted and handed it to him. "Whose picture is that?"

He took it from her, looked at it barely a second and asked, "Where did you get this?" It was the photo of a man at the counter of a car rental agency.

"A box of them was delivered to Mr. Verdun today. He had them separated into six groups and had them picked up by a man from the main office. He was on the phone for over an hour and was very excited about something. When he was out of the room for a minute I went in to leave some mail and picked one out of the pile."

Gill said, "Damn," and looked at the picture again. He could tell it wasn't an original, but had been recopied from a positive print, but for identification purposes, it was as good as the one that had come in from Cleveland. "Who were the photos sent to?"

"I don't know. The packages were unmarked."

"Recognize the guy who picked them up?"

"No. I'm sorry . . . he came and went too fast. I was busy at the files."

"This is good enough."

"Who is it, Gill?"

"A guy they think killed a hood named Holland in Cleveland."

"Important?"

Gill Burke nodded and tucked the photo away. "Your outfit's got a pipeline directly into the police department." He watched the frown pull her face tight. "Don't let it bother you. That's nothing new either." He called the waiter over and gave him a bill with the check, then said to Helen, "Come on, let's get out of here."

Outside, a light mist was blowing in from the northeast, making a halo around the street lights and laying down an oily slick on the pavement. Con Ed had a night crew digging a hole in the middle of the street, a yellow flasher diverting traffic around the obstacle.

Gill said, "Where would you like to go?"

"If I told you, would you really believe me?"

"Sure."

"I want to go and straighten up that clutter you call home."

"Why?"

"Because I just *want* to and I don't know why."

Burke flagged down a cab and they got in.

The man in the restaurant who had made the hurried phone call looked vainly for another cab. There wasn't

any in sight, and the one he had wanted to follow
was turning left at the far corner. He swore softly and
started walking.

Gill wondered how the hell it took a woman two
hours to do something he couldn't manage in a week.
Two hampers and a pillow case of laundry got washed
while she put everything else in order and wouldn't
even speak to him while he sat nursing a couple of tall
drinks, watching the way her body moved under the old
blue oxford police shirt. Her legs were long and athleti-
cally contoured like a dancer's. The shirt was a big one,
but her breasts swelled it tight, the tails just long
enough to be decently indecent.

Helen had pulled her hair back and tied it in a pony-
tail. Her face was shiny with sweat and she hummed
some silly little tune, smiling while she worked. Gill got
one of those odd feelings in his stomach again and went
downstairs to get the stuff out of the drier and when he
got back she had finished.

She pulled the biggest one of his bath towels out of
the laundry bag and told him, "Put your own things
away. I don't know your system. I'm going to take a
shower."

When he had everything sorted and the bed remade,
he went back to the living room and refilled his glass.
The shower was still going and his hand was shaking.
What the hell, he thought, he was getting virgin symp-
toms. He was picturing her naked in there behind the
closed door, her hands soaping her own bare flesh, dry-

ing those luscious curves to a pinkish glow with her image a vivid reflection in the full-length mirror.

How would she come out? Totally nude? The towel knotted like a chenille sarong and a look of subtle desire in those deep, dark eyes? Or would she be expecting him to push the door open, exerting the prerogative of the aggressive male?

Shit, broads never disrupted him before. They'd been there from the cuddly little society blonde in the penthouse who had been crazy about him to the flinty pro who had demanded payment for services rendered and it had all been the same. Physical necessity, opportunity and satisfying, but nothing to have to think about. Now he sat there with a mental tourniquet around half a hard-on, all shook up about a woman behind a closed door.

When she came out the jolt was even worse because she was all dressed and the things he had expected to see still had to be imagined and he wished to hell somebody would loosen that damn tourniquet or untie it altogether.

She looked happy and pleased with herself, and after she took the highball out of his hand to take a long, cooling drink, she handed it back and said, "Thank you, Gill. You may think I'm a ding-a-ling, but I had fun."

He grinned at her. "You're nuts, all right. A little supper sure went a long way."

She let out a deep-throated laugh and picked up her coat. "Home time, big man, and I can get my own cab."

He put down his glass and walked her to the door. She slipped into the coat he held, belted it and turned around. When he kissed her he tried to be just saying good night and thanks for the evening and all the maid work, but the tourniquet was coming undone and the fire was starting to rage and he knew he wasn't going to be able to put it out, so he said, "Now I haven't got any more excuses to lure you back."

"You'll think of something," Helen told him. She squeezed his hand and gave him an impish look. "Or maybe I will," she added.

When he heard the elevator doors close he went back inside and finished his drink, annoyed because his mind always sought a devious answer. She was a cop's daughter who worked for the syndicate and she had done him a favor. But had he done her one too without knowing it?

He opened the drawers of his desk where she had dusted. Nothing seemed out of place. His notepad and wallet on the end table had been pushed back to make room for a coaster for his glass. He couldn't tell if they had been looked at. He thought again and looked at the hidden compartment where the armament was stored. Everything was in place.

There had been nothing in the metal waste basket in the kitchen except the papers he had burned and the empty milk carton he had thrown in later. He should have checked to make sure everything had burned fully, but he had had to leave and had forgotten about it. There really wasn't that much to bother about, but the metal waste can had been emptied anyway.

It could have been simple habit. It could have been something else.

Gill undressed and went to bed, lying there on the cool sheets, his hands folded under his head while he let his mind ramble in idle thought around the bits and pieces that made up the scramble they called a world.

In the Brooklyn garage loft Slick Kevin hung up the phone and turned to the Frenchman. "He did two raps for auto theft and assault with a deadly weapon. Got out eight years ago and nothing on him since."

Verdun nodded slowly and looked at the quaking figure still tied in the chair. A bachelor who lived in Jersey and could have other phony Jersey identities. His boss vouched for him and he made a good living, but he made up his own schedule, didn't have to account for his itinerary as long as the orders came in and had an expense account so low it had to be honest in view of the profits and nobody ever asked for confirmation. He had been in two of the places at the right time, now all they had to do was push a little.

"Get to work on him," he told Shatzi and Bingo.

Shatzi grinned, poured a half can of starter fluid over the charcoal in the pail and set fire to it. When it was going good he slid the irons and the pincers under the briquettes and lit a cigar. Bingo started ripping the clothes off the bound figure and wrinkled his nose in disgust. Between the shit and the piss fright, he stunk like hell.

Frank Verdun and Slick Kevin went downstairs and got in the car. They'd know about it when he talked. Meanwhile, everybody knew what the orders were and all they could do was wait. Only business routine could make the Frenchman tired. When it was time to kill he could stay awake and alert for days at a time. He yawned, ready for a good night's sleep.

Maybe, Gill thought. It was a probability that couldn't be overlooked. They had handed her the dirty end of the stick and it was her syndicate friends who took her off the hook. She was a woman and women can carry a big hate a long time. They could even nurse a little hate until it got bigger than it deserved to be. They could have strange loyalties, like a whore to a pimp who took her money and slapped her silly anyway. Maybe handing him that photo was a sucker trap and her *want* a chance to go through his effects.

If the probability was an actuality he'd know about it soon enough. He wasn't that dumb even though his cock wasn't too bright. He could still picture her in the shower. He put the thought out of his mind and went to sleep.

In the hotel suite the phone jarred Frank Verdun awake. He cursed, picked up the receiver and snarled, "Yeah?"

"It's Shatzi, Mr. Verdun."

"Watch what you're saying."

"Sure. Just wanted to tell you that we couldn't open up that new account. It looked good, and if there was anything to buy, we would've got it."

"What happened?"

"The account decided to cancel out himself."

"Okay, dump it," he said, then hung up and went back to sleep.

6

The previous night's mist had been the overture for a cold front overrunning the East Coast. A driving rain drenched the city, whose towering buildings had their tops clipped off at the twentieth-story level by a lead-gray cloud layer. Cars drove with their lights on and pedestrians fought to hug the sides of the buildings. As usual at times like that, no empty cruising cabs and if one did stop to disgorge a passenger, the city syndrome of bad manners was at its best in the concerted rush to commandeer the taxi. Women might have thought they were equal, but a guy was always bigger and faster in getting to the door and could snarl back the insults as fast as their luckless sisters could give them.

Going downtown, Gill had a half-empty subway car to himself. He got off, fought the rain to Captain Long's office, tossed his wet raincoat and hat on a bench and went in where the captain and Robert Lederer were waiting for him.

"Lousy day, but good morning anyway," he said.

Lederer looked up from the folder he was studying and nodded curtly. Bill Long said, "Coffee?"

"Just had some." He pulled a chair over and sat down. When the assistant district attorney finished his reading he closed the folder and looked up. Gill tossed the photo on his desk. "Take a look," he said.

Lederer only glanced at it a moment. The annoyance showed on his face and in the tone of his voice. "You know we've issued these to all our investigative personnel. If you called me all the way down here . . ."

The captain said, "Let me see that," and took it out of Lederer's hands. He spotted it right away and handed it back. "It's a copy of one of ours."

It took a few seconds for the implication to sink in. Lederer ran his tongue around the inside of his mouth, his lips pursed. "Who had it?"

"The other side's got them handed out," Gill answered. "They're looking for the same guy, so it means you have a big leak in your own wall, buddy. What else do they know?"

"That's hard to believe."

"Oh, crap!" Gill spat out. "What the fuck do you use for brains?"

"Now, listen, Burke . . ."

"If you take that attitude, go screw yourself. You got an organization with an active hand inside of every big city government in the country who can call the shots in a political election or into somebody's head and you find it hard to believe. There's a gang war going on, narcotics turning citizens into corpses, businesses going bust because they can't keep up with the planned thievery and I have to listen to that shit."

Bill Long held up his hand. "Okay, tiger. I know the score. We've only put these out on a limited basis and it shouldn't be too hard to run down. Why the sweat?"

"This is an old hand showing," Gill told him. "It's not going to be that easy."

"So?"

"I want to know how old that hand is."

Lederer didn't like what he was getting at and frowned.

"Like a couple of years, maybe?"

"At least," Gill agreed.

"I hope you're not wasting a lot of time," the captain said.

"No time's being wasted. You always have to start at the beginning."

"Mr. Burke . . ."

Gill looked over at Lederer. "What?"

"Our office has very efficiently and very systematically compiled a great deal of information on the syndicate operation in the past few weeks. It has done so without any help from you at all, in view of the fact that you were specifically recruited to add your supposed store of knowledge to our own. So far you have contributed nothing except this." He tapped the picture with a forefinger, his face grim and accusing.

Burke's face held no expression at all. It was the kind of face too many people had wondered about when they lay there hurting, and a lot of others were forced to talk to whether it was safe or not because they couldn't read what was behind it. After a moment, Gill said, "Let me know when all that efficiency turns into evidence and convictions, Mr. Lederer. When you get that leak plugged up maybe I'll add to your information. Meanwhile I'll just work my end of the deal we made."

Lederer didn't feel capable of arguing against the face that stared at him. He never did feel comfortable inside a police building. There was something about the cold colors, the odd smell and indescribable mien of men who chose to work in an area of crime that reminded him of when he was a college freshman. But he was fortunate then that he had had a rich and influential family. He got up and took his coat off the rack, shook hands with the captain, barely nodded at Gill Burke and left.

"You sure like to rub that guy," Long said.

"If he's lucky, in ten years he'll get some sense. What about that picture?"

"That isn't the only incident."

"Any leads?"

"No, but a few ideas."

"How about the guy in the photo?"

"Our expert in the lab is willing to bet the whole

thing was a disguise. There's even a chance he knew the camera was there and let the picture get taken to throw us off."

"Clever," Gill said.

"Not really," Long told him. "It was pretty sophisticated equipment and the next shot in the sequence took an automatic magnified shot that brought out some detail we might be able to focus on. Scientific advancement is getting to be pretty damn incredible."

"Legwork is a lot better."

"Only when you have the time, buddy. Right now we haven't much of it. This morning we found a body in the middle of Prospect Park that had been worked over until it was a disgusting mess, but originally it could have fit the description of that man in the photo."

"Got a make on him?"

"No trouble at all. He was a former con who had gone straight. For six years he had been making furniture, then switched over to selling upholstery fabrics." Long picked up the photo and looked at it again. "This makes a little sense now."

"How?"

"The odd thing about the corpse was its right hand. There was ink smeared on the fingertips. Apparently somebody took his prints and checked out his I.D. The same person could have lifted this picture and used our files."

"You releasing the picture to the papers?"

"Might as well now," Long said. The phone rang and he picked it up, listened and growled, "Send him up." When he cradled the receiver he told Gill, "Corrigan's on his way in. He's a detective with the Fourth now. Don't waste too much of his time. If you need me I'll be down the hall."

Burke nodded so long, lit a cigarette and had taken his second drag on it when the cop in civvies walked in. Gill said, "Hi, have a seat."

Jimmie Corrigan tossed his hat on the desk and sat down. "What's up, Mr. Burke?"

"How's your memory?"

"Good enough."

"Remember Ted Proctor?"

The cop's head snapped around. "No way to forget that, is there? He was the first, and I hope the last. Killing somebody doesn't leave a nice taste."

"Yeah, I know."

Corrigan flushed and turned his eyes away. Gill Burke's history was very clear in his mind.

"Tell me about that night," Gill asked him.

"It's all in the report, Mr. Burke."

"I know. I read them. Now I want to hear you tell me about it."

"Well, I was an hour from coming off duty. I had called in from the box, crossed over to the south side of the street and continued west."

"On schedule?"

"A few minutes early, I suppose. It was cold as hell that night and I was figuring on a hot cup of coffee in Gracie's Diner at the end of the beat. The Chinaman's laundry and the pawnshop were open and . . ."

"Any incidents?"

Corrigan thought back and shrugged. "I checked an

alley out when I heard a garbage can go over. It was a dog. Right after that some half-lit broad stopped to tell me what a son of a bitch her boy friend was because he had another woman in his apartment when she had helped him buy the furniture."

"Many people on the street?"

"Too cold. I saw a couple, that's all."

"Where were you when you were talking to the dame?"

"By the doorway of the grocery store."

"Lights on?"

"Nope. The place was dark."

"Then if Proctor entered the pawnshop then he couldn't have seen you."

"Guess so. I didn't see him go in, either."

"Okay, go on."

"So I told the woman to forget about it and she left. I went on up the street. When I got to the pawnshop I looked in and saw the owner standing there with his hands up and Proctor facing him. I pulled my own gun out and went in right then and told the guy to drop his weapon, but instead he swung around with the gun in his hand and I thought sure as hell he was going to start shooting and I shot him."

"He say anything?"

"No, but he sure had a crazy look on his face."

"Describe it?"

Corrigan squinted and shrugged. "Been a couple of years, Mr. Burke. I can still see that expression but the only way I can describe it is crazy. Believe me, it was all so damn fast you really can't tell what's happening. You just react and hope you did the right thing."

"You did."

"I wish I could be sure."

"What makes you doubt it?"

The cop rubbed his hands together, his eyes trying to peer at a dim, indistinguishable picture in his mind. "You know," he said, "I try not to, but I keep seeing that whole damn thing over and over again. I even dream about it. There was something there that just wasn't right and I'll be damned if I can figure out what it was."

"Don't you think the follow-up would have spotted it?"

"I keep telling myself so," Corrigan said. "Anything else?"

"No, I guess that's all."

"I thought that was a closed case, Mr. Burke."

"That's what the sign says," Gill told him, "but sometimes closed cases just make room for new ones."

Corrigan said, "That's life," shook hands and left.

Over in records, Sergeant Schneider took Burke back to the files and found the packet he requested. He spread the contents out on the table and said, "There it is. Not much, but we didn't need much." He pulled out photos of three bullets that had taken a life and pointed out the configurations on the enlargements that showed they all came from the same gun, then moved over another verifying the groove marks from the murder weapon. "I wish they were all that easy," he said.

Burke picked up the composite showing the prints lifted from the murder weapon. They clearly matched those taken from the body of Proctor. Schneider pointed out the similarities with expert ease.

"We were lucky here," he said. "The usual cross-hatched walnut stock had been replaced with a clear plastic that picked up those three beautiful prints. The rest were smudged, but even then it didn't matter. The gun was lying right under him where he fell."

Burke jammed his cigarette out in an ash tray, his finger flicking against the photo. "What's wrong with this, Al?"

Schneider took it out of his fingers, studied it and gave it back to him. "Nothing. It's beautiful."

"There's something wrong."

"Like hell."

"Maybe we're just stupid."

"You don't make sergeant being stupid," Schneider told him. "What more do you want?"

"Be damned if I know."

"Why don't you just leave it alone, Gill?"

"Because I don't like to think of myself as being stupid," he said. He looked at his watch and it was closing in on two o'clock.

Just then Trent came in with an eight-by-ten color print and held it out for Schneider to file along with the typed report. "Want to see a beauty? It's the guy they found in Prospect Park."

Sergeant Schneider didn't mind the black-and-whites, but those damned color photographs they were sending down these days made him sick, especially when they were of entrails, mutilated glands and torn flesh. He gagged, and when Burke said, "Let me see that," he was glad to give it to him.

"Who's handling this?" Burke asked Trent after a minute's scrutiny.

"Peterson."

He pointed to an area in the picture where a gaping wound had been gouged into the corpse's belly. "Tell him to check the Minneapolis and Denver files for an M.O. Go back about ten years. Two of the Caprini clowns from the Chicago family were rubbed out by a hit man who liked to tear out belly buttons."

"Why the hell would he do that?" Trent asked.

"Maybe he ate them," Gill said.

Schneider gagged again. Gill laughed and left.

The answering service told him he had had a call from a Mr. Willie Armstrong who didn't leave a number, and after he thanked the operator he fished another dime out of his pocket and dialed the apartment on Lenox Avenue.

When he heard the rumbling hello, he said, "Gill here, Junior, I got your message."

"Where are you?"

"Phone booth. What's up?"

"If you want Henry Campbell he'll talk to you but it'll cost."

"No sweat."

"I promised him no heat."

"Deal."

"He ain't no boy, bossman, and you can bet he's covered. If there's any kickback I'll be the sucker."

"Junior," Gill told him, "right now I'd like to kick your black ass for that remark."

He heard his friend chuckle on the other end of the line. "Sorry, buddy. It's been a long time since we lived in the same foxhole."

"Forget it, ape. Where do we meet?"

"You remember where Perry Chops met his just reward?"

"Exactly."

"Right there at ten P.M." Junior Armstrong chuckled again. "And see heah, boy. Don't play the big white hunter. Yo in Black Panther territory theah."

"Yo bigoted, man," Gill laughed back.

Perry Chops was a long-dead narcotics pusher who bought it in a five-floor fall from a rooftop assisted by the fist of an irate father who caught him about to introduce his two teenage kids into the screaming glories of heroin. The father had a cousin who had a detective on the case for a friend and the fall became a suicide dive on the books. The two kids made the acquaintance of a leather belt on bare asses and both went on to be city firemen with great respect for the parent they regarded as a slob and greater respect for the second cousin and the cop who held them in position while they learned the truth of life the leathery way.

The street hadn't changed any, the buildings were

just as dilapidated and the eyes that looked at him as he parked the car just as suspicious as ever. For a white man to be there at all, far less alone, meant he packed so much power that nobody had better touch anything until it was all spelled out loud and clear and they knew the score.

He locked the car and went up the steps, not even bothering to look at the pair in tailored suits wearing the cocked berets. The tenement was quiet, without the usual odors he knew so well. Too many times Gill had been up and down buildings like this and he didn't have to be shown the way.

Another pair stepped aside at the first-floor landing and three more were waiting at the fourth. One blocked his way with youthful arrogance and said, "You packing any heat, mister?"

Even in the dim light, the kid could feel his eyes before he actually saw them. "You're damn right I am," Gill told him and went on by to the roof. Nobody tried to stop him.

Henry Campbell was an old, old young man who had packed a dozen lifetimes into one and had been worn down by them. He didn't own enough hair to merit the Afro style he kept it in and for a moment Gill didn't recognize him. He was thinner and someplace he had lost a front tooth and the pinky on his left hand.

"Hello, Henry."

"Knock it off. You can call me Mr. Campbell." His voice was strictly New York.

"Fuck yourself. You know my first name," Gill said.

Light flashed on the teeth with the gap that showed through his smile. "Don't nothin' intimidate you frigging cops?"

"Nope."

"Like my boys downstairs?"

"Didn't get to meet any of them on a personal basis."

"One day you will."

"As long as it's not on business."

"Man, you're somethin'. I didn't figure you'd show."

"Like hell you didn't. This isn't the best night in the world to be alone on a rooftop."

Overhead the sky rumbled and the rain was threatening again. Henry Campbell grinned again and held his hand out. "Lay on the bread, officer."

Gill reached in his pocket, found what he was looking for and dropped a penny in his palm. "That's what it's worth."

He got another laugh and the penny solemnly disappeared into a shirt pocket. "You cool, brother. Maybe we're getting to know each other."

"Could be."

"Then ask your questions. I know my rights already."

"Remember when Berkowitz and Manute were killed?"

"Yea, verily, man."

"And you *said* you saw Mark Shelby in the area."

"True. Oh yes, true. I said that to you."

"And later you couldn't remember and you probably had made a mistake?"

"Just too true, man. You are exact . . . exact."

"Which was it?"

"Man . . . Gill . . . damn, here I am calling a cop by

his name . . . or would you like it better if I said Mr. Gill?"

"Want me to start that crap too?"

"No."

"Then which was it?"

"I *saw* him, man. Big as life. He was right there on the street. You think I'd forget a ten-buck tipper?"

"Not in a million years."

"Tell you something else, man . . . even before you ask."

"What's that?"

"You think I'd forget two guys who showed me how they were going to cut my balls off and meant every word they said or the five hundred bucks they laid on me if I knew enough to forget what I saw?"

"That's pretty convincing talk," Gill told him.

"And it's still forgot, Gill, man. It's buried way down deep where nobody can get it out of me because those boys are still big enough to get my balls and without them I am just plain dead, you understan'?"

"Sure."

"There ain't no way to make me remember and I'm just telling you this because Big Willie passed the word on I should, so now you're all told and there ain't no reason for you to be here no longer."

"What was Shelby doing there, Henry?"

"Nothing. All I saw was him *there*."

"He wasn't near that office?"

"Not too far, not too near."

"Going which way?"

"No way. He was just standing there. I never should

have said nothin', but I was young then and didn't know no better. Them fuckin' cops made me feel like a big shot until I damn near lost my balls."

"You working?"

"I got a garage over on Tenth Avenue. Half ownership with a brother. Why?"

Gill pulled out a hundred-dollar bill and stuffed it in his shirt pocket on top of the penny. "I'm a big spender. I just got a tire changed," he said.

Henry pulled out the bill, looked at it and put it back again. "Fuckin' cops," he said with a grin.

"Fucking niggers," Gill laughed.

Henry put out his hand. "Skin, man." They shook hands and Henry said, "The penny would've been enough."

"I got an expense account now," Gill told him. "Hang onto your balls. You might need them someday."

"Hell," Henry told him, "I need them *now*. I just got married."

Artie Meeker liked the hottest Mexican food he could find, so hot that when the waiters watched what he did with the jalapeno chillies, the red pepper and other concoctions he demanded, they made circular motions with their forefingers around their temples to indicate that they had an idiot *Norteamericano* on their hands who owned an iron stomach and they hoped he'd leave a big tip before he died.

And Pedro Cabella was known to serve the hottest food in all of Cuban Miami because he was from Neuva

Laredo where the idiot Americanos loved to wallow in gastronomic volcanic fire and had never seen Havana in his life. Pedro and Artie were made for each other and Artie made the extra miles into Miami whenever the old man let him take his time.

He finished his supper and what was left over Pedro put up for him in a cardboard container to take home and splash over his breakfast eggs in the morning. When Pedro saw him giving the sweet talk to fat Maria he smiled and wished he'd try to kiss her just so Maria would know what it would be like to have her tongue burned off. His devious mind jumped from top to bottom with even a better thought and he could picture Artie eating her pussy while fat Maria screamed from the effects of fresh jalapenos in that sensitive area she would never let him explore.

But Artie had a schedule to keep and all he did was pat Maria on her chunky behind and drop a five-dollar bill down what open space remained between the two great breasts she carried rather than wore and promised her a real treat the next time he came back. The old man would really flip over that ass, he thought.

He got his package from Pedro, paid his bill and picked up his cigarettes before he left. He didn't pay any attention at all to the swarthy little guy in the corner booth who went out ahead of him and was still standing there when he got in the car. After the sedan turned onto the boulevard the little guy went across the street to a pay phone, called his number long distance collect and gave the license number of the sedan, the description of the car and hoped the wheel had landed on his number. Not that it wasn't a useful occupation. He had free meals, spending money and if he found the right car he'd have a big bonus. He could have made a few more calls and gotten extra cash in the mails, but he was afraid of the eyes that belonged to the man who had given him the assignment in the first place. No, that wasn't exactly right. He wasn't afraid. He wasn't even scared of him. He was downright terrified.

Alone with his books, his coded files, two telephones and the new computer, Leon Bray felt safe and secure. There were four and a half million dollars in the Swiss bank account, a luxury apartment in New York, a residence near Las Vegas where forty acres and eight horses were considered a normal backyard to any home, a vacation spot in Baja California where he could relax with one of the showgirls whenever he felt the need for it and the cottage up in the Catskills nobody knew about at all.

His office was his castle, though. The organization had seen to his every need without question because his was the filter through which every facet of the business flowed, to be catalogued, indexed and ready for immediate referral.

Outside, the elite guards kept his castle impregnable, his immediate premises inviolate. Downstairs the faggot Jan and his lover Lucien guarded the portals. The sight of blood was their stimulant and they were always ready to draw it, eager to enhance their sex life. They were the perfect sentries.

Ollie, Matt Stevenson and Woodie were on the next level where they could command every entranceway and trap any intruder in a crossfire.

On the top landing Lupe and the Cobra were playing cards with a miniature deck because it was always dull duty when they pulled a tour around the castle. They were going to be glad when everything moved out to Long Island all on one floor and walled in with a bar at hand and a cottage available so they could sneak in some broads.

Leon Bray felt very secure, indeed.

He didn't know that downstairs Jan was covering Lucien with his bloody body, nor that Lucien's horrified eyes finally knew what it was like to have an incredibly sharp blade drawn across his throat.

Ollie, Matt Stevenson and Woodie never even smelled the gas that touched their lungs with the devastating finger of death. They only knew the fierce spasm that tried to jerk their bodies apart at the same time it reached down their throats with fingers of excruciating pain that grabbed their intestines and pulled them out through their throats. Their weapons made a clatter as they fell to the floor, but not loud enough to alert the others one floor up.

Lupe saw the thing first and since it was nothing like he had ever seen before, just gaped instead of going for his gun, and by the time he thought of it the top of his head blew off when there was a soft *plop* from the landing. The Cobra almost lived up to his name, spinning with snakelike speed, his body lunging to one side while he tried to identify and aim for his target. The apparition had anticipated him and the second *plop* took away his gun, hand and all. The third went into his mouth and made a weird painting in blood and brains on the pale green wall behind him.

He took off the gas mask and wiped the sweat from his face, then put it back on again. No reason to take chances. It would be another five minutes before the ventilators cleared the stuff out enough for safety. He looked at his watch, waiting until the time was up, then slid the mask off and stuck it under his belt.

Ten minutes later the intercom on the stand clicked on and Leon Bray said, "The car ready, Lupe?"

"All set," he said in a voice that matched that of the body on the floor.

The pencil-thin line of light from under the door dimmed, a set of latches clicked and Leon Bray came out, a briefcase under one arm. He used a key to turn one final lock before he turned around, ready to tell his bodyguard to take him home.

He tried to scream, but a vicious backhand chop caught him in the throat and the scream stayed paralyzed in his lungs. He hit the wall, started to slide to the wall, his instinct for survival making him claw the Beretta out of the kidskin shoulder holster he wore. For a moment he thought he had won and felt a flash of triumph deaden the pain in his chest.

It was only the briefest of flashes. The other hand that wrapped around his was too strong and it turned the Beretta in against his sternum and the twisting motion forced his own finger to squeeze off the leaden pellet that penetrated bone and flesh, hit his spine and ricocheted through the aorta.

He knew his keys were being taken from his pocket, but death was too imminent to cause him any concern. The door beside him was unlocked, the three sticks of dynamite carefully positioned and a lit match held to the tip of the length of slow-burning fuse.

Baldie Foreman laid down his cards and said, "Gin."

Across the table, in the shabby furnished apartment, Vito Bartoldi penciled in the score and tallied it up. "I still got you," he told his partner. He picked up the cards ready to deal again, then looked at the cheap alarm clock propped on the empty chair. "What's the matter with them damn fags? They shoulda called by now."

"You better watch yourself with those two, Vito."

"What the fuck did the Frenchman have to bring them up here for anyway?"

"They got talent. I wouldn't wanna mess with them unless I had a chopper in my hands. We had a couple like that in Korea. The pissers usta hold hands in formations and made it in the same sleeping bag. Their Looie never bothered 'em. Damnedest killers I ever saw. Regular butchers and they loved it. Blood got 'em all sexed up. Y'know, they both got decorated."

"Well, they oughta called. They're ten minutes late."

"So Bray's working overtime."

"Bray's a fuckin' machine. He never goes overtime."

"Then call 'em. That's what they pay us for. To check."

Vito threw a nervous glance at the clock again and tossed the cards on the table. He picked up the phone, dialed the building a half block away and heard the phone ring in his ear a dozen times. "No answer," he said.

"Hang up and try again. Maybe you got a wrong number."

He held the disconnect bar down, released it and tried again. The results were the same. "Something's wrong," he said.

They didn't waste time trying to think about it. They both jumped up, yanked on their coats as they ran and cut diagonally across the street toward the building that had been so recently renovated. Nobody answered the bell, so Baldie used his key and unlocked the door, hoping it was a mistake and the fags had forgotten the routine.

But the door only opened a few inches. He had to push it the rest of the way because of the bodies that blocked the way and all he could say when he looked at the horror on the floor was *"Son of a bitch!"* He said it again when they stood on the next landing looking at the inert figures of Ollie, Matt Stevenson and Woodie, who lay there with blank staring eyes and mouths contorted in agony, their hands still clutching their own dead throats. The shattered remains that had once been a paper-thin glass container meant nothing to them and they both crunched the fragments underfoot as they went up to the next level with the automatics in their fists held ready to fire.

They saw the body of Leon Bray too, but it wasn't the deaths that bothered them as much as what Frank Verdun was going to say. They were still thinking about it when they went into the office, hoping that somebody would be there that they could kill that could make up for their own laxity.

Both of them were so tense that they didn't recognize the smell of burning powder until they got close to its source, and just as Baldie tried to yell for them to get the hell out of there the spark hit the charge and the two hoods dissolved into chunks and shreds of multi-colored material mixed with metal and bits of paper.

Ten minutes later the fire department was hosing down the area and the police were herding the occupants of the other buildings to safe places. The only reporter on the scene happened to have an idea of what the building had been used for. He took off for the nearest phone and called the city desk.

7

She was about to open the door of the cubicle in the ladies' room when she heard the two cleaning women come in and the fat one who worked on her floor say, ". . . and that Manny of mine should keep his big mouth shut, I told him. Because he's in that fancy Newhope Restaurant and sees her there with somebody he knows is no reason to call her boss."

When she heard the word "Newhope" Helen Scanlon's hand froze on the latch. That was where Gill Burke had taken her the night before last.

"So four calls he makes and he still can't find the man," the voice went on. "I keep saying, 'Manny, mind your own business,' and he tells me to shut up. His own mother yet he tells to shut up."

No, Helen thought, he didn't reach Frank Verdun because he hadn't been in the office and never gave a number where he could be reached. But he'd be in now because he always got in before everybody else. She waited until they were through changing the paper towels in the racks, gave them a few minutes to be out of sight, then walked down to her office.

None of the others were there yet, but she heard Frank Verdun's voice on the phone in the other room and he seemed all upset about something. She made the decision quickly and when the Frenchman was off the line, she knocked and walked in. "Mr. Verdun?"

He looked at her without feeling. "Yes?"

"Something strange happened that you should know about."

"Oh? What's that?"

"Before I left the other day I had a call from Mr. Burke . . . the one who caused all that . . . damage outside. He wanted to take me to supper."

The Frenchman kept on looking at her, his eyes flat.

"You had already gone, so I couldn't tell you about it, so I went ahead and made the date to find out what he was up to."

"Gill Burke," Verdun mused. His eyes weren't so flat any more.

"Yes. He was quite friendly. We had supper together."

"And did you find out what it was all about?"

"He wanted to know about you."

"Mr. Burke knows about me."

"I gathered as much. He wanted to know more, particularly as pertains to Boyer-Reston—who comes to the office, the nature of your conversations."

"And you told him . . ."

"What I told him was flushable, if you know what I mean."

For the first time Frank Verdun allowed himself a smile. "What did you think of Mr. Burke?"

"One thing," Helen told him, "he's a cop."

"True."

"He's on a definite assignment and that assignment concerns you."

"That's a pretty positive statement."

"Please don't forget that I lived with a policeman father for a long time. I *know* them . . . their ways, their habits, all the little wrinkles they try to pull. I even asked Mr. Burke some questions myself, but he evaded them very nicely. I wish I could tell you more."

"No, that's sufficient," the Frenchman said. "I appreciate your loyalty, Helen. I take it you don't approve of policemen."

She turned on a look he couldn't miss because Frank Verdun was a perfect reader of faces. Nobody could fool him or fake him out with an act no matter how expert they were and now he was absolutely satisfied with what he saw . . . the distaste, the disgust and all the hatred that was inside himself. Her expression was real.

And it was. The only thing the Frenchman didn't

know was that she wasn't thinking of Gill when he asked the question. She was thinking of Frank Verdun sitting on the other side of the desk.

The Frenchman didn't need an answer at all. He said, "Tell me, my dear, did Mr. Burke ask to see you again?"

"Yes, he did. I said I'd think about it. I didn't want to make it obvious either way."

"Supposing you take him up on it the next time he calls."

Helen hesitated, frowning. "Do you think that's very practical? Don't you think he'd suspect I was trying to draw him out?"

"Mr. Burke is a supreme egotist," Verdun told her. "He isn't capable of believing that he could be used by anyone, far less a woman."

She stayed calm and bit into her lip. "Well . . . I don't know . . ."

"There will be a bonus in your paycheck from now on," he said.

She made herself smile and nodded. "All right, but if he comes on too strong I'm going to cut out. There are a few things I don't want to get involved with."

"I understand," he said. "And thank you, Helen."

When she left he picked up the phone and relayed orders for that shithead Manny Roth to get a working over as a reminder to keep his lip shut. Any creep like that who would get the hots by blowing the whistle on one of his people would do it to him too. When Manny got out of the hospital he could start unloading trucks over at the Philly warehouse.

He looked at the closed door and barely smiled again. That Helen Scanlon was some doll. He felt annoyed at himself for even listening to that Manny Roth crumb.

The city editor of the morning paper had taken the gamble after a pair of expensive, discreet and immediate inquiries were made into the probable owners of the blasted building and the early edition hit the streets with a banner *GANG WAR* headline that even scooped the early TV broadcasts. The police hadn't given out any identification of the bodies they found, but a knowledgeable resident of the area knew the score and passed it on in exchange for fifty bucks. With Jan and Lucien spotted, a quick check on the rest of Leon Bray's personal entourage opened up other possibilities and what was hinted as being speculative was actual fact.

Robert Lederer threw the paper halfway across the room and strode toward the leather chair banging his fist into the palm of his hand. "Damn it, Commissioner, how can we help it if somebody pulls the cork like that?"

The burly guy in the black topcoat glared at him. "You should have had that place under surveillance."

"We didn't know it was *there*. It had only been in operation a couple of weeks."

"Somebody knew it was there."

"Look, this can be an internal uprising and . . ."

"Shit, man, don't try to con me. It's a damn gang war like the paper says it is. Something's happening to the goddamn syndicate and we don't know what it is. They got so many frigging bodies laying around they haven't got room to bury them and we got the public bugging everybody from Albany to Washington to go after us for inefficiency." He looked at Captain Long and the two inspectors beside him. "How many arrests have you made?"

One inspector said, "Plenty, but they don't connect up with this mess."

"Nobody knows anything, I suppose?"

"That's right, Commissioner."

"Don't you use informers any more?"

"They don't know any more than we do."

"And nobody even has a single idea. Great, just great."

"We have a lead," Bill Long said abruptly. "Not much, but it's an angle."

"Well?" The commissioner's voice was terse. He was tired of getting excuses for answers.

"That body we got in Prospect Park . . . part of the mutilation was similar to that on a couple of other bodies a long time back. We sent Peterson out to Chicago and he called back with some information he dredged up about a guy they called Bingo who had a thing about people's navels. He couldn't stand them. He hasn't been seen around about six years."

"Beautiful," the commissioner said, "an absolute revelation. You're looking for a guy nobody's seen for six years who hated navels. Wouldn't the papers love to get hold of that."

Bill Long had to grin. It did sound pretty foolish, but there was something spooky enough about it to be true, too. "At least we'll know when we get the right guy."

"How's that, Captain?"

"Because he sliced his own navel off when he was a kid," he told him.

It was enough for the commissioner. He dropped the stub of his cigar in the half-empty coffee cup and walked out of the room. Before either one of the inspectors could speak, Lederer turned on Bill Long sharply. "Where did you pick up that tidbit?"

"From your own boy, Robert." When Lederer didn't answer he explained, "Gill Burke."

"All right. What do you think?"

"It's the only thing that makes sense so far. We've had weirder things pay off before."

"Mr. Lederer."

"Yes, Inspector?"

"What kind of cooperation is your department getting from the other cities?"

"Total."

"But nothing's come in?"

"Everybody's drawing a blank," Lederer said. "Some of the heavies in the mob have hit the mattress, the big names are surrounding themselves with soldiers and a few have dropped out of sight entirely. We do know the big board has called a meeting, but we don't know where or when just yet."

"So the only thing we got is a navel freak," the inspector said.

"Let's hope it works out. Meeting's adjourned, gentlemen."

The three cops said so long and filed out to the corridor. Down by the elevator the commissioner was laughing at something Richard Case had said and they waved so long to him too when they got in the down car. Case's words hadn't been audible, but there was something in the tone the cop couldn't stand at all. The guy was a powerhouse, all right, both politically and economically, and he was always buddied up to people who had the right connections, but there was still something there, a subtle greasiness whose rancidity only an old pro could begin to detect. After the door closed Long said, "That Case is a pain in the ass."

"Don't knock him," the tall inspector told him. "He helped push through the pay raises."

"I still don't have to like him for it," Long grumbled.

Mark Shelby had gotten where he was by combining his knowledge with shrewd business acumen, guided by some primitive instinct and hunches that really were almost instantaneous computations of all the other factors. When he left for Helga's it was always by a circuitous route that gave him ample opportunity to see if he was being followed and he was smart enough to alternate his course so as not to set any definite pattern.

The organization had its own network of internal surveillance and he remembered what had happened to Victor Petrocinni and he wasn't about to take any chances. Being so close to the top of Papa Menes family group, he wasn't expected to expose either himself or the power structure to flaws in his character, especially by establishing a more or less permanent liaison with

Helga. The rules were simple enough. Get laid if you have to, but do it quick and get out. There were plenty of approved whores the family made available in safe quarters where you could douse the flame and get back to business.

But Helga was a flame he couldn't douse, a burning fire that scorched him a year ago and kept getting hotter every day. In the wife he kept at home, comfortably ensconced in the big house with all its expensive clutter, there was no fire at all, just a constantly harping voice that droned on and on from pursed lips set in a flabby face over a flabbier body. She still got undressed in the closet and the last time he had seen her naked, an accidental viewing by way of a partially opened bedroom door and a full-length mirror, he almost threw up.

Helga was his dream. His wet dream, his real living dream, and regardless of the rules, she was an absolute necessity in his life and right then he was on the way to see her.

No one was aware he was leaving the office nor saw where he went. In the basement he put on the padded topcoat, the old hat and picked up the umbrella. It was always easier in the rain with the umbrella shielding his face. Nobody would have taken him for the immaculately dressed executive whose offices took up the entire top floor of the building.

Four blocks away he took the crosstown bus and sat in the back where he had a clear view of the street behind him, got off at the corner where Guido, his cousin, had the grocery store, went in and changed again and took the cellar exit leading to the alley that ran into the adjoining block and walked east until he waved a cab down.

He felt satisfied and secure.

He had paid no attention to the old man with the paper bag under his arm who had been scrounging through the garbage pail in the end of the alley. He never knew it had taken the old man almost six months of patient waiting, step-by-step following and careful anticipation to get this far. But time was the only thing the old man had, that and the monthly check that supplemented his meager pension. Right now he had a little luck going for him too, because he had managed to catch the last three digits of the cab's license number as it went by to stop for Mark Shelby.

When she heard the key in the lock, Helga smiled and lounged back in the couch, arms spread out across the back, the front of the yellow shortie nightgown clasped only in one spot below her half-exposed breasts, her legs twisted so Nils would be able to see all of her in such a delicious pose he would tear his clothes off right there at the door and screw her in a magnificent animal fashion before he even said hello. She was wet and ready and her belly was starting to quiver.

Then she saw Mark close the door and the quiver turned into a monstrous spasm of fear that squeezed out a gentle fart nobody heard but her. But Helga was a good actress. If Mark hadn't been an even better audience he might not have overlooked the flaw in her performance, but that one sight of her, and the way she came across the room to meet him, all tanned thighs and bouncing breasts, to greet him with a tongue-thick kiss, wiped out all his thoughts except one. She was there ready for him at any time and his system was screaming for release.

"You didn't call first," she teased him. "I didn't even make the bed ready."

He nipped at her neck and ear lobe, his hands feeling and kneading her breasts before running down to her buttocks. "Who the fuck needs a bed?"

Helga laughed playfully and grabbed his hand to lead him inside. "Then you need a drink."

"The hell I do."

She pushed him down on the couch. "Not to get you aroused, you beast." She looked down at the swelling under his trousers. "To cool you off just a little. You are always too fast and never enjoy me when you come in like that. The next time I will wear my old ski suit and you won't get so worked up."

Mark grinned at her and said, "Okay, make a drink."

She grabbed him with one hand, fondled him gently until his eyes shut, then picked up the phone and dialed.

Helga had figured out a system too. Nils didn't like it, but it wasn't his choice. Right now she was hoping she would catch him in time. After the fourth ring she began to worry, then Nils' breathless voice came on and she said, "Lowery's Liquor Store? Good. Please to send up one bottle of scotch whiskey and one of vodka."

Nils said, "That bastard. I was just leaving to go over there."

"Yes," she told him. "Quarts." She gave her name and address and hung up.

"How come you ran out of booze?"

She sank down beside him. "How come you drank it all the last time?"

His hand ran up her leg and nestled in the soft, furry place between her thighs. She pushed him away with a teasing gesture. "You wait until we both have our drinks or I won't show you something I thought of."

"Do it now."

"No. The boy will be here in a minute."

It was closer to five minutes and when Nils handed the liquor in as all had been planned out, she gave him a twenty-dollar bill and said, "Thank you, and keep the change."

Nils whispered something foreign and nasty and she closed the door on him. It had been close, much too close. Now she would have to do something distasteful to Mark Shelby she had been saving as a surprise for Nils. She rationalized, figuring that a practice session would help her perfect the trick. Of course, with Nils it would be easier because he was much bigger than Mark Shelby, but it would hurt more, though. Not much, just a little, and it would be a pleasant kind of pain.

"You sure?" the Frenchman said.

Erik Schmidt ran his fingers over his thick, graying mustache and nodded. "No two ways about it, the Germans stopped making that gun in nineteen-forty because it required too much hand work on the components. The slugs were all a special alloy and they weren't diverting any priority metals into the sporting industry. Right now the gun itself is a collector's item."

"How many do you think are around?"

"The factory lists only three hundred produced. I doubt if more than six are in this country. An advertiser in a gun magazine has been offering three grand for a model the past year and hasn't had any offers yet."

"And the bullets?"

"Crocker was the only one who had them. If that ballistics cop hadn't checked by my shop with the spent slug I never would have known about it, but I spotted that special alloy as soon as I saw it. I even ran a spectro test to be sure. I told the cop I couldn't help him and I'll be damned if I know of anybody who can. They were hitting all the gunsmiths and I wised up Crocker to fake them out and started running down that lead right away."

"Tell me again," the Frenchman said.

"Sure." He lit a cigarette and sat back with the butt dangling from his lips, making it bob as he spoke. "Crocker had one box of those shells in his shop since the end of the war. This guy came in and bought six of them at a buck apiece. Crocker tried to talk to him about the gun, but all he said was that he had had it for a long time and the way crime was going up, he thought he ought to put some bullets in it. He remembered him, all right, a tall guy who needed a haircut, had on an old raincoat and wore eyeglasses. The thing that got Crocker though, was that he didn't look old enough to be having a gun after the last war."

"I see."

Schmidt grinned, puffing on the cigarette. The Frenchman wished those damned foreigners would use their hand when they smoke. "There's something even better," Schmidt said. "He had a bandage on his left forearm that came off while he was looking at the slugs. Under it was a scab that covered a fresh tattoo."

Verdun's eyes went bright. "He get a look at it?"

"No, but it was about the size of a quarter and could have been a star. He wasn't sure."

"That's good enough," the Frenchman told him. "You'll be getting a check in the mail."

Schmidt left and Verdun sat down at the phone. It was better than good enough. There weren't that many tattoo parlors around and they'd be able to cover every one of them from coast to coast within twenty-four hours. He picked up the receiver, got his party and issued the instructions. The wheels of the great machine ground into action.

It was hot, humid, the damned air conditioner in the sedan wasn't working right, and Papa Menes was aggravated at having to go to Homestead to get tied in on a conference call with the big board where he had to listen and talk instead of being able to see people face to face and challenge expressions that could reveal motives and desires. He reached the coin booth five minutes before the prescribed time and went in and made believe he was making a call, his finger on the receiver cradle so nobody could tie up the line.

The call lasted twenty-five minutes, during which time he learned where the shaky areas were with the new generation of punks, who, sensing the disruption of the organization, had disregarded the respect they should have shown, put away the fear they should have known, and had begun edging in where they didn't belong. No one group had shown its hand yet, but it was beginning to take off its glove to operate more sensitively. The board wasn't at all pleased with the New York affair. The loss of Leon Bray and the infinite amount of information he had had at his command was immeasurable and they hoped Mark Shelby would be able to duplicate everything with the help of Papa Menes, and their *hope* was tantamount to an imperial order of a tyrant ruler with only one penalty for failure.

Papa Menes assured them Shelby would have no difficulty. He was, after all, their own protégé, with a remarkable memory, and although he never kept any incriminating records, he would have sufficient coded notes to work from. He, Papa Menes, would see to it. Meanwhile, the whole thing might break wide open faster than they realized since the Frenchman was personally conducting a search for the person who could point the way.

When he hung up he spat out something dirty at the phone wishing the bastards at the conference table could hear it. Fucking pigs, he thought. The New York operation accounted for as much as all the rest put together and he had run it efficiently for more years than most of them had lived and here they were laying the threat on him. Those cocksuckers wanted to try him out and they were going to get a mouthful bigger than they could handle. Ten years ago he had seen it coming when they gave him that birthday party in Chicago and he had prepared for it. He had his own people right inside their most protected places and they still didn't know about it. Let it come to a showdown and they'd know what a gang war was really like.

It's just too bad, he thought, that he didn't let Joey Grif fire a bazooka rocket right into that damn room while he was on the phone with them. Joey was right across the street on the top floor of a building just two stories lower than the one where the conferences were held in supposed safety, but the angle of elevation had already been carefully calibrated and Joey sure wanted to shoot that bazooka.

Papa Menes smiled at the thought and felt better. He was still in control and could prove it with one call to Joey at the right time. They were pretty close to Miami and he wondered if they ought to go into the city and look up a couple of girls. That last one had been pretty damn good. On second thought, he wasn't all that young any more and had to ration his hard-ons. He'd hate to get all mentally aroused and only have a limp dick frustrate him. Yeah, he'd wait another day or two, then really stuff it to that broad. She really liked it up the ass and when they liked it, he liked it better too.

He told Artie Meeker to take him home.

"You thought fast, Helen," Gill told her.

"I had to. I was pretty sure somebody had already reached him and I didn't want him putting it to me. Right now he thinks he has a loyal company girl working for him."

"Has he?"

"As long as they pay my salary I keep the legitimate workings of Boyer-Reston confidential. Nobody has subpoenaed me or has me on a witness stand."

"That's the way it should be."

"But I don't have to live with them."

"You don't have to stay there either," Gill said.

"Don't be funny. What would I offer anybody else in the way of references?"

"Guess you have a point there. Any action in the office right now?"

"Not the kind you would expect. Mr. Verdun came in long enough to get something out of the safe and left. He didn't say when he'd be back. He had no calls and no visitors since. All we've been doing is sending out invoices and taking orders." She paused, her eyes worried. "Gill . . . what's happening?"

"You read the papers."

"Is it . . . really like that?"

"People keep saying there is no Mafia. No such thing as organized crime either." Burke let a wry grin play around his mouth and took a long pull on his cigarette. "I wonder why all the biggies have their armies out while they stay in the bunkers. They've been chewing up the phone lines trying to find out which one of them is doing the pushing and all the alliances are being strengthened. They have couriers and spies strung out from one coast to another and you can damn well bet there is one hell of a price up for the brains behind the revolt."

"What's going to happen?"

"You can never tell. They'll probably close their ranks on an individual basis until they know for sure what's going on. Otherwise they'll just hole up somewhere while their pros tackle the job. Nothing different from any other revolutionary tactic."

"But the police . . . they're protecting them. The papers said. . ."

"Protective surveillance to forestall any trouble. Too damn many citizens can get in the way of stray bullets if they start shooting, and believe me, it'll start before long."

"Gill . . ."

"What?"

"Take me home. Please?"

"Okay," he told her. "Mind if I make a stop first?"

"No, I don't mind."

When he pulled up at the curb outside the pawn-shop, she glanced at him curiously at first, hiding a smile. "Are things really that bad?"

He patted her thigh with a laugh. "Cop business, honey. I'll only be a minute."

"I was only kidding."

"You'd better hope so."

The broker was selling a battered guitar to a long-haired kid and Gill waited until the transaction was completed before he walked over to the counter. "Evening, Mr. Turley."

A natural suspicion clouded the owner's eyes and his tongue ran over his lips. "Officer . . . do we have to go through that whole thing again? I was just about to close up and . . ."

"A little early tonight, aren't you?"

"My wife wants to go out."

"Well, I'll only take a minute of your time."

"So take."

"It isn't easy to forget details of a holdup, I guess."

"No? You ever get held up? You get somebody waving a gun and you're supposed to remember?"

"How was he waving it?"

"Like he was going to use it, that's how!"

"Okay, take it easy. Just what did he say?"

"Oh, mister, come on."

"He didn't just stand there."

"For me to give him my money is what he says. He's all drunk and I can hardly understand him, only that gun says plenty."

"Don't you usually hand it over?"

"What else you expect with somebody pointing a gun?"

"You've had a pistol license for ten years. Where do you keep it?"

The guy shrugged and pointed with his thumb. "On the bottom shelf."

"Not very handy, is it?" Gill asked.

"My neighbor, Mr. Koch, he says I should have it. So I get it and there it stays. It's better I just give over the money. Guns I know nothing about."

"But Proctor was drunk, you said. You couldn't fake him out or anything?"

"You think I wanted to *shoot* somebody?"

"You thought he was going to shoot you. It's a good

enough excuse to make a try to save your own skin."

"Mister . . . that cop came in. I didn't *have* to. Maybe if he didn't . . ."

He made a "who knows" gesture and Gill said, "Yeah, I guess you're right." He turned toward the door, seeing Helen in the car reflected in the angular glass window and wondered why the hell he was bothering with it all anyway.

When he started the engine she asked, "Do any good?"

"I think I drew a blank."

"Think?" she queried.

"It looks like that," he told her.

She laid her hand over his on the steering wheel. "Then it's because it is, or it's supposed to," she said.

For a few seconds he just sat there, then his mouth worked itself into a grim smile and he looked at her. "That's the kind of talk that can get you kissed," he said.

"Can we wait until we get home?"

"Just barely," Gill told her.

A rising sense of annoyance had Helga on edge. She had given Mark Shelby everything he had demanded of her, plus a little extra, and instead of leaving as he usually did, he had slept for six hours making it impossible for her to keep her date with Nils. Not only that, but after he had called his answering service and gotten a message, he was aggravated enough to give her two solid smacks across the face to get her out of the bedroom while he phoned in private. The inside of her mouth was cut and she was hoping that she wouldn't get another black eye.

For once she felt like picking up the extension to see what it was all about, but she knew very well that if Shelby even suspected her of doing that he'd whip her hide raw with his belt. Or worse. There was something about Mark Shelby that really terrified her but why a wholesale grocer from Trenton, New Jersey, could do that, she couldn't understand.

Instead, she went to the bar and made herself a light drink. She sure would like to do something nasty to him, though. Maybe someday she'd light that damn candle under the religious statue on the back bar that he made her keep there. She'd burn it all the way out and . . . then a smile cracked across her swollen lips and she looked at the mirror behind the bar. She had a better idea. She'd take his holy candle that had such an interesting size and shape, maybe round the end off a little and lubricate it well, and when Shelby wasn't there she'd use it on herself while she conjured up her sexual fantasies and make herself come a dozen times, at least. Then, when she was good and mad, she'd tell him what she'd done with his religious paraphernalia and walk out with Nils.

She reached out to touch the waxen form and didn't hear him come into the room until he said, "Get the hell away from that."

Her smile and pert glance completely eclipsed her thoughts. "It reminds me of you, my love."

It appeased his male ego enough so he let the matter

drop when she brought him a drink. A fleck of blood still stained the corner of her mouth. "I hurt you?"

She reached up and patted his face. "You know I like it when you beat me. Only aren't there better places to hit than my face? It makes it difficult for me to do best what you like most."

He yanked a couple of hundred-dollar bills out of his pocket and shoved them in her hand. It was the only answer he knew how to give. He knew how stupid he was to treat her like that, but he was sure one fucking lucky bastard to have a broad like her around who could take it. Without her he'd flip, and right now, of all times, he had to stay cool as ice and just as slippery. Even the trouble was working for him and if things kept on, and went even a little bit further, he'd be at the exact positioning of time and place to attain the goal he had set for himself that evening ten years ago.

When Shelby finished dressing he kissed Helga on the side of her neck and took the elevator down to the street. He walked to the corner, waited until a cab came by and gave the driver the Frenchman's address. Let Frank Verdun issue the orders and if anything got screwed up, Frank could take the responsibility. Frank would want to use his own men and that would keep him out of it altogether. Hitting a cop was a delicate job.

8

She relaxed on the bed in total languor, naked and satisfied, feeling Gill's hand stroking the smooth contours of her body. She murmured and rolled her head to lay in the muscular hollow of his shoulder. The lingering pleasure of the past hour made a tremor go down her thigh and his fingers, sensing it, kneaded her flesh gently.

Never before had it been like this, she thought. Never so beautiful, so good, so strong. Never had it been her own emotional demand . . . no, that was the wrong word . . . her desire that led her into the wild gyrations of love that were so incredibly sensuous she could hardly believe that it was part of her own self.

At fourteen she had been indoctrinated into sex by a street punk who liked to be called Killer Miller, who had attacked her in the vestibule of their own apartment. When Joe Scanlon caught up with him in the parking lot of the supermarket it took four men to drag him off a pulpy body so mutilated and so brain-damaged that when Killer Miller was released from the hospital seven months later they all called him Silly Millie.

There were no screams of police brutality in those days, either.

At eighteen sex was something Kiernan said was part of love and she fought down the horror and the sickness because she believed him until he dumped her for the big-chested nymphomaniac who ran the liquor store on Broadway.

At twenty-two sex became a necessity to sign a contract, see her name in the gaudy lights outside the theaters or any place the agents and managers decided to book her and she learned to accept it as she would a bad dream, closing her mind off from the experience and completely forgetting about it afterward. She had neither wanted it nor sought it. Actually, she had avoided it, learning all the tricks possible that could void a man before he could culminate his intent, even to the point where they blamed themselves for their own overexuberance rather than her expertise.

Never, never before had it been like this.

The wetness was still there, the satisfied glow in her body that centered directly in the full brunette triangle that was the apex of all her immediate being. Her breasts quivered with delight and a dreamy exhaustion seemed to flow from her fingers to her toes.

Gill felt it too, letting his thoughts drift through the smoke from his cigarette. He didn't know whether he liked it or not, because for the first time there was an infringement on his perfect sense of independence. Always, he had been alone, capable of independent and solitary action, accountable to no one. He had never known a *want* that he couldn't dismiss, never known anything he couldn't do without.

Now there was something clawing at him he didn't understand and wondered why her warm flesh felt so damn good under his hand and why he was beginning to get a fullness in his groin again when he should have been completely worn out.

No, he told himself, it had happened much too late. The button had already been pushed and the missile was flying. You don't try to board after the launch. If you did, you'd be dead, and he didn't want that to happen to her.

He stubbed his butt out and took his hand away slowly. "I have to leave, Helen."

She put her arm through his and held on tightly. "It's too late." Her voice was drowsy.

"I have work to do."

"Tomorrow."

He kissed her gently. "Now, you gorgeous doll."

She let her eyes drift open and looked at him. She wished she could see more than just the outside. She wanted to know everything about him, everything inside his mind and body. But too many years had gone into building the same kind of facade her father had had and the inscrutable mask that shielded all those things was too opaque to dislodge.

"Say it again," she asked.

"Now?"

"No, the rest."

"Beautiful doll."

"I like that," she said.

She watched him get dressed, snap the holster on his belt and slip into his jacket. In the half light of the room he looked huge and she could still imagine the weight of him on her and inside her. It was all new and so different that she quivered again.

"You'll be back?"

"How can I stay away?"

"You could if you wanted to."

"I don't want to. In a way, I wish I did, but I don't want to."

"I understand," Helen said.

"No, you don't at all."

The delightful quiver suddenly had a cold chill to it and she knew how Mother must have felt when Joe Scanlon had to get up in the middle of the night to do what he had to do.

Nobody had to tell the Frenchman the score. What he didn't know already he had been briefed on, but when events that should have stayed buried came back to throw a ghostly shadow over the vital workings of the organization his life was dedicated to, he felt annoyance turn to wrath at the bunglings of the incompetents who tried to take on assignments better left to the experts.

Half the night had been spent going over the details until he was satisfied that everything was in order, and now the scotch was beginning to blur his vision and make him forget he was in New York for a more primary purpose than having one ex-cop eliminated.

As long as Gill Burke had been off the force he hadn't constituted a menace, but now he was a fucking badge-carrying piece of officialdom whose death could initiate an investigation they didn't need at all. He was a nuisance when he had directed all his efforts at getting the top syndicate men, but the ones he had nailed they could afford to lose and twice they had dropped pretty well-known troublemakers in his lap. If they had stopped there and promoted him to a desk job like they thought they would have, there would have been no more trouble at all. Paperwork can grind any machine to a halt. But they didn't and Burke kept pushing until he hit such a sensitive nerve in trying to nail down Mark Shelby that they had to take away his teeth. Luckily, he provided his own grease and built his own skid. All they had to do was give him a shove and bureaucracy did the rest.

Now he was back pushing again and that fucking overeducated Shelby was getting the jumps because Burke had picked up where he left off and Mark didn't trust the cover they had laid out for him. Frank Verdun didn't like Shelby in the first place. Him and that *Primus Gladatori* shit because he had punched a few holes in a handful of guys. The old dons liked it, but he had quit counting the bodies so long ago that Shelby looked like a damn amateur.

Asshole. The Frenchman thought. Knocks off two Jew photographers because he thought they had taken pictures of him and some cunt. They had plenty of that stuff in their files, but Shelby wasn't in any of it. They were working in the room next to his in that fucking flea-bag hotel and that hole in the wall came from a slug that drunken sailor had let loose the week before.

Now they had to tap out Burke before he could get too nosy. That was always the trouble. No matter how you tried, you couldn't kill everybody involved. Somebody always had a little piece and if somebody was nosy enough and smart enough, he could put those pieces together. It was law-and-order time with soft courts and liberals all over the place protecting this right or that, but with a guy like Burke all that was a lot of garbage and if he was satisfied the pieces fit he'd go in shooting and take his chances with an explanation later.

And they couldn't afford to scratch Mark Shelby. The dons still had the power and they raised him from a pup to mind their affairs. He had made his bones and made their millions and he was still their boy and boys had a way of getting into trouble once in a while and he was supposed to take care of it.

He'd like to give Mark Shelby, *Primus Gladatori,* one swift boot in his tail and shove a gun barrel down his throat far enough to make him gag. Except that Papa Menes or the big board might order his balls dipped into a pan of boiling water for his arrogance and he didn't want that at all. Not since he had seen it done to Malone, his Irish upstart predecessor.

The Frenchman picked up the phone and tried to call Slick Kevin for the ninth time. The phone rang until he tired of the buzz in his ear and he slammed it down, cursing. He didn't need it, but he was annoyed as hell, so he poured a shot of scotch over two cubes of ice and sat down in front of the TV set that was running the late, late movie and thought about his plan for killing Gill Burke.

The more he thought about it, the less he liked it. Then he remembered something special and smiled to himself. Yes, the board would like this one. He could walk Burke right into an open grave and he'd never know how it happened . . . nor would anybody else.

Soon he'd speak to Helen Scanlon. There was no better bait than a big-titted broad with an inviting pussy who was all for the company and had such a yen for show business she'd do anything to get back in front of an audience. In due time she would disappear into a hole in the desert outside of Vegas and that would take care of it.

He picked up the phone and tried Slick Kevin one more time.

It rang for two minutes before Verdun gave up.

He could have let it ring for an hour without doing any good at all. Slick Kevin was lying on the floor not five feet from his desk where the phone was, but Kevin was dead with a single hole between his eyes, an unfired automatic in his hand and a huge section of skull like an obscene ash tray propped up against the wall near him. Stuff still dripped from it.

The move came from a strange quarter. It was premature and stupidly overt because the insurgents didn't recognize the time, money and effort that had gone into establishing the fairly new Arando family. All they saw were the openings because the big board had called in the button men from Sal Roma's territory and they filled in the vacuum with what they thought was pure, ripe power and muscled the lucrative businesses outside the pale of legality into their own sphere of influence.

They were tough, kill-happy and working in their own backyard, the kind of punks Capone used in the beginning, who didn't know how to be afraid. They were the new Gallos toppling the established thrones that had been ruled too long by age and outmoded experience. They wanted their share and they wanted it big . . . and *now*.

So they made their move and they were able to hold because the flux of Miami jelled under their hands in its newness, and they couldn't care less if Pasi Arando had been given the territory because his cousin Steve was ruling over the northwest sector or his Uncle Vitale was on the big board itself.

Herman Shanke, the big-muscled, wide-shouldered punk who hated himself because he was only five feet seven, ran the revolution with a brace of nine-millimeter Lugers, a hatred of the world and a burning ambition to revenge a paperhanger who had been dead a long time.

He liked to be called Herman the German.

Luckily for the public, the winter crowd was moving out and there were fewer bystanders around.

Uncle Vitale got a call from the big board and phoned his son Steve to tell his cousin Pasi that if he didn't put the insurrection down he'd be in trouble. By trouble he meant that he would be dead, and in this case, family connections didn't count.

Now that the big board knew where the trouble was stemming from, they were able to put things in their proper perspective. A month ago Herman the German's best friend had left for New York, the killer who had taken those independents from Cuba and eliminated the witness in the Lindstrom Company case. He had a private collection of guns, the natural instincts of a hunter and the physical abilities of a chameleon to adapt to the enviroment for protective coloration.

His name was Moe Piel.

When the various families heard of Slick Kevin's death they put the word through the right channel and every police department was alerted to look for Moe. A fifty-thousand-dollar contract was let out on Herman the German who laughed when he heard about it and tightened the reins on the Miami operation. Bevo Carmody came in with a cardboard carton of money he had lifted from the garage where the Cuban refugees had been collecting it for another assault on Castro and after giving Bevo five grand, he parceled out the rest to his few associates to begin a reconnaissance in the area of Manhattan he knew so well. Ever since that old son of a bitch

Papa Menes had had his head beaten bloody and tossed for dead in that Newark garbage dump, he had been figuring out how he was going to get even.

Now he knew.

And it was going to be easy.

They all thought he was behind the big trouble.

He wished he were.

The district attorney had taken charge himself. The pressure had blown the lid off and he was passing it on down the line. The commissioners were feeling the heat the press and TV commentators were laying on and wore an edge that was ready to slice into anybody. Robert Lederer was acting as spokesman, since his boss had run out of expletives and was sitting there glowering at the assembly of police brass and the sardonic face of Gill Burke.

"We've had two informers in Chicago for seven years," he told the group. "They were holding for something like this and nothing else. The one who passed the information on about the Miami uprising made the mistake of calling from a windowed booth where a deaf-mute lip reader we suspect of being connected with the mob could see him. He was dead an hour later. So far, they don't know about the other one, but he isn't connected high enough yet to get inside things."

The tall inspector from uptown said, "Who else has this information, Bob?"

"At this moment it's confined to this room."

"How about Miami?"

"We're assuming they're taking the same security precautions. Right now they have special detachments out covering all areas. They can't move in on Herman Shanke because they haven't anything definite to go on and they don't want to provoke a shooting spree."

One of the other inspectors asked, "Any outsiders moving in yet?"

"That's the trouble, right there. The airports and other terminals are covered, but nobody's showed. If they go in, they'll probably go by private transportation and that won't be easy to spot. It's between seasons and there's enough travel activity to conceal anything. With all the living quarters available it's going to be one hell of a job to check everything, especially if they have their own safe places to stay in."

"Chicago and St. Louis called," Bill Long told him. "They're missing some top soldiers they thought they had under surveillance. Evidently they saw this coming and had things set up."

"Miami's going to blow," Lederer said solemnly.

Gill Burke's voice was flat and quiet. "Miami isn't the place."

All the eyes swung toward him, waiting for the rest.

"Miami's just the teaser," he said. "A smart vulture waits for the beast to die before going in for the remains. The young stupid ones make an early try and get their feathers full of claws, then get eaten themselves."

"This isn't exactly the place for analogies, Burke," commented Lederer.

"Look at it this way. The action is where the money is and the money is in New York."

"The facts don't . . ."

"Frank Verdun is in New York too."

"Burke, I think . . ."

"Mark Shelby is in New York too."

Irritation drew Lederer's face into a flushed scowl. "This is not a personal affair, Burke. Damn it all, so far you haven't . . ."

Gill didn't let him finish. "How about the belly-button man, Mr. Lederer?"

Captain Long had been waiting for that and smiled. He opened the folder on his lap and said, "Denver gave us the lead and the F.B.I. confirmed it. They had three other mutilations with the navels torn out and we have an APB out for a white male caucasian, age forty-five, medium build, slightly balding, with a slightly crossed left eye. The only name we have is a probable alias of Shatzi. A definite identifying mark is a large scar where his navel formerly was. That last bit of information came from a woman he cohabited with."

"I suppose you'll have spotters in the turkish baths to look for the scar," Lederer said sourly.

"Sure," Long told him. "We're checking all the whores, too."

"When you find him, there'll be an easy way to make him talk," Burke said.

"Oh? And how is that?"

"Tell him you're going to sew his belly button back on."

The laugh that went around the room broke the tension, except for the boiling anger inside the assistant district attorney. He let it ride with a grim smile and went back to the briefing. They finished an hour later and when it was over everybody agreed they were still up in the air.

Everybody except Gill Burke, and when he had Bill Long across the table in the coffee shop he said, "One, there's a leak in the department. Two, we have a lead with this Shatzi character. Why not concentrate on those angles?"

"Why not swing at the wind? Hell, Gill, we're doing all we can, you know that."

"The lab get anything from Bray's office?"

"Plenty. Two truckloads of junk. The explosion and the fire destroyed everything. What was left of the tapes didn't make sense because they were all coded, nothing we could tie together at all."

"Well, you got something there, haven't you?"

"Like what?"

"Supposing another mob *was* moving in. They'd rather have all that information than destroy it. Bray was a key man in the organization and what he knew would give them access to practically every phase of their businesses. The syndicate is big business, pal. They don't do things in their heads any more. It's all down on punchcards and tape like the records of any other cartel."

"You got something there, kid. Got any answers to go with it?"

"Just plenty to speculate about," he said. "You ought to try it."

Long stared past his head at the faded yellow wall. "Yeah, I think I will."

The other girls in the office had been sent out on business matters and Helen Scanlon was alone when the Frenchman called her in. "Helen . . . can you take dictation?"

"Yes, certainly, Mr. Verdun."

"Good. Then get your hat and coat and we'll do it at lunch. That is, if you don't mind?"

"Not at all." She closed the door behind her and went to the coat hanger. She thought about it a minute and shrugged. It seemed a reasonable enough request, and if there was anything behind it, she'd know soon enough.

Verdun had his driver take them to a chic cosmopolitan restaurant in the mid-fifties where an accented maître d' led them to a walnut-paneled booth, took their orders for drinks and disappeared silently across the plush carpeting. Concealed speakers radiated soft semi-classical music and the conversational hum of the other patrons was almost inaudible.

Before the drinks were even served, a messenger came in, delivered an envelope to Verdun, and less than ten seconds later a waiter brought a phone to the table and told him he had an incoming call. He spoke rapidly about a Boyer-Reston venture in a new plastics industry, gave instructions to complete the merger and hung up. He told the waiter to hold all calls and lifted his drink to Helen.

"Now you see why I must combine lunch with business," he said.

Helen tasted her drink. "Yes, I certainly do."

When they ordered their meal he dictated several letters in answer to those she had put on his desk that morning, then finished when the waiter arrived with their food.

"Good?" he asked her.

"Lovely, Mr. Verdun. I've never been here before."

"One of my favorite spots when I'm in town," he said. "Tell me, how are you making out with your policeman friend?"

This was the reason, she thought. Now she could really find out.

"He's still curious, but I guess all cops are."

"Is he charming?"

She had to smile at that. "It isn't easy for a cop to be . . . charming. I've never known one who didn't have rough edges."

Verdun let out a chuckle. "They can be pretty devious, my dear."

They can be pretty direct too, she thought again. She looked at the Frenchman, busily engaged in buttering his bread, wondering what he knew. There was only one way to find out.

"I tried being a little charming myself."

He lifted his eyes quizzically. "Oh?"

"As far as I know, he's all wrapped up in this syndicate thing. All those killings."

"There isn't supposed to be a syndicate," Verdun said casually.

"Not according to him. But he didn't say much about it. We had supper, then his idea of fun was to visit a hock shop before he took me home."

"Policemen are notoriously underpaid," Verdun said. *But his mind was telling him something else. Burke*

166

had to be hit fast. He'd sure as hell like to make it a two-for-one and get that stupid Shelby at the same time, but that part was out.

They finished the rest of the meal with just a little small talk and while they had coffee he remembered one more letter and she took down a reminder to the main office to update the billing machines and install two more phone lines. The driver took them back and he disappeared behind his door where she could hear him in occasional conversations. One of the other girls transcribed her dictation while she filed the invoices, delivered envelopes from the messenger service and admitted the clients who had appointments.

At four-thirty Frank Verdun came out with a client, talking about a promotion in Arizona, walked over to her desk. "Did Mr. Clough's airline tickets come in, Helen?"

She picked up an envelope delivered by one of the messengers and handed it to him. "Ten minutes ago. The eight-ten out of LaGuardia."

The heavyset man checked his flight and stuck them in his pocket. "Thanks. Saved me a lot of trouble. Sure hate to leave this soon." He looked at Verdun, fished around in his coat and brought out a pair of theater tickets. "Maybe you can use these, Frank. Took me a month to get them and Sadie is gonna be mad as hell about missing it, but the trip is more important."

Verdun took the tickets and shook his head. "Tomorrow I'll be with the auditors." He tossed the tickets down on Helen's desk. "Here, see if anybody can use them."

When they walked out she looked at the tickets. They were good seats for the top show in town. She asked the other two girls if they wanted them, but one had seen the show and the other had a heavy date, so she stuck them in her pocketbook.

Maybe she could charm Gill Burke into taking her.

A clammy sweat beaded Mark Shelby's face. It was bad enough having to try to put back all the information that had been destroyed and the job would have been impossible if the orders hadn't been so explicit and direct. Between the old Mustache Petes and the new breed bucking their way in, there were no exceptions, no excuses, and if you couldn't cut it, they'd cut you. The more he thought about it the more fierce his anger grew, the only satisfying aspect being that the pressure wasn't going to last forever and one day they were all going to fold like deflated balloons and be swept into the fucking ash can where they belonged and he'd be the one with the pan and the broom. Damn their hides . . . they with no class, no education, no natural ability except enjoying a total lack of conscience that enabled them to let death do the ruling. Pricks. That's all they were. Fucking pig pricks. They held onto Old Country ties when they couldn't even locate Rome or Naples or Sicily on the map. They sure were going to make some funny faces when they went down. Maybe they'd even do that crazy breast-beating routine.

The thought made him feel better, but only for a second. Oh, he could put everything back together again because he had his mind and more notes than they thought he had. He'd even get bigger when they learned how it had all been accomplished and it was even conceivable that he could accomplish his goal without using his original plan.

What was screwing everything up was that damned Gill Burke, that bastard cop they should have hit and been done with instead of just shuffling off into nobody-land. Now he was back at the pawnbroker's asking questions and that lousy slob might not be able to take the pressure any more and say more than he was supposed to.

Maybe he already had!

The thought made him sweat again. He never underestimated Gill Burke, not even once, and he wasn't about to now. He had kept a check on him all the time he had been off the force and there had been no repercussions, but there was always the chance that Burke had figured it that way too and had been a little more artful than he had been. There had been time for him to puzzle it out, too, and he could have reached the right answer. The whole big board had investigated too, and they even had access to the police probe, but they had been satisfied with his story.

Nevertheless, he, the *Primus Gladatori,* wasn't completely satisfied and until he was he couldn't concentrate on what he was doing. Shelby picked up the phone and dialed Helga. He knew she had a beauty shop appointment and she was just getting ready to leave. All he did was confirm the fact, exchange a few pleasantries and tell her he'd call tomorrow. He looked at his watch, waited fifteen minutes and took his own special way out of the building.

The little old man who just seemed to be shuffling along picked him up at exactly the last point he had lost him and this time everything was working in his favor. It was no trouble at all to tail Mark Shelby to the building where he kept Helga in her luxurious apartment and when he was satisfied he found the nearest phone and made a call. A tape recorder answered and he left his final message innocuously disguised and felt a little sad that his assignment had come to an end. It had been a lot of fun, had used up his idle hours and made him a lot of friends in odd places. It was now going to bring him a sizable bonus that would finish the payment on the orange grove in the middle of Florida where he would sit in the sun until he mummified.

Mark Shelby made sure the apartment was empty and while he was checking the rooms, automatically looked through Helga's personal effects too. Whatever she had, he had given her. Except one thing. A new packet of three rubber condoms was in the back of the drawer in the nightstand table. For a second his fist clenched because if she tried fooling around with some punk on him . . . then he grinned because it was a new pack, discarded in the back, just in case her coil fell out or something like that and it was for him, not some punk.

He went out to the living room behind the bar and lifted the candle from the holder, not paying a bit of attention to the religious statue at all, took it in front of a strong light and tried to peer through it. It was too opaque to see anything, so he inspected it carefully. After five minutes he was sure that nobody had ever touched it since he had put it there.

A great weight was lifted from his mind.

He looked at the statue guarding his treasure and wondered why he didn't feel the need to genuflect or something. Maybe make the sign of the cross.

Screw that stuff, he thought. His faith was in the candle, not the statue.

He went back downstairs to retrace his route.

At that moment the message on the tape recorder was being decoded.

9

Moe Piel had come to New York again in an old panel truck that bore the labels of a Fort Lauderdale television repair service. He had driven within speed limits, stopped overnight outside of Myrtle Beach, South Carolina, and the only incident had been a flat on Route 13 in Delaware. A state trooper had even stopped to offer assistance, but when none was necessary, had driven away after a perfunctory license check.

Had he inspected the truck he would have found a tool box full of cash destined for delivery to another dealer in arms and ammunition with a warehouse on the Lower West Side of Manhattan. Unfortunately, the Delaware police had, at that time, no want out on Moe Piel or the truck, but that wouldn't have mattered anyway since his license, registration and occupation were all phony anyway. Besides, he looked like any typical television repairman having to make an emergency trip to New York to pick up parts that would take too long in shipment.

Unfortunately, too, the organization knew that if Herman Shanke were to hold on to the bite he had taken out of their Miami operations, he was going to have the weaponry to do it with and the police had clamped down in Miami to such an extent that nothing was available in that area.

Which left New York, and the organization knew about the unscrupulous dealer in arms and ammunition with his warehouse a stone's throw away from the West Side Highway.

And Bingo and Shatzi were waiting for him when he parked the panel truck in front of the old converted garage that supposedly dealt in used car parts, which wouldn't even attract a junkie burglar.

Since Moe Piel had never met the dealer, he didn't recognize that Bingo Miles didn't fit the description at all until Shatzi shoved a gun in his ribs from behind and he didn't even get the chance to go for the rod he kept in his belt to impress the city slickers when they were culminating the transaction. All he could feel was embarrassment, because down there at the tip of Florida he was one hell of a hotshot killer with his own inexhaustible supply of weapons and suddenly he was nothing but a stupid shit.

What made it worse, they thought he had dumped a whole fucking handful of big wheels and were treating him with a little respect when he didn't even know what the hell they were getting at. All he knew was that they thought he was an idiot for going out of his league to hustle ammo for Herman the German when some slob could have done the same thing. He heard them talking it over and the conclusion was it was simply a matter of expediting matters. Except that Herman wasn't *family*, nor was Moe, and they couldn't be expected to know any better.

The place wasn't soundproofed or isolated, so after they tied him up, they taped his mouth and Shatzi took out the pan, charcoal, poured in the starter fluid and stuck the irons in the works. They gave Moe Piel a pad and pencil to write with when he was ready to talk and put in a call to the Frenchman.

You really couldn't tell when Frank Verdun was mad. It was even better when you *could* tell, but when you couldn't it was worse. He had killed the best when he was at his happiest moments, savoring the ebbing away of life, his face placid and the tiniest of smiles playing around his lips. He was looking at Bingo and Shatzi like that right now.

"Look, Frank, I swear, neither Bingo or I touched him. No shit, Frank. We were waiting for you and when we looked he was like that, all drooped over and hell, the irons didn't even get hot yet."

The Frenchman yanked Moe Piel's head back by the hair and stared into the lifeless eyes. "You dumbheads!"

"Frank . . ."

"Shut up." It wasn't the first time he had seen this happen. Twice before it had happened to him and he had made a doctor explain it all in detail, and now he went through those details until he was satisfied. "The fucker's had a heart attack."

"Aw, shit Frank . . ."

"Stupid bastards. You have to put on the full show before I get here? You like it that way?"

"We only thought . . ."

"Who the hell ever told you to think, you dumb pricks? You know what this bum could have told us? We could have the backup man, the rest, the head . . . and you lousy assholes blow the whole deal."

"Come on, Frank, we was expectin' a driver. Who else? So when we see this punk we're gonna set him up for you. It always works. You know . . ."

"Shit." He looked at the two guys and let the anger ebb from him. All they did was the job the way they were used to and they couldn't be blamed at all. "Where's the dealer?"

Bingo said, "I killed him. He's in the back."

"Okay, dump them both."

"What about the truck, boss?"

"You rig it up right and send it back. Let that fucking Herman the German have some ammo, but make sure it blows up in his fucking face. You think you can do that right?"

"Sure, boss," Bingo said.

"Hey, Frank . . ."

"Now what, Shatzi?"

"Ah, nothing, boss."

The Frenchman nodded and went out in disgust. Shatzi smiled. No sense asking for something so simple. He pulled the knife out of his pocket and while Bingo was rigging the truck he cut the navels from the two bodies, looked at them with horrified eyes, then flushed them down the stained toilet.

They dumped the corpses in the Jersey meadows and sent the truck back to Florida with the big surprise for Herman the German.

The big board in Chicago was duly notified and approved the procedure, even though they didn't appreciate it. The only thing they didn't know about was the navel surgery.

She had enjoyed the show, but Gill had sat there silent beside her and never even cracked a smile, even during the most hilarious scenes of the performance. He didn't look at his watch or squirm or complain, so that's the way he probably enjoys a stage show, she was thinking.

But Gill Burke was occupied by the two bodies the Jersey police had found because they were searching the area for a lost kid, and the lab had turned up physical evidence of particles that indicated they had both been in a garage, a very old garage that stored number-one cup grease which had been out of style since World War I.

That fracas had been a long time ago and the garage had to cater to renovators of antique automobiles, or their parts, or just be plain old. They hadn't gotten a make on the corpses yet, but that would come and when the performance was over he'd have to call Bill Long to see how far they had gotten. He had tried once at intermission and they were still working on it. Well, another fifteen minutes and maybe they'd have it.

He didn't realize the curtain had come down until everybody started to leave and he remembered the present and looked at Helen. "Enjoy it?" she asked him.

"Great."

"Later I want you to tell me about it."

"Why?"

"Because I think you sleep with your eyes open."

"You know better than that."

"Do I?"

"Maybe if I had you next to me . . ."

Helen let a slow smile drift across her mouth. "He told me you could be charming."

"Who?"

"Mr. Verdun. He gave us the tickets."

The crawl started down between his legs and crossed up his belly. Everything was there and she didn't even have to tell him how accidental it all looked. Damn, he was dumb! He should have asked, should have done something. He was too preoccupied with his own thoughts and let everything go by the board.

"Helen . . ." He looked around him. The aisles were emptying fast. "Don't ask questions and do exactly what I tell you to do."

"Gill?"

"Just do it. Come on." He took her arm and edged out of the row of seats, then fought his way into the throng heading for the exits. When they were firmly surrounded he spotted a group of eight, joined them in their frenzy to flag down a cab, then beat them out with a hard shove of his left hand and shoved Helen in and got in behind her.

He told the driver where to go, kept checking behind him, but the streets of Manhattan at theater-closing time are nothing but cabs anyway and he couldn't tell if they were being followed or not. When he dropped her at her apartment he told the driver what else to do and got out four blocks away.

By the time the cab that had really followed him had reached the point he was at there was a basement stairwell handy and he dropped into it before the tommy gun went off and took the windows out of the lower floor right beside his head.

Only this time he had a two-handed grip on the .45 and let one slug off and saw the driver catch it square in the side of the head and the cab went halfway down the street before it crashed into the row of parked cars at the curb.

He wasn't fast enough to get the occupant of the back seat, but Bingo Miles was sure as hell dead in the front one.

Two hours later the disgruntled lab technicians who

had been summoned from their quiet homes had certified the fact that Bingo Miles had the same microscopic particles in his clothing that had been found on the dead men in the Jersey meadows and Robert Lederer was blue in the face because Gill Burke wouldn't tell him what it was all about.

All he'd do was grin and he couldn't even fire him, since Burke was the only one who had any inkling of what was going on. That son of a bitch renegade ex-cop was holding all the aces.

Until now, the Frenchman could never understand fear. He had seen it in others, heard it expressed, saw it demonstrated, but he never could understand it, because until now it had been part of somebody who was fearful of him. He didn't like the sensation at all. In fact, he didn't even recognize it until he vomited without being sick. He just stopped on the street and vomited like a fucking pregnant woman.

So what if that idiot Miles got himself shot? He had it all set up and instead of letting it happen he gets himself shot and that fucking Shatzi is all hyped up because his buddy gets knocked off and he's all shook because he thinks the setup went the other way. Damn it, you couldn't trust a freak when the chips went down and why he used Shatzi he'd never know. Maybe he was getting too old. He used to be able to handle the freaks, now they blew up on him and if he didn't squash that crazy bastard he'd have the whole big board climbing down his neck. He should have remembered what Lulu told him one day. "Freaks speak," she had said. He should have listened.

Okay, Shatzi, you are on the hot list now.

But Shatzi Heinkle had already figured that one out and had packed up his stuff and changed hotels. When the soldiers came to look for him, the room was cold and empty. The night clerk had not seen him go, neither had the doorman, who was half drunk.

Frank Verdun felt another quiver of fear when they told him. He didn't like what was outside there. Gill Burke was bad enough, but there was something else too.

The whole fucking organization was falling apart, he thought.

"Let's have it again," Bill Long said.

"They set me up," Burke grinned slowly. "Verdun tossed the tickets in her lap and they were able to spot my movements."

"That right, Miss Scanlon?"

"I don't know. Mr. Verdun said I could give the tickets away. I choose to keep them."

"Then you could have made the deal work."

"If you look at it that way, most likely, yes."

"Fuck you, Bill," Burke said.

"All right, it's a possibility, damn it!"

"And it stinks."

"Not from what you told me."

"You got no schmarts, pal. From the neck up, you're dead."

"What will a good lawyer make of it?"

"Nothing," Gill said. "The prosecution won't even take it into court and you know it."

"That leaves you on your own personal vendetta."

"Balls, I never had much to do with the Frenchman."

"This is now, buddy."

"Now I'll kill him," Gill said. Then added, "If he gives me the chance."

"You won't even advise him of his rights?"

"Screw the Miranda or the Escobedo decisions."

"Just like the old days, eh?"

"Correct, chum."

"Fine cop."

"Shit."

"Maybe Lederer doesn't need you any more."

"He sure does, my friend."

"Why?"

"Because I'm not the one who is running scared."

Bill Long took a deep breath and settled into his chair. He should have known better than to get into a hassle, but things weren't the same any more. "Tell me," he said, "why with all this crap and all these kills are you suddenly being the target? The whole damn Mafia doesn't suddenly pounce on you when they have something like this other thing happening to them."

Burke stood up and lit a cigarette. When he had a couple of deep drags he looked outside toward the night of the city and said, "You should have asked me that a long time ago. Or do you still want me to goad you into further speculation?"

"You know what you can do?"

"Sure," Gill smiled. He looked at Helen in the big leather chair. "But why do it myself when I have somebody else to help?"

"Out," Long snapped. "We're straining our friendship."

"How about that?" Gill told him.

In the cab, Helen reached over and took his hand. "I can't stay there any longer, Gill. I guess you know that."

"I wasn't going to let you anyway." He yanked the cigarette pack from his pocket, found it empty and tossed it out the window with an angry gesture. "That slob was just a little too cute."

"Gill . . . he *didn't* tell me to use those tickets."

"No?" He turned and studied her face a moment. "Figure it this way. He probably knew his office staff pretty well and you were the only one uncommitted. Women don't generally change their plans at the last second even for good seats at a prime show. You were a natural, baby."

"But why would he want to have you *killed?*" she asked him.

"I'm in their way."

"So are all the rest of the policemen."

"Not like I am. They got trouble enough without me."

"That's an awfully big chance they were taking then."

"And that's how they live. With the odds. They got rid of me once before and I didn't stay down so they had to rig the game again."

"Captain Long still thinks I had something to do with it."

"Not really. He's grabbing at straws. He knows the whole story."

Her hand tightened around his and her teeth nibbled at her lip. "I don't know, Gill. I think I'm beginning to get scared."

"Forget it."

"Gill . . ." She looked at him anxiously again. "It'll happen again, like last night, won't it?"

He shrugged, his face unmoving. "Maybe. But it can end the same way too."

"Oh, Gill, isn't there any way out . . . just for a little while?" There was a strange note of pathos in her voice. "Everything is going too fast. I . . . I have to get away from this!"

He ran his hand up her arm and cradled it around her shoulders. "Sorry as hell you were caught in the middle, Helen. I know that session with Bill was rough, but he had to have your statement. Look, you're finished with that damn job and all the rest of the crap. Get it out of your mind."

"Fine, but what will I do now?"

"You're going to sit back and let me take care of you."

For a second she didn't move, then she turned and looked up at him, her eyes soft. "Gill . . .?"

He fought with himself a full minute, telling himself all the things that were barriers, reminding himself of what could go wrong. He wasn't a kid any more and she had had enough of a cop's life years before. He still had something big to do that could get him killed and the whole business could expose her to something worse than she had ever known.

But that other feeling he had, the one he didn't think would ever come to him, was even stronger and he looked at her and grinned. "It's a hell of a way to put it, sugar, but that's the way it is."

She laid her head on his shoulder very gently and said, "I love you."

Gill kissed her hair, saying the same thing without words.

"Gill?"

"What?"

"It's Saturday night."

"Yeah, I know."

"Can we go somewhere for the weekend?"

He looked at his watch and frowned. "It's nine-thirty now."

"There's an awfully nice place in Jersey where it's quiet and the food is good. All the rooms have patios that look out at the hills."

"Honey . . ."

"Please?"

His arm squeezed her gently. "Okay, pest." He glanced at his watch again. "I'll drop you off, go pack some of my own things and pick you up in half an hour."

She came off his shoulder and shook her head pathetically at his ignorance. "Lover," she said, ". . . and if that's what you want to be, you had better understand women just a little better. It *has* been a rather harrowing experience and I *would* like to look my best for this particular assignation, so please, please give me an hour and a half at least."

Burke laughed because she was so damn right and he was so damn stupid. They were almost at her apartment and he leaned over to kiss her softly on her mouth. "I'll learn, kid."

She patted his cheek. "I hope so."

"But you'd better learn something too."

"Oh?"

"I wasn't thinking of this as an assignation. My suggestion of keeping you was motivated by a more permanent and basic reason."

She felt her face flush and wondered when she had ever been more happy. Never, she concluded, and went upstairs to her apartment feeling tingly all over.

Papa Menes didn't know whether to feel good or bad. All he knew was that the big board knew he was in the area where the trouble was and now they had to speculate about him turning the pot over. Miami was where the trouble was, he was only an hour's drive away, and if he weren't the instigator, then he could be the stopper in the drain. He was on the big board, but not present when the decisions were made because he had a nose for blood and he didn't want his to be part of the smell. It was much nicer to screw a tender broad up the ass and enjoy himself than to have to go through all the mayhem that had been part of his formative period and on into the chairman's seat of power where torture and murder were only spoken words you never saw executed at all.

He was there through accidental choice and now he had to take care of a jerk German who thought he could buck the power of the organization and since he knew the odds and the way, they were asking him to complete a totally menial task. The dames were on the way down and he could take care of Herman the German any time he wanted to. His soldiers had arrived, were ready to operate, and even though the Miami police were covering the whole area, his people were the only ones capable of going inside to make the hits. They were completely equipped, excellently skilled and totally dedicated.

Why the big board wanted Herman the German rubbed, he didn't know. That was an operation for any local *capo,* not the boss. But, if they wanted him to handle the deal, it was fine, fine. Very fine.

Up in New York that bastard cop Burke was giving the Frenchman all kinds of hell and he liked that too. Every time the board brought in a sex creep like the Frenchman they always had trouble. Shit, just let him have his own button men and he could do it alone, but no. They brought in Frank Verdun and ever since, the trouble got worse.

Well, they couldn't blame him. Two days, a week from now, that bum the German would be dead and the trouble would be over. A whole fucking month of trouble over a stupid German and that dead Moe Piel. Assholes.

The word brought him back to the present because

Artie Meeker was driving up with the two broads from Miami and now that he knew she really liked it, he was really going to lay it to her. No more baby oil to lubricate the thrust. This time he'd use spit and if it hurt, so much the better.

Frank Verdun had an animal instinct. He knew when he was being stalked. He could feel it in his bones and even as he walked his hand was on the gun in his pocket. The feel of it used to quiet him, but this time it didn't. It felt cold and inadequate, and no matter where his eyes went or his mind turned, there was never anybody there. He remembered Vic Petrocinni and the others, suddenly knowing how they had felt, and his stomach turned sour.

When he reached the safety of his apartment he vomited again, kneeling on the shag rug in front of the toilet bowl so as not to get any of the slop on his person. Not much came up because he hadn't eaten anything, but the terrible retching was there in his bowels and he had to let the spasms take their course. When they were over he took his clothes off and stepped into the shower.

The Frenchman came out with a hard-on like he always did after playing with himself with the soap, and feeling better, never saw the knife slash through his enlarged genital member at all. All he could do was stare before he sucked in his breath to scream. He saw the face without being able to pronounce the name behind it and the next slash of the knife took his throat completely out from beneath his chin.

He even had the terrifying experience of living through the excruciation of dying, looking up at a complete improbability and knowing no majestic reason for it at all, wondering why the hell one little worm could eat through stone walls and make them crumble like sand. He was still alive when the knife went through his certain parts with the wildest impact any mind could conjure, and all the fear blended with the pure knowledge of what he had done to those other people and he tried to scream.

But it wasn't any good at all.

What came out of that gaping slash in his throat was a big sigh and he started to die knowing, but not being able to tell.

For a long time Shatzi stared at the pool of blood that bathed the naked body, his face warped with some deep inner thoughts. In life, Frank Verdun had been a terrifying person to be obeyed or avoided, and after what the Frenchman had had done to him all those years ago, Shatzi had remained truly loyal to every whim and demand of the top enforcer. Not because of respect or devotion, but plain, unmitigated, unreasoning fear.

Now he was enjoying what he saw and a dry cackle that passed for a laugh rasped from his mouth. "You didn't have to set the soldiers on me, Frank," he said. "Verdun, you dirty bastard, Verdun, you shithead, you're finally gonna get it."

He thought he detected a slight movement of the eyelids, but he couldn't be sure. Too bad, he thought. He'd never done it when anybody had been alive before. He took his knife and carefully scooped out Frank Verdun's navel from his stomach, holding it up on the point to study it. When he looked down at the Frenchman's face his shoulders gave an involuntary twitch. Verdun's eyes were open, all the way open for one horrified second as he saw his tie to life being raised on the blade of death and his eyes filmed over as the feeble heartbeat stopped altogether.

Shatzi grinned when he saw it, pulled a dirty handkerchief from his pocket and wrapped the grisly souvenir in it. "This one I'll keep, Frankie boy," he said. "This one is special."

Gill picked up the phone on the fourth ring and barked a short hello. Bill Long said, "Thought you might like to know, we got a line on Shatzi Heinkle and it looks like it's going to pan out."

"Where is he?"

"Running, buddy. He's in one hell of a big hurry too. He cleared out of the place he was staying and right afterwards some guys came looking for him. The description we got on them matches a couple of hard cases from Brooklyn."

"Uh-huh. They got him marked. If he was the guy in the cab with Bingo they'll want him out of the way. Right now they can't afford any kinky characters going loose."

"Would Verdun let out a contract on him?"

"It sure as hell sounds reasonable."

"That's the way I figured. They should be getting there just about now to see what the Frenchman says about it."

Burke felt himself frowning. "That guy can move in a hurry too."

"Hell, we've had his place staked out all night by one of the detectives. You want in on it?"

"Not tonight, old buddy."

"What's wrong with you?"

"If I told you, you wouldn't believe me."

"I'll believe."

Gill nodded to himself. "I'm spending the weekend with Helen Scanlon. If you want me I'll be at the Clipper Inn over in Jersey."

"Oh, brother," Long said quietly as he hung up.

Burke picked up his overnight bag and went downstairs to grab a cab to pick up Helen.

Papa Menes woke up thinking of how he had penetrated the blonde from Miami. A nice willing victim, that one, fleshy and limber and hard to hold onto in that position. He knew she had loved it and he figured she was putting on an act with all that yelling and twisting, but she really didn't try too hard to get away and the few times he had given her a belt across the tanned flesh of her buttocks she had whimpered properly and had held fast while he accommodated himself.

The girl was a real pro and knew how to adjust to the customer's demands. When she realized his preference she adapted to them and performed in a proper manner, but the old fart was a real bat with a half-limp cock that couldn't go in all the way and she wasn't getting half the pleasure out of it she thought she would. Too bad, if she was like her friend who was in there with Artie Meeker getting laid in the missionary position or doing her simple oral bit, it would be much simpler. One shot and Artie was finished for a few hours, but this old fart kept plowing and plowing and he'd never get that row hoed if he didn't get his rocks off and right now she was beginning to get sore. At least he could have used the baby oil.

So to distract herself she raised her head and looked over toward the dresser. She saw the gun, but that was nothing new with these Yankee pricks. What she saw that really bothered her was the crumpled telegram on the floor below her eyes and the one word that made her anus contract so hard that Papa Menes reached his orgasm was *VERDUN.*

Her grandfather had been killed in a battle of that name. Then she remembered a guy with the same name who had almost killed her.

She was young then, much too young to have left home, but the group had convinced her she was square and above all things she didn't want to be a square so she had climbed aboard the battered Volkswagen van and handed her sixty dollars to Glen to put in the communal fund and they had taken off from Decatur to go to the lush riches of California. But somehow they had gotten pointed in the wrong direction and went southeast instead until the van broke down. They had sent her back to a garage a mile away, but the garage had been abandoned a year before and when she got back the van was still there. Not the little family, though. They were gone and they had taken her things with them too.

For an hour, she cried, then she started to walk. That was when the convertible stopped and the suave man in the sharkskin suit invited her in. She was feeling too miserable to refuse. The nearest town was twenty miles away, and the remote asphalt county road she was on didn't show any signs at all of carrying traffic. For a few miles she sniffled in self-pity and told her story.

She screamed in pain not long afterward, but the barn was a long way from anything and its walls were thick. She lay there naked, the ropes biting into her flesh, forced to do whatever pleased him, escaping the pain only by being totally submissive to his wishes, then writhing in agony as he reverted to the painful things again.

When he cut her loose she tried to crawl away, but there was no place to go and she cowered against the side of the stall where he had hung his clothes. He had dressed quickly, not paying any attention to her at all. The only thing that happened was the letter dropping from his pocket and before he retrieved it she saw the name on the envelope and that name had been *VERDUN*. She remembered being told how her grandfather had died in that place.

Until now, she had never remembered the name again.

This time she knew she'd never be able to forget it again.

10

Driving across the bridge to Jersey, Gill was quiet, enjoying the sensation of breaking free from the incessant noise and frantic activity of the big city behind him. In a way, it was like walking through a door and he felt himself wishing he didn't have to go back again. Luckily, he could adapt. There were a lot who couldn't. The city was their lifeblood, their entire being. To him it was a place he had to be until he decided he didn't want it any longer. He had been born and raised there, worked there until New York was more than just a city, it was an intimate, animated mountain of masonry with every canyon, arroyo and wash etched into his mind. The people who lived there he catalogued, cross-indexed and filed in those hidden recesses of his brain and sometimes he felt the weight of their numbers lying there like a cancer. The ones in his file were the cancers. The others were simply the reluctant hosts that fed and nourished them, only to be consumed in the end while the cancers kept growing.

"You look awfully serious, Gill."

He turned his head and let a smile flicker across his mouth. "Thinking, that's all."

"Big thoughts?"

"Not very." He stared out through the windshield. "Someday I'm going to get away from all this mess."

"When?" Helen asked softly.

"After it's all over."

"Will it ever be?"

"No. It will slow down, that's all."

She rested her hand over his on the wheel. "That's what my father used to say too."

"That's what they all say."

"Why don't they do it then?"

"Because cops are strange people, kid. Why the hell they get into that line of work I can't figure, but they do. It's something you know you're going to do long before it happens. Some come in after high school, others spend a fortune on a college education and are happy to walk a beat. They were born cops and they die cops. It's their life, I guess."

"Yes, I know," she told him.

"You don't approve, do you?"

"Somebody has to do it."

"That didn't answer my question," he said.

After a few moments passed by she nodded thought-fully, feeling the words rise she knew had been buried too long. "Yes, I do approve, Gill. It was a life I hated because I lived through too many worried days and nights until the inevitable happened. When I think back, it was always me who complained, never my mother. She knew and approved all along. She . . . she *helped* dad. She did every damn thing possible to make his life easier because she only had the fear to face, not the actual conflict or the pain or the physical experience of death." Helen paused, let her fingers squeeze his hand again with a comforting gesture and said, "I approve of you no matter what they said you did."

Something twisted at his stomach again and he stared hard through the windshield. The years of being a loner were screaming at him to stay silent, but there were years still to go and they wanted him to speak. He turned his head briefly for a quick look at her and that one, stolen glance was almost too much. He said, "If I had met you earlier things might have been a lot differ-ent."

"It wouldn't have changed things any," she told him.

"Could *anything* change things?"

Her fingers squeezed again. "No," she said simply. "I think we both know that."

"I got a stupid feeling."

"Like what?"

"Damn it," Gill grated, "you know like what."

"Would you believe I have that same stupid feeling?" Helen asked him.

He felt that twisting in his stomach again. "Love is supposed to be for kids."

Her laugh was low and rich and she laid her head against his shoulder. He could smell the subtle fragrance of perfume and feel her body heat on his arm. "I guess we're a couple of kids then. We sure picked a silly place to bring it out into the open."

"I don't know any better places."

"You could have tried when we were sharing the same pillow."

"Then it would have sounded phony."

"Not coming from you," she said.

Mark Shelby heard the phone ring, put down his drink and looked at the big clock on the wall. They were getting old in Chicago, he thought. It had taken them over two hours to double-check the information he had relayed on, convene the board and come to a decision.

When he said hello, there was no exchange of names, but he recognized the voice on the other end of the line. Now that they knew the Frenchman was dead they'd remember he had always been the *Primus Gladatori* and they'd put the matter where it belonged.

"We just talked over the situation," the voice said.

"Yes?" Mark's voice was firm and dominant.

"How far along are you on the other matter?" It was a

reference to the information fed the destroyed computer system.

"A few more days will do it."

"Can you handle something else?"

"Naturally." His voice was even more certain this time.

The one on the other end gave a satisfied grunt. "Okay, we're giving it to you."

"How much?"

"While Pop's away, you're in charge. You handle it good, okay?"

"My pleasure," he said with a smile in his voice before he heard the connection break.

But there was no pleasure in his face at all. *Shit*, he thought, all they were laying on him was shit. He had the Frenchman's job to do now while that fucking Papa was kicking around in his supposed hideout. Hell, he knew where he was in Florida. Maybe nobody else did, but he made a point of knowing these things because one day when he sprung the trap he didn't want the jaws of it to close on empty air. The only trouble was the big board would lay on the assignment to mop up that stinking Herman Shanke in Miami and Papa would toss in the soldiers, then take all the bows for slamming the opposition.

How the hell an unknown like Shanke could pull off a coup like he did was damn near unbelievable, but when you looked at it closely enough you could grasp the possibilities. He *was* unknown, killing didn't bother him and the ambushes he set up weren't really all that complicated. Some pretty stupid soldiers he knew had minds devious enough to work a setup like that . . . but then they'd be stupid enough to brag about it to some bitch and be laid out an hour later.

He picked his drink up from the file he had retrieved from the Frenchman's office before the cops got there, smeared the wet ring the glass had made onto the table top and flipped the folder open again. There was something there he had glanced over casually that bothered him and he shuffled the papers until he found what he wanted.

It was a report on the sale of bullets that matched a murder weapon to a guy with a fresh tattoo on his left forearm. A penciled note indicated Eddie Camp had been put on the job of tracing the inked art work.

Mark looked up Camp's phone number, dialed it and got a sour-voiced woman who said Eddie was gone and not expected back at any certain time. He told her to have him call the minute he checked in and hung up.

There was something about that tattoo business he didn't like at all. He couldn't figure out why not.

Before he put the phone away he made three more calls to keep abreast of the situation. All he found out was that Miami was a sealed-off area with the boys closing in, the word being that any hits were to be quiet and unspectacular, a silent massacre with all the bodies removed and the evidence cleaned up so it looked like Herman the German and company had simply decided to ease themselves out and keep any public outcry down to a minimum. The big board and Papa Menes had hand-chosen the best soldiers available, all experienced professionals, and the job shouldn't be too difficult.

Too bad, he thought again. The more trouble now, the better he could work the rest of his master plan. He came to a decision quickly. The money was there, he knew how the delivery could be made and he picked up the phone again with a self-satisfied smile.

An hour later a packet of money changed hands. Forty-five minutes after that the material was loaded and sent on its way. Herman the German was going to get his arsenal without Moe Piel's help at all.

He finished his drink and was about to get ready to go to bed when the doorman downstairs buzzed his apartment and told him a Mr. Case was there. He told him to send him up, wondering what the hell Little Richard wanted at this time of night.

When he came in, Case didn't waste time on pleasantries. "You know who bumped the Frenchman?"

"Suppose you tell me."

"That fucking Shatzi, that's who. The cops spotted him coming out of his apartment building but he got away before they could get to him."

"Shatzi?"

"Yeah, Frank's own boy, that's who. He missed carrying out the contract so Verdun lets out the word to have him picked up and Shatzi runs for it. All he thinks is Frank's going to have him knocked off and that lunatic flips."

"The late news . . ."

"Hell," Case almost shouted, "nobody's got the story.

The cops are making the papers and the TV bunch keep quiet about it. He cut the Frenchman's cock right off, scoops out his fucking belly button and slices his neck. The doorman identified him, the cop recognized him, now they got every bull in town looking for him."

Shelby made two drinks and handed one to Case. "Like you said, he was Frank's personal man. He can't be tied in to us."

"Look, Mark, nobody knows how much that loony could have picked up. We just better find him before the cops do, that's all."

"Frank's orders are still in effect, aren't they?"

"Damn right. I called in another dozen of our bunch to go at it too." He paused, exasperated. "What the hell is going on any more? Here we're all riding fat and easy and suddenly the fucking building is crashing down on our heads!"

"Relax, it's happened before. We take care of these things."

"We didn't have any idiot navel nippers around before either."

"Who told you about the Frenchman?"

"I was there when Lederer was blowing his top. I could hear him right across the hall. City Hall must have leaned on him because he's gotten all leaves canceled, got the detectives working overtime and eating the ass out of Bill Long because Burke's disappeared someplace and nobody can find him."

"Okay, finish your drink and go on home. Chicago dropped the whole thing in my lap until Papa comes back and I'll take it from here. Tomorrow we'll get some action."

He locked the door behind Case and stood there a moment thinking of Gill Burke. He didn't like for that bastard to be missing. He wanted him right where he could get to him.

Only Bill Long had gotten to Burke and told him about Shatzi.

Gill said, "You sure?"

"Positive make. Doorman and the cop. The medical examiner confirmed that Verdun died just minutes before the cop saw Shatzi run out of there."

"So you got a break finally."

"No two ways about it. He mutilated the Frenchman like he did the others, only worse. Cut his damn pecker right off. He even left bloody prints in the elevator."

"He was pretty damn dumb about it."

"Hell," Long said, "Verdun knew him, let him in and got it right out of left field. He never expected Shatzi would even try to take him."

"One mistake is all it takes," Gill said.

"And Lederer wants you back here. He wants to have a long talk about Verdun with Helen Scanlon and you'd better be ready with some fast answers or you are strictly up the creek. He's beginning to think you're tracking around dung on your shoes, old buddy. He's even got a couple of his own men running a check on you."

"Let him go screw himself."

"You said that before."

"Then what else is new?"

"When you coming back?"

"Monday morning. And in case you're thinking of coming to get me, remember that this is New Jersey."

"Come on, Gill, I didn't tell him where you were."

Burke laughed into the phone. "Keep up the good work. A guy needs a rest occasionally."

"You're not getting any damned rest," Long told him as he hung up.

When Gill put the phone back, Helen was grinning at him. "You're not going to get any, either. Come back here, you big pig."

Burke leaned back against the pillow, his arm around Helen's warm shoulder. But something had happened to him and he wasn't there with her at all. His mind was back in New York and suddenly little things began to come together, not swiftly, but swirling in like the first flakes of snow in a gusty wind, twisting and revolving while they looked for a place to settle. One would alight, stick a moment, then blow on into another place until it adhered, then waited for another to come and attach itself. It was forming now, and when the pieces stopped coming together everything would be covered and in place.

She knew he had left her and didn't disturb his thoughts, content to be there while he tunneled into secret places after the hidden things only cops look for, wishing she could help, but knowing she couldn't. The only thing she could be sure of was that tonight was all she had of him until it was over. She closed her eyes and tried to blanket herself with sleep.

On the top floor of the cheap hotel on Forty-ninth Street, sleep was something that couldn't come to Shatzi Heinkle. He kept looking at the chunk of flesh in the pickle jar of rubbing alcohol that was beside him on the night table and felt a thrill of excitement unlike any he had ever experienced before.

Alive! He had done it to somebody who was alive!

He licked his lips and took another pull on the bottle of cheap whiskey he had picked up downstairs and grinned foolishly. Outside they'd be searching the city for him, but right now he couldn't care less. The fleabag hotel was a safe place for him as long as Bert was at the desk, but tomorrow he'd move on to another safe place until he reached the clapboard shanty halfway across the United States where he was born, and he could live there happy and peaceful all his life with his trophy in the bottle of alcohol and know that he finally got back at the world. Oh, he was too damn smart for them. Or too dumb for them, maybe. They never could think like he could and that's why they never tagged him. And who would look in a place that didn't even have a post office?

One by one, he went over the moves he would make and how he would make them, knowing his escape route was perfected. The only thing that bothered him was the bottle beside him and the wild excitement he felt. Hell, if just one of those things could make him feel so good, how would he feel if he had two or even three in the bottle? His mouth went dry from pleasure and he wet it down again with the whiskey.

Sure, there was that big wheel Shelby, the fat guy from downtown they called Little somebody. There was Remy who had told him to get lost once when he was waiting for Frank outside the office. Damn, but he could go back to that safe place with maybe two bottles full, knowing he left behind the story of what a really big man he was after all, and that kind of food would sustain him forever.

He could always leave, but if he left now, he could never add to the bottle. And he was much too smart for them anyway.

Or dumb. Either way was just as good.

11

The years of professional whoredom had left Louise Belhander with a total callousness, an absolute lack of sensitivity and, until she saw the name *Verdun* again, an almost complete forgetfulness of her past. But that one word had brought it all back to her again, even the moments when she unconsciously went through the V listing in the phone book while she was making a call. Wherever she had been, she had never found the name, and now all she had was a terrible sense of stifled rage burning in her mind as she remembered nearly every detail of her sordid life that began that day in the barn.

Even if the old bastard and his friend had paid them well for their services, they were somebody who knew a man named Verdun and if it were the same Verdun she was going to see that they all paid even more.

When Artie Meeker drove them back to Miami she said she was going to stay at a friend's house and stopped in Homestead to make a call. What she did was arrange to have a car ready for her use and when Artie dropped her off she got in the waiting sedan, followed him while he let out the other girl, then headed back to the Keys with him. Artie never realized he was being followed because Louise stayed well ahead of him, and on the Florida Keys, there is only one road. At a gas station along the way Artie stopped for a good ten minutes at an outdoor phone booth, then practically ran back to his car and drove like hell. When she saw the lights of his car slow down, then turn, she swung around, spotted the cottage, parked in a deserted driveway and ran back to Papa Menes' cottage.

She squeezed into the clump of bushes outside the open window, oblivious of the insects that welcomed her, watching the small living room, listening to every word they said, feeling the shock waves bounce through her brain at what Artie was telling Papa Menes.

Only once in his life had Papa ever felt a curdling in his stomach and felt the inside of his thighs quiver because he was afraid. Now he was feeling it again and he squeezed the arm of the chair so he could control himself and when the spasm passed he said, "Now, give me that shit once more."

Artie Meeker stopped his pacing and swung around.

"It was like I said, boss. Verdun's dead. That Shatzi cut his button right outta his belly and even took it with him. Blam, just like that and the Frenchman's outta it. The big board's got Shelby handlin' everything up there and they're raising hell because nothing's getting done down this way."

"Shelby ain't handling nothing," Papa said nastily.

"I'm just telling you what they told me."

More to himself than Meeker, Papa said, "The board's a pack of nitheads. If they think they can cancel me out with Shelby they're crazy."

"Boss . . ."

"Shut up, Artie." He stared at his hands, clenched them, then opened his fingers. "Those asses sent Verdun in themselves. They called him over my head without even asking me and now they're screaming."

"Boss . . . you were the one who brought the Frenchman in the first time," Artie reminded him.

"And once was enough. What else did they tell you?"

"Everybody on the cops in New York is looking for Shatzi. Our guys want him first and the lid's ready to blow. That damned D.A. . . . Lederer . . . is really laying on the heat. They want you to clean up here, then get back to the city."

"Just like that."

Meeker shrugged. "They said you got the soldiers down here, now use 'em. They want that Herman punk hit like right now."

"Didn't you tell them how I was playing it?"

"Sure, boss. Real cool, I said. No excitement. The board said to screw the fancy stuff and get in there."

"Fucking idiots," Papa said.

"So what do you do, boss?"

For a minute or so, Papa Menes didn't answer. He sat there thinking until his mind was made up, then turned his head toward Artie. "How many of our boys are down here?"

"Only four."

Papa nodded. "Call them off. The rest are all the ones the big board sent out themselves. When it hits the fan we'll let Chicago catch it. That damn bunch of westerners need to get burned. Maybe the coast families'll wise up and get back in line then."

"Want me to do it now?"

"No. Tomorrow's time enough."

Artie picked up his beer, took a long pull and made like he was studying the label on the can. Finally he said, "Hey, Papa."

"Now what?"

"Who the hell you think knocked off all our guys?"

"Somebody who wants to take over, that's who."

"Herman the German ain't got that much smarts, Papa."

"Yeah, I know."

"Then it's gotta be somebody else."

"I know that too."

"Who do you think then, Papa?"

"Hit this Miami prick and if it happens some more I'll sure as hell know."

Artie nodded thoughtfully, still looking at the can. "One thing screwy, boss . . . Verdun was careful. He wouldn't let a slob like Shatzi walk in and tear him up. Shit, the Frenchman could tear him apart. He got it right by the shower so whoever came in had a key and he wasn't about to give no key to Shatzi." Artie shuddered and his mouth twisted. "The fucker cut his pecker right off and chopped out his belly button."

"Knock it off," Papa barked. He didn't want to hear about it again either.

But outside the window Louise Belhander felt a warm glow of satisfaction wash over her and she savored the mental image with pleasure. Verdun was dead then, and that was all right. But here were two others he was associated with and they'd do just as well. She watched Artie Meeker pick up the old man's beer can, then hugged the wall while he walked outside to toss them in the trash can. When he went back inside she stayed in the shadows, crept to the can and retrieved the two empties, handling them with the tails of her blouse.

There were things she wanted to know.

What she found out came from an ex-cop now in private business specializing in divorce cases. He lifted the prints for her, had them identified through a friend in the department and didn't ask her any questions at all.

But being a cop he recognized the local brand of beer, photographed the stamped price marking on the lid and noted the distribution numbers on the label.

Louise Belhander spent all the next day reading old newspapers at the library and was a little stunned at what she discovered. That one time with Verdun in the barn was going to cost an international organization plenty.

Only a short haul to retirement, Bill Long thought, and all this crap would be out of the way. At that minute retirement still seemed a lifetime off and the concern of the present was etched deeply into his face.

He looked at Burke and said, "Helen Scanlon didn't tell them anything they didn't already know."

"She couldn't, Bill. All she did was work there."

"Lederer doesn't think so. He'll press her until she busts."

"And I'll bust his ass. If she had anything I would have known about it. Don't think I didn't figure her to be tied into the organization in the beginning too."

"What made you change your mind?"

"I didn't. I just let it play out until I knew for sure."

"Just the same, when he's done harassing her she won't be finding many job opportunities."

"She won't have to. I'm planning on taking care of that end myself."

Bill Long looked at him carefully, then frowned. "I detect a note of reservation in your voice, Gill."

"Because my occupation carries a high risk factor."

"You're still a survivor type."

"Sure. And if I don't survive she can inherit my estate. I haven't anybody to leave it to anyway."

"Okay, rich man."

"A bachelor with no high spending habits can pick up a lot of bucks over the years, buddy. Now let's get off my personal life and back to business. Want another coffee?"

"No. You get one."

When Burke sat down again the captain leaned back in his chair and lit a cigarette. "The Los Angeles cops just came up with some results."

"Oh?"

"On Stanley Holland."

Gill stirred the sugar and milk in, nodding.

"They located the doctor who did the plastic surgery on his face."

"So?"

"He was owned by the mob. Treated bullet wounds without reporting them . . . all that kind of stuff. Apparently he handled plenty of abortions for them too, but never got rapped for them."

"Great, but where does it fit in?"

"Well, those L.A. boys know how to put the pressure on his kind and he started to talk. One of the things he mentioned was that the photos he took of Enrico Scala after he turned him into Stanley Holland were lifted from his files along with the negatives."

"Who knew he was having the job done?"

"The same people who always okayed work approved by the syndicate."

"So it's somebody on the inside?"

"Not necessarily. One of the detectives started taking it from another angle and worked on the death of the guy they thought was Scala, you know . . . the faked car wreck and all that. So he finds out there was somebody else poking around the scene everybody took to be an insurance investigator, except the company who held the policy never did anything more than take one look at the wreck and pay the bill. The other guy wanted to see the remains of the body, all the identification and even checked into the funeral arrangements."

"Find out who he was?"

"Too long ago. Nobody could give an accurate description."

"Who was the dead guy? All I remember were photos of the smash-up. I was out in California for Compat Company when it happened."

"They still don't know." He took another pull on the cigarette, still frowning. "You know anything about Scala at all?"

"Only from the old police fliers. He was a West Coast hood all the way."

"Coming up fast too . . . until he got nailed. The mob had big plans for that boy."

"They can forget that now."

"Yeah. They got Miami to worry about."

"Now what?" Gill asked.

"Somebody ran a load of guns and ammo into the city and Herman the German's bunch are having one hell of a shootout the past two hours." He looked at the narrow-eyed expression on Gill's face and added, "You ought to check in the office more often, friend."

"How many down?"

"Two of the German's and three soldiers from the Midwest area."

"Anything on Papa Menes?"

"If he left the area, he didn't go by our security. He still pays for his hotel suite, except it's occupied by a couple of hoods named George Spacer and Carl Ames."

"Menes had a driver . . . Artie Meeker. Dumb but faithful."

"He's gone too."

"They use a car?"

"Papa's big limo is still in the garage."

"He'd have a spare someplace."

"They haven't located it." He snuffed the butt out. "Now I'm really getting worried."

"Why?"

"Because it's too damned quiet here in New York. It's like knowing a fuse is lit and you can't find the frigging bomb. All you can do is wait until it goes off and hope you're not sitting on top of it."

Mark Shelby had the same feeling too. The action had started in Miami and no matter which way it turned out, all hell was going to break loose. Even if Papa Menes came out on top, he was going to be marked lousy with the big board and his position was going to go down. Nor would the heat from the public and the police let the old-liners there in Chicago off the hook either. They'd be coming at them from every direction possible and the whole organization was going to be shaken to the roots.

He smiled silently, because if they had stayed in all their illegal activities they couldn't have cared less, but those many years ago they had diverted their hot money into legitimate enterprises that made up a billion-dollar structure, and whoever came out with those in his hand owned the organization too.

It could be done. It was just a matter of time.

He looked at his watch and thought about Helga. He

needed her badly, but he had to wait for that call about a guy with a star tattoo who had bought those foreign bullets.

Fifty minutes later it came in. The job had been done right there in New York in a bootleg shop on a man about thirty who had wanted a star initialed in the middle with the letters DS above WV. The star looked like an old-fashioned sheriff's badge. When he took his shirt off to get the job done the operator had noticed the bullet-hole scars in his left shoulder and lower right side.

He put in a call to Remy and after a brief conversation Remy suggested that the initials stood for Deputy Sheriff, West Virginia and the guy had been recently invalided off the force, but proud enough of his job to want to wear its insignia permanently. It wouldn't be a hard job at all to check on.

After he told Remy to get busy on it, he called Helga to tell her he was coming over and went out his usual route thinking of all that wonderful skin waiting for him.

Burke had to wait until six o'clock until Myron Berkowitz got home. The lawyer was a tall, scared, skinny guy who started sweating the minute Gill popped his badge on him and he wondered just what kind of legal practice he had. Myron tried to pleasant it out and invited him into his apartment and even seemed surprised when Gill accepted the drink he offered.

When he finally squirmed into his chair he tried to look businesslike and said, "Now, sir, what can I do for you?"

"Your aunt told me how you handled all her husband's effects after he was killed."

"Yes, yes indeed, I did that. Of course, there wasn't much of an estate. . . ."

"I saw the papers in the basement."

"Luckily, my uncle had insurance."

"Did you get everything down on that inventory list?"

Myron didn't have to think about it. "Everything," he said.

"If they were making stag movies, how did they sell them?"

The question didn't seem to fluster the lawyer. Obviously, he knew what his uncle's business actually was. "Direct. No rental sales if that's what you mean. They weren't all that good, and besides, with the new pornography in the theaters in full color and sound his seemed a little old-fashioned. He sold copies of one-reelers cheap so he stayed in business." He paused and made a wry face. "That's what I couldn't understand."

"What couldn't you?"

Myron shrugged and sipped his drink. "How he could think about buying a house in the country and a new car. He didn't have anything saved up like that at all."

"Maybe it was a pipedream."

"Not with him," Myron stated positively. "My uncle didn't waste time with the impossible. He told me he was going to move to a new house in the country and wanted me to get a price on a new car for him . . . a big new car."

"When?"

"Not a week before he was killed."

"Then where do you think the money was coming from?"

Myron looked a little worried. "Could be he made a decent picture for a change."

"Friend, that's not exactly what you're thinking."

Myron couldn't meet his eyes this time. "Well . . ."

"Say it."

"He might have shot some film on somebody who would pay a lot to get it back."

"Would he?"

Very slowly, Myron nodded. "Once before. In Boston, it was. Some people wanted to photograph a party they were having. For their own use, of course. They made him give them the negative."

"But he kept a copy for another sale later."

"Something like that. Remember, I'm just guessing."

"He kept a work diary?" Gill asked.

"Yes, and there was nothing there that I could find. I even checked his film against his work sheets to be sure."

Gill grinned at him slowly. "Thinking of going into business for youself?"

"Of course not!"

"But someplace you found a discrepancy in the whole bit, didn't you?"

The instant consternation in Myron's eyes made Gill sure he was right. He kept looking at the lawyer and his face wasn't a pleasant thing to see. Myron gulped at his drink and said, "There was an invoice for a piece of equipment that wasn't there."

"What kind?"

"Mr. Burke . . . I'm a lawyer, not a photographer."

"Don't give me any shit, kid. You checked it out and it's all likely to backfire in your face if you don't spill it."

"Well . . . it was a microfilming device."

Gill gave him another tight smile and put his glass down. When he stood up, Myron said, "That's all?"

"That's all," Burke told him. "From you, anyway."

Down on the street again, Burke looked up at the evening sky and felt a drop of rain hit his face. It wasn't the snow he was thinking of the other night, each flake a bit of the puzzle, but it would do. It was all there, hanging just above his head, and now it was getting ready to come down.

As he walked he separated the puzzle into its separated pieces, putting a label on each one. Berkowitz and Manute, dead photographers. Mark Shelby in the area. Why would Shelby use . . . or kill . . . photographers? Yet, Berkowitz had purchased microfilming equipment and expected a big chunk of money. A theory could be put together damn quickly there.

Trouble was, it exploded when Ted Proctor comes in. Gill frowned and went over it again. If Proctor somehow knew about Berkowitz coming into dough and thought he had it, he could have tried a robbery that turned into a murder, and when there was no money, he held up the pawnshop instead. Logical, but somehow it didn't fit Proctor's nature at all. He wasn't the type who could hold together for two jobs . . . or kills.

One thing for certain . . . Jimmie Corrigan was as square a cop as lived and there was no denying the accuracy of his report when he walked in on Proctor holding a gun on the pawnbroker. Corrigan's service record was impeccable, he had had plenty of experience and wouldn't have acted with undue haste unless he thought his life was threatened.

Enter the next squirrely point . . . Corrigan knew the facts as well as he did, but he felt something was wrong too. Some crazy little thing was all out of focus because it was either too complicated or too oversimplified for anybody to see it.

But it was sure as hell there.

Henry Campbell *had* seen Mark Shelby in the area there even though he'd deny it publicly. Mark Shelby was there and denied it completely. Ergo . . . if Shelby *wasn't* implicated, why all the fuss?

More rain splattered against Burke's face and he shrugged into his raincoat. A taxi slowed for him, but he waved it on. Right now he had to think.

The landlady of Proctor's rooming house had never seen any evidence of stolen goods, nor a gun, yet the investigating team had uncovered wallets hidden away, half of which had been reported stolen, apparently by a pickpocket.

For a second Burke stopped, a sudden thought in his mind. The rain was coming down harder and a slow grin came to his face. A couple passing by saw it and edged to one side, a nervous look in their eyes.

Burke said something very softly under his breath and went out in the street to whistle down a cruising cab. He gave the driver the number downtown and settled back into the seat.

Sergeant Schneider was just getting ready to leave

when Gill Burke walked in. He took one look at Gill's face and said, "Aw no, not you again."

"Won't take long, buddy."

"Look, I'm an hour late for supper already. Can't it wait?"

"What's the matter, don't you want to be a hero?"

"Who can be a hero in the records section, you kidding?"

Burke just stood there until Schneider threw up his hands. "Get the files on the stuff they found in Ted Proctor's room," he said. "I want to see the complaint sheets and the names and addresses of the owners of the junk that was hoisted."

"For Pete's sake, Gill!"

"Come on, it won't take all that long."

With another resigned look, Schneider pushed himself out of his chair and nodded for Gill to follow him. Thirty minutes later he had everything Burke had requested and watched while Gill went through them one by one. Seven persons had reported their pockets picked with a total loss of four hundred and eighty-six dollars. The notation made said that the wallets and remaining contents had been returned to their rightful owners. Gill jotted down their names and addresses in his pad and closed the folders.

Schneider gave him an annoyed look and asked, "That's all?"

There was something bright in Burke's eyes. "We all missed something there, buddy."

"Like what?" The sergeant didn't get it.

"Those complaints were all filed within two days."

"So what? You get a guy hoisting wallets on a good day and he isn't about to quit."

"Proctor was a two-bit drunk. He didn't need over four hundred bucks to satisfy his kind of thirst."

"Then you've forgotten your drunks," Schneider told him. "He'd get rolled himself before he could spend it and with the kind of a need he'd have he'd go try for another score."

"Maybe."

"Maybe hell. You've gone ape over this crap, Gill. I don't know why you bother."

"Because this kind of crap got me booted off the force."

Schneider just looked at him.

"And it is crap, friend. The whole damn thing is a phony."

"You can prove that, I guess?"

Gill nodded. "Yeah, if I'm right, I think I can."

It was simpler to bypass the government bureau and get what he wanted from the newspaper office. The guy at the city desk was having a slow hour and was glad to escort him to the right department and open up the files. He looked up the dates, handed Gill the two detailed sheets and let him read them over. When Gill handed them back he said, "Find anything?"

"Beautiful," he said and thanked him.

He went back outside, walking toward the corner in the rain that came slashing down from the roiling sky that churned about the towering spires of the city. He was alone on the street and he was smiling again in spite of the downpour, because the two nights all those pockets were reported picked it had been raining the same way as this one and not the kind of night a pickpocket would be working at all.

12

The explosion in Miami came within two hours of the arms shipment to Vigaro's Outboard Motor Outlet. Neither Vig nor Herman the German bothered checking the source of their bounty, fully believing that Moe Piel had somehow arranged it all. They didn't even bother to consider that the value of the arms they received was far greater than the cash Moe had carried. The mere sight of grenades, Army issue submachine guns still packed in cosmoline and cases of ammunition was so exhilarating that all they could think of was the power it brought and Herman the German had a sudden vision of a new order with himself in the seat of power being instituted in the peninsular state with an even more satisfying picture of at last having the means to wipe out a certain old Don named Papa Menes whose guts he hated so badly it made his bones ache.

Unfortunately for the two out-of-town soldiers the big board had sent in, they had figured anything outside their own city was Hicksville and, after making a hit on one of Herman's men, didn't cover their getaway trail well enough, never suspecting that a fifteen-year-old girl on a motor scooter was the one tracking them to their hideout. A grenade through the living room window of the cottage they occupied kept them from having any regrets.

Another group making a pass at a drive-in hamburger stand where one of Herman's top lieutenants had been reported to be having lunch was chopped up in a cross-fire of rapid bursts from three tommy guns and only the driver escaped alive, the other two in the car being cut to bloody pieces.

The shock wave that went through the organization that considered itself invincible took hours to subside, then they realized that the enemy they considered such an upstart was far more formidable than they had supposed. He was operating in his own territory, an area of absolute necessity to syndicate operations, he had all the equipment for defense and offense he would need, the manpower to handle it, and with the flush of success he'd be getting new recruits all the time. But more important than anything, he had the temerity to hit hard and the intelligence to remain obscure while he did it. Already he had decimated the brains of the organization with bold strikes across the country in a manner so unpredictable as to make a defense impossible.

What the big board could not quite understand was how they could have underestimated or overlooked a person like Herman the German. Anybody with any sense at all should have picked up his potential long ago and either alerted them or had him knocked off.

It was Florio Prince who remembered the incident of Papa Menes having him beaten up and kicked out of New York, and after a short consideration they determined that it was that indiscretion on the part of Menes that had terminated in the near-destruction of everything they had so carefully built up. So, even though Papa Menes was the head of the structure, the mental reservations were there on the part of the members and unless he fully redeemed himself, he would be invited to step down.

Taking no chances on having Papa Menes learn he was the instigator of his demise, Florio Prince informed him of the board's inclination, wondering, at the time, how the old man could be so calm when the others wanted his ass and his realm.

Papa Menes was far from calm. He chewed on the end of an unlit cigar, something he hadn't done for years, his hot eyes roaming over the six *capos* assembled in the back room of The Red Dolphin Grill, boiling mad because a revolt like this should have been handled at the local level without having to bring in the head of the entire structure.

He didn't admit it, even to himself, but the main reason for his anger was something else, a haunting fear that Miami wasn't the answer to it at all, and someplace out there was a gun waiting for him to expose himself so it could go off inside his skull. He kept remembering Victor Petrocinni, Teddy Shu, Slick Kevin, Stanley Holland and all the others and a little trickle of sweat ran down his back and he was glad he wore his seersucker jacket so they couldn't see the fear stain on his shirt.

They gave him the details of the layout, the number of men involved and certain possibilities of attack. It was going to have to be done completely within the organization because their political connections had all gone sour and there wasn't a single official contact they could count on for cooperation. The police would hit them as quickly as they would Herman's men and there was always the probability that the FBI would find a reason to enter the scene and reinforce the local department.

But Miami wasn't new to Papa Menes. It had been his second home for half his life and he knew every street and business in it. Those things never changed. They expanded, or were renovated, but they never really changed. The only thing that changed were the people and that's where the trouble always came from.

The meeting lasted a little over four hours, and when it was done, the assembled group murmured with pleasure at the sheer genius of Papa Menes and realized why he was the Boss, completely understanding how he got to that position, and already feeling sorry for anyone who tried to challenge his authority.

Because of his age and position, Papa was not expected to have a direct hand in the operation, but it would proceed according to his detailed plans and he would remain in the background if any alteration of the scheme seemed necessary.

When they adjourned, Papa got in the car with Artie Meeker and started on the circuitous route back to the cottage in the Keys. His part of the job was over and he felt good. Those bastards in Chicago would see how it was when the real expert came in and he'd sure as hell lay them out at the next meeting. A few heads were going to roll just to set an example for the rest of the pricks who thought he was finished. Shit, there wasn't a one of them he couldn't outthink or outfuck anyway.

He felt his belly stir at the latter thought and decided he'd have Artie pick up that little blonde that night for a celebration. Artie didn't mind the driving at all as long as he had his own broad to bang. Poor Artie, he thought. No imagination at all. Just a mechanical piston going up and down exactly so many times before exhausting. A pause for cooling and refueling, then another energizing. He never bothered to notice the bored look on the broad's face. Now with him, Papa, the dame *always* had an expression and it sure wasn't boredom. It could range from pain to pleasure, but it was never boredom. He might be old, but he certainly was imaginative.

Back in New York, Mark Shelby had come out of his controlled rage because Little Richard Case had met him in an out-of-the-way bar on the West Side, and from his expression, the news was good. They had their drinks served at a table in the back and when the shoddy bartender had gone back to his post Mark said, "What did you get?"

Little Richard shifted his bulk in the chair and tasted his drink. It was lousy, but something he needed. "The cops have Shatzi located somewhere in a two-block area uptown. They got the whole section cordoned off and are doing a house-to-house search."

"How'd they find him?"

"The slob brought some dame into his room and you know what? He's got the Frenchman's belly button in a damn bottle. She spots it right away and cuts out because she's terrified of weirdos. The broad's only a five-buck hooker, but she's been rousted plenty, so she tries to make points and tips the cops."

"Shit."

"They don't want to scare him off, so they moved in the plainclothes bunch. No lights, no sirens . . . just a lot of manpower."

"Who we got in that area?"

Case gave him a small smile. "Marty and his cousin Mack. They're in the next building. They've been living there four years."

Shelby nodded, waiting.

"I told them to take him," Case said.

"Good."

"Neither one's got a record and they both got jobs. The cops won't shake them any."

"You tell them to get him over to the place in Brooklyn."

"Might take a while."

"Doesn't matter."

"You know, Mark, that loony isn't going to stand still and be taken. If the cops knock him off . . ."

"We don't take any chances, you know that."

"Hell, what could Shatzi know?"

Shelby made a sour face and shook his head. "Come off it, Case. They always know something and Verdun was close enough to the top so that things could rub off on even the punks. Supposing he always did have it in for Frank. Supposing he had been planning a shot like that and backed it up by grabbing some of Frank's papers?"

"The Frenchman didn't make notes, Mark."

Over the drinks, Shelby's eyes narrowed as he looked at the other. He was thinking of himself when he said, "You never can tell."

"Guess you're right."

"Keep me informed. You going back downtown?"

"Yeah. Something else is stewing. That fucking Gill Burke is moving around after something and he's got Lederer hopping mad. He put on pressure to get some people assigned to him and the D.A.'s office couldn't stop it."

"What for?"

"He won't say, that's what got Lederer boiling. That guy would do anything to dump Burke even though he brought him in in the first place."

Shelby felt his fingers tighten around the glass and cursed inaudibly. Gill Burke was the only one he really feared. The bastard wouldn't let go of anything. They gave him something really big to play with and instead he goes right back to the original bit. Not that he was worried. He had covered his tracks completely and the years had completed the job.

"Screw Burke," he said.

"Don't play him down."

Shelby knew Case had more to say and waited for it.

"Remember that cop Corrigan?"

"Yeah."

"Burke's been talking to him. He's been back to that pawnshop too."

"He was there before too, remember? What the hell can he find out after all this time? You think that shylock is going to talk?"

"Burke doesn't give a shit about squeezing somebody. He'd never make the courtroom."

"You think Burke would give a damn? Look what he did to Bennie and Colfaco eight years ago. He saved the state plenty of money and they couldn't prove he tossed them over that rooftop."

Shelby put his drink down and rubbed his chin thoughtfully. "You know, you might have a point there. That guy's the only weak point. Maybe we ought to get him out of the way."

"Sure . . . and Burke would figure it out right away."

"Not necessarily. He's been robbed enough to make it look kosher. This time he gets hit."

"Don't stick your neck out, Mark."

"When I want to order something done, don't you tell me not to."

Case finished the rest of his drink with disgust. "Okay, it's your show for now, but Papa Menes isn't going to like it."

"Papa Menes is too busy with his own problems to worry about it."

The quiet tone of his voice made Case feel uncomfortable and he squirmed in his chair. Shelby had his own kills behind him while he never had been called upon for any direct action. His position in the organization was undercover and so far, good enough so that nobody had ever suspected the liaison between the officialdom of the two governments.

He shrugged his big shoulders and said, "I better call Marty before Shatzi spots any of those cops. You coming over to Brooklyn when we take him?"

"Not if we have to question him, Little Richard." Shelby grinned at the look of horror on Case's face. He knew what was going to be done and the thought of it made him sick.

"That's your job," Case told him. "I'm just the delivery boy this time."

"Every time, Little Richard," Shelby said mockingly. He waited until Case had left, then picked up the phone and dialed Miami. For a full minute he listened, smiling slightly, a callous, bemused glint in his eyes, then said a curt, "Okay," and hung up.

Papa Menes was having it rough. It wasn't like the old days any more. The years had piled up on the old man and he just didn't have it. Those punks would bust him down and if he didn't fall easily the big board would give them an unwilling hand. They didn't tolerate failure at all, even amongst their own.

And that was why the big board had to go too so that when the *Primus Gladatori* took over the helm there would be nobody to stand against him, at least no one who could command the troops. The power would be his alone, the rest would be easy.

Up there in Helga's apartment, buried in the wax of the sacred candle, were the numbers, facts and details that would make it all simplistically possible. The numbers would open the Swiss accounts, the facts and details gave him the reins of influence over the areas of the establishment where control and corruption were needed. The surplus information, delivered to the proper authorities, would eliminate any opposition who chose to cross him.

There was just one loose end that had to be tied up first. It wasn't something he could leave to somebody else. This time there would be no slip, no necessity for having to pull out all the stops to squeeze Burke out into the pastures of ineffectiveness. This time he'd walk him into a permanent corner with a six-foot drop beneath his feet.

While Marcus Shelby was contemplating the scene with pleasure, another truck was pulling into Miami, approaching from the west. For half the trip the driver had been plagued with engine trouble, but because of the load he carried, he couldn't trust anyone to make repairs, so he had to do everything himself. It wasn't that he was a bad mechanic. Trouble was that he didn't have the right tools and had to make do with crescent wrenches and an old pair of box-end jobs. He wasn't sure how they had booby-trapped the heap to blow and he didn't want to trigger any mechanism accidentally. The old mill was gradually sputtering to a halt when he got to the area he was told to park it. He got out, walked back two blocks, out over to the highway and spotted an outdoor pay phone. He made the single call Frank Verdun had told him to make and one more to a taxi company. A half hour later he was on an interstate bus heading north and he was able to read the first news in four days. What he saw made him almost choke on his own spit. Verdun was dead and he didn't have anybody to cover for him now at all. Son of bitch, he'd have to move faster than he ever did before. When that truck went off . . .

13

For a while it looked as if the rain would stop, then the wind freshened, got a chill to it and got behind the rolling clouds that tumbled overhead in the night. Abrupt flashes of lightning streaked the darkness and Helen Scanlon watched the reflection in Burke's eyes. For the past hour he had been so far away from her she couldn't get through to him at all. Like her father, she thought.

When Bill Long came back from the phone he had tied up the past fifteen minutes, he dragged out his chair, sunk into it wearily and passed Burke a sheet of paper. It had a single name on it. "Know him?" Long asked.

"Yeah," Burke finally said. "Former deputy sheriff. He had to retire when he got shot up. Why?"

"He got shot up again and now he's retired permanently. It looks like somebody tried to take him and never expected the kind of battle he put up. He knocked off a pair of torpedoes and apparently wounded another who drove off." The cop paused and studied Burke a few seconds. "He had your card in his pocket."

Burke didn't show any emotion at all. "So I'm head security officer at Compat. The guy approached me for a job at home, I gave him my card and told him to apply out at the plant."

"Gill . . ."

"What?"

"Shit, nothing, that's what. What the hell would they cut this guy down for?"

"Knowing me, maybe."

"There an angle to this, Gill?"

Burke stared back at him, his mouth a tight, hard line. "I hope not, friend."

"They found his furnished room. He had three oddball automatics in a locked suitcase, all loaded and wrapped as though they were ready for delivery."

"As far as I know, he still carried a deputy badge. Under his state law those rods could be perfectly legal. Check it out."

"Maybe I will."

He had more to say, but the waiter came up to him and said, "Phone for you, Captain."

234

"Thanks. Be right back," he told Burke.

When he left Helen pulled her hand out from under Gill's palm. "There *is* an angle to what you told Bill, isn't there?"

Burke's eyes barely moved to meet hers. "Oh?"

Helen turned up her hand so he could see the blood oozing from where his thumbnail had dug into her flesh when Long showed him the paper. "Your reaction was immediate and a little painful. It surprised me. I really didn't think you'd show emotion when it came to the job."

"He was more of a friend than I explained to Bill. He was the kind of guy you hate to lose."

"I don't think you fooled Bill at all."

"I never try to."

"Don't you think cooperation . . ."

"Screw cooperation. You start working in committee and everybody concentrates on the same line of thought. I stay diversified." He stopped and looked up at Bill Long. "Now what?"

The big cop had to lean on the table to keep his hands from shaking. Lines of anger and frustration seemed etched in his face and he had to take a couple of deep breaths before answering. "We had Shatzi holed up. We had the whole fucking area closed off and moved in to nail the crazy bastard and he wasn't there. We got one corpse with his throat wide open and his belly button almost sliced out and that's all. Damn it all, Gill . . . are these loonies so fucking smart they can . . ."

"Who was the dead guy?"

"Marty Stackler. Just a guy who lived there. Worked over in Brooklyn. No record, nothing. He must have walked in on Shatzi and . . ."

"Stackler's a plant, Bill. They keep them all over the place, but they keep them in pairs. He have anybody with him?"

"They said he's got a cousin . . ."

"Mack? Mack Ferro or Berro?"

"It's Ferro. How the hell did you know?"

"Come on, Bill, that's my old territory."

"You think Shatzi's got this Ferro too?"

Burke shook his head. "No, I think Mack's got Shatzi."

"How the hell did they get out of there?"

"You've forgotten your origins, buddy. Those old tenements are like rats' nests. They have areas of entry and escape you'd never believe."

"Maybe you'd know where they were headed too?"

"I might."

"Burke . . ."

Gill let his mouth relax in a hard grin. "Stackler worked at a warehouse in Brooklyn that belonged to the old Statto family. It's been legit for a long time now, but it's still available for a holding operation if the mob needs it."

"Supposing Shatzi . . ."

"Was that bottle with the Frenchman's belly button still there?"

"On the table. And the dead guy's button was half . . ."

"They should have hit them together," Burke told him. "They probably split up and Stackler missed. Shatzi didn't. His mistake was trying to mutilate the body.

That's when Ferro probably coldcocked him and got him out of there."

"Hell, what for? Why not hit him right there?"

"They want to speak to him first, Bill. They're not about to take any chances."

"Yeah," Long said. "You coming?"

"No, not on this one, Bill."

"Look, Lederer . . ."

"Screw Lederer. How many times do I have to tell you that?"

"Then where're you heading?"

"Right now I'm going home and get my ass out of these wet clothes. After that I may make a few official inquiries and take a few official actions to justify my position on the staff of our great crusader."

Long gave him one long disgusted look. "You know, I stayed on past my retirement day just to help out. I shoulda said the hell with it."

Burke waited until he was gone, then tossed a bill on the table and followed him out. For a few minutes he huddled under the canopy until a cruising cab caught his wave, then they got in and Burke gave the driver his address.

Neither he nor Helen said a word until they were inside, and while Gill was changing into his other clothes Helen idly flipped on the tape recorder that was built into the base of the phone. An odd voice strained by age came through reciting words that made no sense at all, then a few numbers and finished with a chuckle.

She hit the rewind button and was playing it back again when Gill said, "It's a code."

"Important?"

"Could be. Just something I've been working on a long time."

"You're not going to tell me about it though, are you?"

"Nope." He finished buttoning his shirt and grinned at her. "Mad?"

Her shoulders made a gentle shrug. "My father did the same thing. He never wanted to worry my mother. Where are we going?"

"To intimidate somebody, sugar, and it isn't we. It's just me and I want you to stay right here until I get back."

"But . . ."

He walked over and took her by her arms, his fingers kneading her gently. "We got this far, Helen. Let's stretch it out as far as we can. It's a lousy business and I can handle it better when I handle it alone."

"Gill, Gill . . ." She smiled up at him, her eyes moist. "I love you, Gill. Be careful for me."

"I'm a pretty good survivalist."

"The odds are terrible."

"Not when you can manipulate them," he told her.

He leaned down, kissed her damp lips and let his fingers drift through her hair. "I won't be long."

The strident ringing of the phone interrupted her answer. He picked up the receiver and heard Bill Long's voice say, "Burke . . . get your tail over here now. A prowl car will pick you up downstairs."

"You get Shatzi?"

"We got better than Shatzi, soldier. Now get here before Lederer does so you can get a story ready. None of his boys had this location on the books at all."

"The beat cop coulda told him."

"Uh-uh. He's a new one. The old regular retired out three months back like I should have done. Now get moving."

"Yeah." He hung up the phone and grabbed his raincoat. "I'll have to do the intimidation bit later."

"You still want me to wait?"

"It'll help hurry things if I know you are."

"I'll be here," she told him.

The strange part was, he could slip his forefinger as far in the hole as it would go, yet it didn't hurt at all. There was a tingling sensation around the edges of the wound, something like when your hand falls asleep and down below there was a creeping numbness, but for Shatzi, it was all very pleasant.

He coughed and leaned up against the side of the building a moment to rest. He still had the thing in his hand and he looked at it again, a puckered obscenity indented in a little hill of fat. He frowned, trying to remember what had happened to the other one, but the thought didn't come and he shrugged it off.

That stupid fat Case and the other guy. They must have thought he was a pushover. He could remember the sudden impact of something against his skull when he was bending over that guy in his room, the one who tried to jump him with a billy. So he was dumb there, but he was smarter when he woke up because he was on the floor in the back of a car and that guy Mack was wanting to kill him right there and Case wouldn't let him do it. Twice that bastard Mack wanted to see if he'd come around and stuck a knife in his leg, but he didn't move or let out a groan and when Mack went back to arguing with Case, Shatzi had slipped out the foreign switch blade from his sock and when the car pulled into the alley between the buildings he reached up and almost cut Mack's head off before sticking the blade into Case's chest. The slob was so fat he had to slam him three more times before he collapsed and as he did the grisly remains of Mack stirred, the head trying to twist with the shoulders and not quite making it, blood pumping and squirting like somebody squeezing a gory sponge. Then the little gun in his hand spit once and Shatzi felt the tiny fist action a little above his belt on the right side.

It hardly bothered him when he performed his ritual surgery on the two bodies.

Now he had to follow his plan. He had had one, he knew, but it wasn't easy to remember. He was going to a place out west . . . a shack in a tiny town nobody knew about and he could look at what he had in the bottle and know that once he had been bigger than them all. But he didn't have the bottle any more. All he had was that sticky thing in his hand. He coughed again and sat down. He could hear police sirens in the distance, but they didn't mean anything to him at all. He felt the hole in his side again and wiggled his finger there idly. There was a burst of rain that felt cool on his face and he tilted his head upward. Three other faces were looking down at him, but little by little they dulled to pale ovals and he felt himself toppling over.

The four police cruisers and the rain were enough to keep the curious back. Not being a residential area, only a handful bothered to see what the flashing lights were about, but since there wasn't any apparent action, they kept moving. Only one who knew the diverse uses of the warehouse bothered to make a call that would be relayed to the higher echelon.

Gill Burke walked away from the two bodies in the rubber sheets and waited until the other morgue wagon drove up. A uniformed attendant hopped out of the back still shaking his head. Until now he thought he had seen everything. "What's with that one?" Gill asked.

"Dead as hell. Took him a while, but he never had a chance. That slug turned his insides into muck. You know what he had in his hand?"

"Yeah, I know."

"Son of a bitch. What're we supposed to do with it?"

"Guess you sew it back on the right party."

"Beautiful. Just great."

He heard Captain Long come up behind him, heard the terse, angry voice of Bob Lederer and spun around to give them both that bold, flat look that was so much a part of him again. Before Lederer could talk, Burke asked, "Got it figured out yet?"

"Not for public consumption," the D.A. said softly.

Burke glanced around and scowled. The only two reporters were talking to the coroner's men with not much success. "You going to keep Case in it or out?"

Lederer sucked his breath in, held it a second, then let it hiss out slowly. "Mr. Case was a very public-spirited man. He happened to have a C.B. radio in his car and probably was alerted to Shatzi's whereabouts when the call was put out."

"Not bad," Burke agreed.

"His car was seen parked not too far from the building, so that when an escape vehicle was needed, his was commandeered."

Burke let out a little laugh and lit a cigarette. "Who's going to buy that crock of shit, mister?"

"Gill . . ."

"Oh, Captain, come on, you aren't buying that stuff, are you?"

"No, but we're hoping somebody will."

"Richard Case was your security leak," Burke said. "How much will it take to tie him into the mob?"

"Probably not too much, Gill," Long said, "but it could be better if we left it alone."

"Bullshit. Their whole structure is coming apart right now and you want to handle this one with kid gloves."

"Look, Gill, that's the way we're going to play it, so stay cool, buddy."

"Sure. Okay. So now what? You got enough here to go out busting heads on. What do we do?"

"We sit tight. We go home, have a drink and let all the great brains get together and come up with an official attitude and issue orders and all the usual crap and try not to make waves."

Burke barely turned his head and looked at his friend.

The captain felt something cold run down his back. It wasn't the rain or the wind. It was just *something,* and in those few silent moments of stark contemplation, Bill Long was remembering about those items in the paper datelined somewhere in South America and his mind began it's own analysis of the details of the past months until a hardness slipped into his eyes. "Just do what I told you, Gill," he said.

When Herman Shanke got the message he sent out two of his least valuable dummies to bring in the truck. He wasn't that stupid not to figure a plant by the enemy, and after they had alternately driven, towed and pushed the truck into several preselected areas, Herman the German got a look at himself and gave an approving grunt to three of his lieutenants and said, "How do you like that balls of that Moe Piel! Son of a bitch, whatever kind of deal he made he sure cleaned house!"

"Wonder why he didn't call us?"

"What for? The thing was to get this stuff bought and on the road."

"Moe shoulda brought it himself. He shoulda been here."

"Moe's got more to do than play war, dummy. He's a hustler."

But Herman's lieutenant just wouldn't leave it alone. Everything had to be black or white without a touch of gray showing, otherwise it left him edgy with the little hairs on the back of his neck and hands standing straight out. "I don't like it, Herm," he said.

"You don't like what?"

"How come we got that other truck first, Herm?"

"Come on, man, this one got a sick engine."

"You sure that's Moe's truck?"

"Look, shithead, I can see the plates from here. I know the rig, get it? Now go check it out and if it's okay, get it back of the hotel. Once you get in the alley we seal the place off."

"Sure, Herm. How come Moe didn't show?"

"Maybe he's making another deal. Who the hell knows? He'll be back."

Twenty minutes later the truck turned into the back alley, pushed by the old four-door sedan, eased down the incline after a gentle bumper nudge and was braked to a stop in back of the old hotel that was the new headquarters for the rapidly expanding Shanke organization. The move from the old place had been subtle, clever and expertly carried out. At that moment six of Papa Menes' torpedoes were raiding the old place. What they didn't realize was that the guns inside belonged to police officers investigating the emptied building and they had already called for reinforcements on their walkie-talkie radios. Within ten minutes, the cream of the Menes armed forces was about to be eliminated.

And so was a square block of the city. The troops of Herman the German had moved in all but four cases of armament from the truck, gloating over their new acquisitions, reveling in the power of powder and steel, then the critical case was lifted and a wild inferno of flame and smoke erupted with a terrifying roar that dismantled everything within the perimeter of its destruction and threw the wreckage in mad, burning arcs into other city blocks where they could create their own little holocausts and in a single microsecond there was no army led by Herman the German.

But within thirty seconds news of the ravaged section of Miami flashed out on radio and television and five minutes later confirmation was made by a charred, staggering Shanke supporter that everything was lost because the Menes forces had suckered them all.

In Chicago, it was an hour before the big board could convene. Every one of them was aware of what had happened in Miami and silently cursed Papa Menes for jeopardizing the entire organization with one stupid move. Right at that moment, every civic organization, every governmental agency was getting ready to mount a massive thrust against the underground empire that was their life's blood. One spurt of true public indignation and their present and future, families and selves, would be wiped out of existence.

There was a single redeeming factor. Papa Menes was in the Miami area, it was his operation to conduct and his responsibility to assume. Throw Papa Menes to the dogs, the public would be satisfied and they could go back to business as usual.

Since the decision wasn't all that imaginative, they appeased their lack of originality by a lengthy discussion and parceling out of public relations assignments designed to focus attention on Papa Menes while detracting from their own notoriety.

All in all, it was a very harmonious meeting, with much drinking and shaking of hands.

All in all, it was a very stupid meeting because they underestimated the very person who had put them in their relative seats of power. When Papa Menes heard the news of the Miami destruction he put in an immediate call to Joey Grif, who sat across and down from the meeting room of the big board with a fix-mounted, precalibrated bazooka.

Joey answered the third ring, knowing who was on the line because nobody else knew the number, and said, "Yeah, boss."

"They meeting tonight, Joey?"

"Yeah. Big deal. This time everybody's there."

"You ready?"

Joey Grif felt a wave of the most incredible excitement he had ever experienced in his life wash over him. It was like being drenched with boiling oil that didn't even burn, but just made you feel good, so good it was even better than when you made it with a broad. He didn't want the boss to call it off because he seemed excited or overanxious, so he kept his voice even and said, "All ready, boss. Tell me when."

"How well can you see them from where you are?"

"Not too good. They're all sitting down. Talking, I guess."

"When they get up, they'll have drinks. Then do it."

"Got it, boss."

"Good luck, Joey. You're well taken care of."

"I know that, boss." He heard the receiver click and he hung up. Downstairs his car was waiting, the house was ready up in the mountains with the money safely stashed. No one would be able to trace him or the equipment, and with a satisfied smile he made an adjustment on the rubber gloves he wore, loaded the bazooka with a rocket projectile especially designed for this single shot and sat down to watch the windows of the room where the big board convened for the proper moment.

At precisely the right moment, Joey Grif triggered the bazooka and a moment later a cascade of searing flame roaring in front of a deadly hail of explosive pellets that churned inside a hellish explosion wiped out the heads of the crime syndicate in the western two-thirds of the United States.

Papa Menes was quite satisfied with himself. Reconstructing the empire wasn't really that much of a challenge, and this time he'd shape it in the manner he personally desired. He grinned inwardly and patted the naked body of Louise Belhander. She looked up at him, her eyes shining with some wild abandon, cheeks flushed and her breath coming deeply. He could feel the slight tremor in her body and his own blood surged through his veins.

Damn, she was hot for *him*. That crazy blonde was all worked up for real and she was sure as shit panting for his body. Well, by damn she was sure going to *get* his body and it would be something for her to remember. Whores ought to carry union cards, they were such great actresses, but this piece wasn't putting on any act at all. Papa let his hand roam over her breast and could feel the frantic pace of her heart and when she moaned the fire came back into his groin and he began to tremble himself. When her hand touched him the sensation was so intense he almost came right there. Oh, Papa wasn't fooling himself any. He'd had these crazy feelings before, especially right after he knocked somebody off personally, or read about their death in the paper. There was some wild sexual excitement that murder induced and he didn't realize that he still had it. Well, by damn, he did and he was sure going to keep it. This little bitch was all right too and damned if he wasn't going to take her right along with him. Anybody who could respond to the fire in him like she did wasn't going to get paid off and forgotten.

Except that Papa had misjudged the force that stimulated her.

It was identical to his. Death. And soon it would happen.

The thought of it allowed her to work a sensual magic on the old man, banking, but never putting out his fire, and when he proposed that she join him in a trip up north she agreed readily, knowing already exactly how she was going to kill him.

14

The events in Miami and Chicago commanded the attention of the entire nation. The regular TV and radio network news programs gave the affair exclusive coverage with special bulletins interrupting the other programs at irregular intervals.

And Mark Shelby was worried. No, that wasn't quite the feeling. He was scared, and if he really admitted it to himself, he was scared shitless and didn't know why.

He poured himself another drink and paced the length of his living room, staring blankly while he tried to figure it out. Sure, he had expected the big trouble in Miami and knew it would be laid in the old man's lap if it went sour, but where the hell did the big blast come from? The cops had found evidence that a truck had been turned into a massive bomb and they were tying it right in with the mob rebellion in progress.

Shelby shook his head impatiently, annoyed at the lack of conclusion. Okay, so it was a blast. It could have been a freak thing. Maybe that crazy Herman Shanke had gotten a load of explosives from someplace else and it went off by accident. That was the most likely explanation, but as far as the public and the police were concerned, it was part and parcel of organized crime and the lid was going to get clamped down tight enough to put a crimp in everything.

But even that wasn't the scary thing. It was the way somebody took out the entire brains of a once mighty organization with one lovely, well-planned, perfectly timed and executed hit.

Just like all the others, Shelby thought, *but he didn't do it singly this time. He went for broke on this one and made it!*

Where the hell did the guy get the information? The big board had only used that meeting room for a couple of months, using a series of fronts to rent it. It would have been changed before the next meeting . . . yet somebody had set up a gun position opposite it the same time they began using the premises.

Who?

Thirty-two men wiped out. Two more critically injured and not expected to survive. Six were unable to attend the meeting due to bad health, one other couldn't make it in time . . . and one was very busy in Miami.

Shelby stopped his pacing, finished his drink thoughtfully and went to the bar and made another one. For a minute he stared at himself in the ornamented mirror. Could it be possible. . . .

Papa Menes was getting old and even though he was the titular head of the whole group of families he didn't have that iron grip of sole control that he once had and like in anything else, the new ones were coming up and crowding, forming their own alliances, pulling their own power plays, anxious to squeeze out the very ones who had begotten them. Oh, it had been rumored around more than once that Menes had to go. He had opposed too many of their moves and they couldn't tolerate the interference. All they needed was an excuse.

Well, he, Mark Shelby, had tried to give them that excuse, and just before the blast went off Jerry Dines had given him the coded word, by phone, that Papa Menes had been voted out the hard way.

The trouble was that old tigers didn't take easily to dying. They might not be as agile, nor as strong, but they had the years of experience to augment their natural instincts and could beat the challengers to the kill every time.

Papa Menes was a tiger, all right. Shit, he knew damn well what the pattern was. He had his own pipelines into any area he wanted and he wasn't the type who would give up anything graciously. He was as tenacious and as mean-tempered as any old jungle tiger and pulling a coup like the Chicago wipe-out if they tried pulling the cork on him would be just his style.

But . . . was it possible?

And if it was, that meant Papa was the logical one behind the killing of all the others. He was getting ready to reorganize all over again and this was just the sort of shithead senility the organization was always worried about.

Shelby was thinking back to the early days. It had happened like that in the early forties, but Papa wasn't Papa then . . . he was *the* Man and the total tiger who took over everything and had kept it.

With a grin creasing his mouth, Mark Shelby took a long sip of his drink. So . . . the old man was determined to still keep it.

Like hell.

All the cops had to see was certain pertinent pieces of information he had collected and verified over the years and Papa Menes would be an automatic candidate for a life sentence in a federal prison if somebody didn't pick up the contract for his immediate demise, issued by the remaining handful of family heads in the country.

Poor Papa, Shelby thought. All done and didn't know it. Hell, they were *all* finished and he was in the catbird seat now. He alone knew the vital details of the intricate processes of the organization and if there were any complainers there were other details that would take them right out of action into an unmarked grave or a maximum-security cell.

Shelby finished his drink and winked at his image in

the back bar mirror. Damn, he felt good. He had it all figured out and now he felt damn good. He started to make another drink, but shoved the glass back and corked up his bottle. Booze was the last thing he needed to celebrate. What he wanted was one big blonde with big tits and a pussy like a vacuum cleaner and he'd celebrate his head off in high style and maybe when he took over he'd tell her who he really was and move her right into the apartment with him and live it up the way he always dreamed about and if his wife bitched about it a little accident could be arranged or he'd get Pete the Meat to put it to her in front of a photographer and he could dump her on an infidelity charge.

His hand reached out for the phone to call Helga, but he stopped before his finger touched the dial. With all the heat on they'd be watching everybody like a hawk. Helga would just have to wait a few days until everything relaxed a little. He went back and made the other drink after all and sat down, wishing Little Richard would call. So far there hadn't been one word on the news about Shatzi being pinned down, or if they had broken him loose or whatever. There was no answer at the warehouse, but that was to be expected at this time anyway. He'd just have to wait, that was all. He didn't like waiting because he always felt vulnerable when he wasn't taking the offensive, but right now that was all he could do.

Once the decision had been made, it took Papa Menes a short half hour to complete his arrangements. He rode in the back seat behind Artie and Louise up to a side street in Miami where they exchanged cars, took on a single suitcase of Papa's personal valuables, then drove on to Jacksonville in the north end of the state. Although his name was mentioned on every news flash, the announcers hinting that he was either missing or dead, no police accosted them, nor were they recognized.

At the airport Artie bought Louise a one-way, first-class ticket to New York, told her where to stay until they arrived and gave her five hundred dollars in cash to keep her happy in the interim. She had wanted to drive up with him, but Papa kept remembering how they yanked old Tommy Hazelton out of action on a Mann Act rap, and he'd be damned if he was going to take a fall for transporting any dame across a state line no matter how old she was.

Back at the car Artie said, "Boss, I don't like to say nothin', but you sure about that broad?"

Ordinarily, he might have gotten a fast backhand across the mouth, but this time Papa Menes only smiled. "The day I can't read a dame right," he told Artie, "is the day I'll go back to my wife. That kid is absolutely nuts about me."

Artie nodded reluctantly. He had seen the looks she had given the old man and the way she was with him and she wasn't faking a bit of it. He wondered what the hell the old guy had to turn a chick on that way. He even wished a little of it would rub off on him.

He said, "Sure, boss, but if anybody says anything . . ."

Papa's voice had a deadly chuckle to it. "Who's to complain?"

Artie grinned silently and turned the key on. When he was clear he pulled out of the parking lot, got back on the highway and turned north. This was the part of the job he liked best, a long straight drive where he could do nothing but listen to music and think about the broads back there on the Keys and the ones who would be waiting in the city. He would drive at speed limits, stopping only for gas and snacks, letting the old man get his sleep in the back seat. It was a twenty-four-hour run and he was going to enjoy every minute of it, especially those times when he saw some sucker pulled over by the local cops on a traffic violation. Yes, sir, anybody who broke the law on the road ought to get everything they could lay on him. Serves the bastard right. Artie let out a contented grunt and patted his pocket where he kept his wallet. He'd never even had so much as a parking ticket in his whole life.

Behind him, Papa wasn't sleeping at all. His eyes were closed, but he was looking at a screen of events in his mind, trying to view them as he would a movie. At times his vision would be documentary in effect, then take a fictitious angle and explore its possibilities, then he'd wipe it all out and start from the beginning.

Finding the beginning wasn't easy. It didn't start with all the sudden deaths of important syndicate personnel . . . it had to start long before that. There had to be scheming and planning before the first death right up to the last magnificent holocaust in Miami.

Everybody had been so damn sure that Herman

Shanke had been the answer when all that horse's ass did was take advantage of the situation. He sure had the artillery, though, and he wasn't good enough to latch on to that kind of equipment unless he had one hell of a connection. The screwy part was that fucking explosion that tore a hole in the city. It could have been an accident, but those kind of accidents took a lot of preparation and he could smell a shadowy hand moving around to stir things up. And preparation was one thing he, Papa Menes, believed in. If he hadn't been such a believer, the big board would have a contract out on him right now, never knowing how nicely he had been framed into looking like an incompetent old fool who finally needed dusting off.

So . . . who did that shadowy hand belong to? First, who was left in positions of authority? There sure weren't many, but when it came to control it was Mark Shelby. Who knew the total workings of the machine beside himself? Why, Mark Shelby . . . of the living ones, that is.

Papa smiled grimly to himself and leaned his head back against the cushions. It was a game he liked to play with himself. A long ride ahead and he could dwell on all the points, major and minor, separating and analyzing them, bring back to memory all the things that didn't seem to have importance at the time, but when fitted with the rest suddenly took on genuine significance.

And if it spelled out Mark Shelby, *Primus Gladatori*, old Primus was going to be a *Finis* gladatori.

With the repercussions still echoing from the South and Midwest there was enough material to keep the news media satisfied and there was no trouble at all getting them to delay releasing the news of the death of Richard Case and company. As far as anyone was concerned, the dead had simply dropped out of sight temporarily. Case had been separated from his wife for three years so it wasn't likely that she would make inquiries and his business associates had already been notified via a faked call that he'd be gone for a while.

Robert Lederer and his staff augmented by select personnel from police intelligence units had been going over the reports for the past five hours, trying to make a complete picture out of what had happened, but despite the detailed accounts the final version was more speculation than anything else.

It wasn't until fifteen minutes ago that anybody had known the whereabouts of Papa Menes. He had voluntarily made an appearance with his lawyer and witnesses who verified that they had been on a vacation in a mountain cabin far upstate, completely out of touch with current events.

Both Burke and Bill Long gave Lederer a sour grimace when he made the announcement and the captain asked, "How far are you going to push his alibi, Bob?"

Lederer shrugged and spread his hands. "All the way, but we're not playing with a kid. Menes'll have all his tracks covered. I'm not getting enthusiastic about breaking his story down at all. Besides, there's just the possibility that he's telling the truth."

"Balls." Burke's tone cut right across the room and heads turned to look at him.

"Okay, Mr. Burke," the D.A. said, "you've been coming up with all the believe-it-or-not kind of details around here, but if you've got something to say about this matter, keep it factual."

"Why should I? It's more than you can do."

"Because we're the ones who are going to draw the conclusions from whatever we get, fact or fancy . . . not you, Burke."

"All right, we'll stick with the facts then." He shook a cigarette into his hand, stuck it between his lips and lit it carefully. "You have what's left of the syndicate sprinkled around the country with their best men shoulder to shoulder in the morgue. You have public indignation at its peak and no matter what move you make against the fucking mob, you can't be wrong as long as you're quick. Everybody's sitting in a political rose garden where everybody can suddenly look good from the uniformed police to the big-shot politicos."

"That last part is pure speculation, Burke."

"In the pig's ass. You know it's true. The only thing that's got everybody bugged is the mob's chain of command and the disposition of their legitimate enterprises. Their billions in business can take one hell of a chunk out of the economy if it falls and nobody quite wants to get stuck with that label.

"Which brings us to another fact. The head man is right here in New York. The next in line is right here too. Everything is up for grabs with winner-take-all and there's going to be one hell of a war when Papa Menes and Mark Shelby get their troops in line . . . and you can bet your sweet behind that right now they're burning up the phones to every torpedo ready to hire out. The old man's got money stashed and ready for delivery and so has Shelby. They'll pull the cork, step back and see who comes out on top. They won't be around and you'll never get enough evidence to connect them to the hassle, but it will sure be one hell of a hassle. It's going to make that fracas in Miami seem like a teen-age rumble in the park."

"Don't get carried away, Burke."

Gill gave him a tight grin. "Hell, buddy, I'm trying to *understate* the case. If you think I'm blowing wind, ask your advisers here. Not all of them are yes-man types."

A quick glance told Lederer that Burke was right. "Of course, you have the solution to this whole thing, I suppose?" His voice was filled with acid sarcasm.

Burke nodded sagely. "Sure."

"Go on."

"Kill them," Burke said.

Bill Long handed Burke the plastic cup of steaming coffee and sat on the edge of the table staring out at the city on the other side of the window. Tiny lines seamed the corners of his eyes and he didn't so much as grimace when he sipped the scalding drink. That same thought was trapped in his mind and he couldn't lose it. In fact, it kept growing and building, but it was like a tree growing in the darkness. The substance was there, but you just couldn't see it.

Burke said, "We done for the night?"

The captain nodded, still looking out at the city.

"I'm taking off then. I'll give you a call tomorrow."

Bill Long heard his feet cross the room, but before Burke got to the door he said, "Gill . . ."

"Yeah, Bill?"

"You meant it, didn't you?"

After a moment Burke asked, "Meant what?"

"Upstairs . . . about killing them."

Burke's laugh was deep-throated and hard. "It's the only realistic answer, friend. You're damn right I meant it."

Long turned and looked at him, his face bland, but his eyes cold and hard. "You considering doing it too?"

For a few seconds, Burke said nothing, his eyes probing those of his friend. But both had their screens up and the walls were too thick to penetrate. Burke said, "Yeah, I've been considering ways and means."

"Find one?"

"Maybe. When I'm sure I'll call you."

15

His careful reconnaissance located only the single stakeout that had been there all day, replaced on schedule every four hours, so Mark Shelby decided that his physical needs justified the risk, and without bothering to call first, he took his usual circuitous route out of the building, picked up a cab two blocks away and gave the driver Helga's address.

Mark needed the diversion badly. He had to get his thinking straight, his efforts organized so that there would be no chance of anything going wrong.

Tangling with the old man always left him edgy, even when he had everything going for him. The trouble was, there wasn't any big board any longer and nobody to back him up in a power play. Papa Menes didn't give a shit if they had handed him the operation. Right now Papa was the big board, the little board and everything else. At least he thought he was. Mark glanced at his watch. By this time he ought to be having a few doubts himself. Mark had gotten the best bid in on a dozen of the top guns in the business and Papa could settle for second best. He knew Papa was making his own contacts, and given time, could come up with a bigger and better army, but Mark didn't plan to give him any extra time at all. Papa Menes could fall gracefully, his pockets well lined, or he could fall hard and empty.

On the West Coast most of the shattered families had tossed their lot in with Shelby. Instinctively, they knew that Papa Menes had ordered the nearly total destruction of the organization heads, and although they knew he was justified, their resentment was too great to accept the old man as their head.

Besides, Mark Shelby had intimated that he had everything wrapped up the way he wanted, and knowing Mark for the shrewd manipulator he was, they saw him with a handful of aces. Not wanting to be cut out of the pot, they readily threw in behind him.

The old Midwest bunch still had the mustaches and wouldn't even spit on somebody who couldn't converse in the old tongue. Even though they had all been hurt in the upheaval, they threw their weight behind Papa, expecting the conflict to push and shove a little bit, then resolve itself the same way it always had when the big dons were up there where they belonged, until the time came for them to personally hand over the reins of control to someone of their choice.

Shelby had sat in on too many intraorganizational squabbles not to know how it would go and who would throw in with whom. It was a new era this time and the name of the game was money. Hired guns didn't give a shit one way or another who ran the factory as long as they got their pay. The more you paid them, the greater their allegiance and they could smell where the money was. Mark had it all wrapped up and when the sides were chosen and he knew exactly who to cut off, he'd select what he needed out of his vast horde of details, see that it reached the right police agency and the opposition would fall completely and permanently without his hand having been seen by anyone.

Undoubtedly, the old man would have an ace or two up his sleeve, but it couldn't beat a royal flush. He smiled silently to himself, remembering the way Papa Menes had sounded on the phone earlier. He sure was one pissed-off old fart, but he was a smart old fart too. How the hell he managed to find out he had sent that extra load of artillery down to Herman the German, Mark couldn't figure. He thought he had covered the deal pretty carefully, but it was a hurried play and the exposure really didn't matter at this point anyway. Not that he admitted it outright. He had simply laughed and reminded the old man of a few things he could document that would turn a couple of those old-line loyal families against him completely. He finished by saying, "Stalemate, Papa."

"You think so?" Menes asked.

"All the way, Papa."

"Mark, you keep forgetting something."

"And what would that be?"

There was a chuckle first and Mark felt himself frown. It wasn't the time or place for anything to be funny at all. The old man said, "It's all there waiting for who-ever's big enough to take it, right?"

"Correct, Papa."

"And plenty big enough for you to try to get and me to try to hold onto, right?"

"Absolutely, Papa."

There was another chuckle and the old man said very slowly, "You fuckin' shithead, you think you know everything and maybe you do, except for the one big-gest thing of all."

Shelby felt a shudder run across his shoulders, then relaxed and smiled. Papa Menes always had that effect on people and now he was trying to psych him out too. With the old man, it was an instinctive thing, with Shelby, it was deliberate, so he made his pitch. "What's that, Papa?"

But the old man won. He chuckled again and said, "If you can't figure it out by ten o'clock, give me a call, shit-head, and I'll tell you something that'll tie a square knot in your cock."

Before Mark could answer him, the old man hung up. Mark grinned at the dead phone, stuck it back in its cra-dle and felt good because the days of the whip the old man held were past and dead and the whip would be in his hands now. The only annoying part was that he couldn't figure what the old slob had been talking about. Hell, it was pretty damn plain now who was the instigator of those initial raids on the organization. Only one hand was behind it . . . an experienced old pro who knew everybody's move and could hire and train outside guns to carry out every damn detail with only one man to each kill. No wonder they could never put it together. But the original premise that came up at the meeting was correct. Only one hand that trained many. Only one motive . . . complete takeover of the organization. Government, even the underground one, was being confiscated by a dictator.

And Papa Menes was the only one who could have accomplished it so beautifully. For a second Mark felt the irritation come back again. The dirty old son of a bitch probably even figured his, Mark's, own reaction and tried to use it against him. Only something went wrong. He was still alive and kicking back from topside.

That was always the trouble with revolutions, Mark thought, some lousy little thing didn't stay in place, or somebody was late, or somebody decided to take a crap before going to the office and the big scheme never quite came off.

What was the most beautiful of all though, Mark told himself, was that his own plans had gone into operation years and years before Papa Menes had felt his own position jeopardized and decided to do something about it.

The pleasure of the thoughts he had just reviewed was making Mark Shelby horny and he felt himself starting to bulge against his pants. He squirmed so he wouldn't be so uncomfortable, took a five-dollar bill from his roll and when they reached the building he handed it to the driver and told him to keep the change.

He hoped Helga had some crazy innovation ready for him. This had to be a very special night.

A very special night.

When he turned the key in the lock and pushed the door open he knew it was going to be the wildest night of all, because Helga came off the couch in all her nakedly amazing glory, ran at him and jumped in his arms so hard he almost tumbled backward and while he was still struggling to regain his balance her mouth was all over him, her fingers tearing at his clothes, and he was fighting to hold her back before she ripped him apart. It was as if she were trying to rape him and the thought shocked his loins into an immediate erection too sensitive to tolerate and he locked his arms around her and carried her into the other room and tossed her into the middle of the king-sized bed.

She bounced back before he could get a single button undone, her fingers clawing, little mewing sounds coming from wet lips that kissed every inch of flesh that became visible as she undressed him.

Finally he stopped resisting the aggressive demands she made and let himself go into a completely passive state, being the recipient of all the things she gorged herself on, lolling in the total splendor of absolute sexual fulfillment. He was asked to give nothing. All she wanted was for him to enjoy, to take, to spend, to rise to the heights of screaming physical pleasure where everything becomes blanked out in those nerve-shattering waves of orgiastic abandonment that left the body spasm-wracked and helpless.

He knew then, why it was called the *little death*.

His mind was too satiated to wonder what had encouraged the superb performance on her part. He lay spread-eagled on the bed, his formerly stiff member a humorless blob, his eyes slowly closing until he was asleep.

From the doorway, Helga watched him until she was sure he was in the exhausted embrace of sexual fatigue and let herself shiver finally, her body tight with fear and anxiety.

She had thought it was Nils coming in and she had prepared herself for her lover with all the ardor she could muster. Her bath had been scented, her hair had been carefully arranged and the handsome young man with the fluttery hands and falsetto voice had been skillful enough to electrify her mind and body with all the erotic technique he had accumulated over the past four years so that when he had left she was at an emotional peak that only a woman sensitized in the arts of sex could understand or a man so practiced and appreciative in its application could enjoy.

It had all been arranged for Nils and then that stupid lout who paid the bill walked in and she had to waste it all on him.

Draining the bastard wasn't the hard part. Any five-dollar whore could have done that. It was hiding her own fear that tore her insides out and depleted any emotion she thought she owned. Oh, it wasn't the little gun he always carried. He had money enough on his person to warrant the protection it offered . . . no different from the jewelry salesmen she used to know or that real estate broker from Phoenix she once serviced who only dealt in cash deals.

What scared the hell out of her was that magazine she had picked up with the paper . . . the special edition rushed out to capitalize on the monstrous things that had happened in Miami and Chicago . . . the one that carried the candid shot some itinerant photographer, dead now, had taken of the syndicate leaders coming out of a conference in the midtown hotel, and there in the nearby obscure background was the man she had thought to be an innocuous wholesale grocer from Trenton, New Jersey, when, in reality, he was Mark Shelby, suspected head man of the mob.

And Nils' plane was late. He had been due in an hour ago. The apartment belonged to the naked man on the bed. He could have bought off the doorman so she couldn't try to alert him. All she could do was play it by ear and hope to hell she wasn't caught in the middle.

Helga was far from dumb. She had so much time on her hands she had to read everything to occupy the idle hours. She could think and she could speculate. Her past had incorporated enough diverse activities in the area outside the legal concept of normal living so that she could put fact and fiction together and glean a strip of truth that was enough to make brave men quake, and being only a woman, she not only quaked, she went to the bathroom when she didn't even have to, like a kid watching a horror movie, and evacuated her emotions into a toilet bowl. While she wiped, she considered getting Shelby's gun and killing him.

That was too risky. Helga wasn't all that brave, either.

She could wait for Nils and let him kill Shelby.

But Nils wasn't that brave, either. A great lay, a big talker, a fabulous body, but guts for a shootout he didn't have.

All she could do was wait and hope some hidden gene inherited from their forebears, a gene with spunk and determination, would show up and between the two of them they could get away from the terror who lay limply on the bed for the moment, and trust that their mutual anxieties and knowledge of cowardice wouldn't interfere with all those lovely sex games they had planned on playing.

Helga looked at the clock again.

Where the hell was that fucking airplane?

What would she do when it got here?

She could feel it all around her, an invisible force as though someone were stretching the air too tight. There was a tension in the city, in the way people moved, unconsciously nervous. Unreleased energy was back in the night sky again, rumbling with displeasure and spitting intermittent belches of heat light night, waiting and daring anything to trigger it into celestial madness.

Helen Scanlon looked at the two of them, Burke and Captain Long, sensing that something had happened to their friendship, challenging it so that whatever had matured in all the years was balanced on a knife's edge, and no matter which way it fell, both of them would lose.

She knew she shouldn't have been there. It was a time

for men alone, yet in a way she was like a catalyst whose action could temper or instigate a cataclysm. Inside each of them was a locked secret and they probed each other to bring it out . . . not overtly, but just a single word or expression that would satisfy their own conclusions.

For a second she felt a flash of hatred for the whole world, the entire stinking system that could turn men into animals and the earth into a laboratory of destruction to benefit a few warped minds.

She looked at her watch. It was a quarter to nine.

Bill Long put down his coffee cup and took the cigarette Gill offered him. "If you're right it makes the entire department look like it's pretty damn stupid or on the take."

"Not necessarily."

"No?" Long leaned into the match and blew a thin stream of smoke across the table. "You realize how many men we had working that deal?"

"Sure."

"Top guys, not rookies. Guys all pulling for you, yet the kind of guys who would lay the evidence on the line no matter what they found."

"They found plenty of it, didn't they?"

"Nothing you could refute."

"Oh, I refuted it," Burke told him. "I just couldn't prove it."

"Why didn't you stick around and sweat it out?"

"Who needed the aggravation. Things kept piling up against me and there was no way out. There was enough basis of truth so that the whole package looked good. All I could do was make matters worse and you damn well knew it. There wasn't a chance in the world when it became a public issue the politicals could capitalize on and I'll be damned if I was going to take any more of a beating from those pricks. The committee at Compat knew the score better than you did and offered me the job. I didn't have to think twice then. I made more in a month than I did in a year on the force without having to face a rule book that worked against me or a crowd of cop haters and superior officers running scared to protect their pensions."

"Don't hand me that, Gill."

"What could you have done, buddy?"

"Kept your case open until we got the break, that's what."

"That sounds good, but I don't like starving or having to eat the shit I was having thrown at me." He stopped, took a drag on the butt and shook his head. "The other side was just a little too good for your boys. They didn't have any rule book to fight against. They could pull out all the stops. They yanked my teeth very effectively and saw to it that when I was gone, everything settled back to normal."

"But it didn't, did it?"

The smile Burke gave him was almost frightening to Helen. There was something about his eyes over the hard slash of his mouth that sent a shudder down her spine.

"No," Burke said, "it didn't."

"In fact, it got worse."

"For some people, perhaps." Burke had stopped smiling and was watching Long.

The cop nodded. "When you look back at it, the whole thing seems to have been a well-engineered deal."

Burke's shrug was enigmatic. "Who knows? In this business, anything can set off a chain reaction."

This time it was Bill Long's face that had a peculiarly strained expression. "True. *If* . . . and only *if* . . . you know where, when and how to touch off the original action."

"It could be accidental."

"Accidents," Long said, "are like coincidences. In this business they don't happen. They're planned."

"A lot of things are planned, kid. Then suddenly they get unplanned and the shit hits the fan." He looked at his watch and tossed a bill on the table to cover the coffees. "And right now we're about to plug in the fan."

The captain's face got tight again, his words sounding clipped. "Suppose you brief me on this bit, Gill."

"Suppose I just let you see it happen and explain as I go along. You haven't got much choice anyway."

Helen saw the tendons in Long's hand stand out against the flesh. Finally he said, "Okay, it's your show, Burke."

She reached out and laid her hand on top of Gill's. "If you'd rather . . ."

He didn't let her finish. "You've been there before, doll. We're simply going to make an inquiry, that's all. Maybe an intimidating-type inquiry, but no rough stuff.

You see . . . it's partially because of you that I began to understand how it was done."

Whenever Mark Shelby recovered from the effects of an orgasm he was a hollow shell forced to look inward upon himself and disgusted at what he saw. What he thought was manhood expended itself in a fiery gush leaving nothing at all to disguise the self-contempt, the loathing and the bitterness of having been a gutless, wanton puppet whose prowess lay, not in his own ability, but in the hands of those who owned him and twitched the leash to make him respond to their demands. There was nothing brave or daring about the way he had killed. Anyone could shoot or knife from ambush, or in the back, or under the guise of being a friend. He always knew what he would do if faced with an adversary who didn't fear him at all and came at him with a death weapon in his hand. He'd run. He'd hide. He'd wait until somebody else destroyed the enemy before he would reappear with a logical explanation and claim credit for the victory.

Alone, Mark Shelby was a weak thing who could hate himself to death.

Fortunately, he was never alone. The power was still with him, outside there in the other room, a cylindrical waxen tower of power.

He wiped the bitter taste from his mouth, got out of bed, showered and dressed. Outside in the living room she'd be waiting for him, all vibrant, active sex ready to relieve herself in a dozen more climaxes, ready to bring him into the heady rapture of a gut-wrenching spasm . . . and again, like almost all the other times, he was going to have to make some excuse so he would not have to participate in an act that would expose his incapabilities. Maybe he never did fool her, but he couldn't be sure. At least she understood and gave him the benefit of the doubt.

That was why he was so damn crazy about her. She was all his, from the top to the bottom with all those good parts in between. He was strictly one hell of a big man to her and nobody could come near him for sheer physical magnetism. She let him know it, too. He grinned and sucked in his stomach a little. When he had the operation in the palm of his hand, he'd let her know just who he was, take her right in with him and tell the old lady to fuck off. Then he and Helga would really swing.

But it wasn't at all like it should have been. She wasn't bare-assed naked at all. She was sitting cross-legged on the couch with her dress hiked up around her thighs and she was smiling, but there was something forced in the way she did it and the drink in her hand was heavy with scotch and half empty. There was enough animal in him to smell the nervousness in her.

He was about to yank the glass out of her hand when the phone rang and she almost dropped it. Then his fingers beat hers to the receiver and he said in a soft, deadly voice, "I'll get it," and watched her eyes go wide and scared for a brief instant. Shelby said, "Yes?" then grunted and handed the phone to Helga. "Some broad for you."

There was no doubting the relief in her eyes at all. Her voice had the quick, staccato tone of relief as she went into a vivid description of the dress she wanted altered and she didn't look at him at all while she was talking. She hung up almost reluctantly and was staring at him when he came back from the bar with a drink in his hand.

He was just about to accost her when he saw the hands of the wall clock standing at ten and without taking his eyes from hers at all, he dialed Papa Menes' private number, waited until he heard the old man's voice and said, "It's ten o'clock, Papa."

The old man let a laugh ripple out of his mouth. "Figure it out yet, shithead?"

"You're acting senile, Papa. This call is only a courtesy now."

"Is it, Marcus? Not as long as you believe I was behind all the trouble, punk."

A cold chill ran down Shelby's neck. "Why would I believe that?"

"Because," Papa told him, "I was almost stupid enough to think you were. Then I sat down and ran it all through my mind until I was sure you never did have the guts or the brains to pull it off. You just waited behind the scenery and let it all happen. It wasn't what you planned, but as long as it happened you let it alone, then even helped it a little bit. Only like I said, you forgot something."

"Papa, listen . . ."

"Lay off the shit, punk. I know it wasn't me and I know it wasn't you. What you forgot was that someplace the one who started it all is still out there waiting and we both got to be on his list . . . and you're in a tight spot."

"I'm . . ."

"Don't shit me, Marcus. You're not at home, you're not in the office, so you're someplace where you can be tagged real easy. You see, I'm smarter than you, shit-head. I'm holed up tight in a safe place with twenty guns all around me and I can wait it out for a year if I have to. By then you'll be dead anyway." He chuckled again and added, "Besides, if you ain't dead, you'll be doing one hell of a lot of hard time. That cop Burke was back around the pawnshop again. He was looking for some blond tramp. He won't have much luck because she's long dead, but he sure as hell might figure something else out."

The phone was dead in his hand with the old man's laugh still ringing in his ears. When Helga smiled with phony sweetness and asked him if everything was all right his stomach churned up into his throat and stifled the scream he let out as he threw his fist into her unprotected face and knocked her sprawling back against the couch. There was no stopping the madness that made him tear into her, his knuckles grinding into her ribs and head, his feet kicking huge welts into her skin until she was a bloody, discolored mess on the floor.

When he finished he was a breathless, disheveled figure with wild eyes and skinned fingers and all he could say came out in a panting hiss. "Lousy, stinking bitch. You're waiting for a guy. You fuckin' two-timing whore, you won't be any good to any man again. You're

276

going to be dead, you and him both. I'm coming back and you're going to be dead."

Shelby would have waited, but there was something more important he had to do, then he'd kill them both. The insane fear that one single guy could blow up his entire scheme was so staggering that he even forgot what Papa Menes had told him.

He was back on the street when he remembered, but by then it was too late to change his mind. He flagged down a cab, told the driver where he wanted to go and sat back.

Maybe luck was on his side again. To help it along he changed cabs three times until he reached his destination, certain now that he wasn't being followed.

The fear had ebbed out of him, and now he was at his deadly best, ready to kill again from ambush.

Gill Burke parked the car a block away and sat there with Helen and Bill Long. The rain had turned into a fine mist, greasing the streets and throwing halos around the street lights. They looked up the empty block where only a few stores still waited for late business.

Burke said, "I'm going to lay out the background for you, Bill. It isn't a big story and after we check it out you'll find nothing but circumstantial evidence . . . except for one critical piece."

"I'm waiting."

"We go back to Mark Shelby again."

"You're kidding yourself, Gill."

"Am I? Let's see if you think so."

"Okay, go ahead." There was no confidence in his voice at all.

Burke said, "Think of it this way . . . Shelby was in a position to know everything about everybody, the workings of the business, personal details . . . everything. He always had been an ambitious guy, but he kept it hidden pretty damn well because the syndicate didn't like ambitious people in sensitive places.

"Shelby didn't want to be a target, either. He was planning the ultimate takeover and wanted to make sure he stayed covered, so besides gathering all the data on the organization, he had evidence on everybody inside it that could keep them out of circulation permanently.

"Hell, it's not an old scheme, Bill, but he was able to make his work. He couldn't keep reams of paper around, so he found a couple of unknown and unscrupulous photographers to microfilm his collection. Unfortunately, one or both were a little too unscrupulous and realized what he had. They tried to hold him up for a little blackmail and Shelby killed them on the spot. He had probably stayed on the spot while they did the filming, but one of those guys could do a duplicate of something to hold over his head. The poor slob didn't realize who he was playing around with and that was it. Shelby picked up the dupes and walked the hell out.

"It was a sleazy neighborhood and he probably never expected to be recognized, but one guy spotted him . . . even spoke to him. He was a lucky kid. When they put the heat to him he wasn't about to talk . . . and he still won't . . . but it put Shelby in a position of not being able to take any chances. He could have ditched the gun, but he wanted those two kills solved fast and to everybody's satisfaction. After that, whatever the kid said wouldn't matter anyway.

"He found a perfect patsy, an alcoholic named Ted Proctor. He made up a story the guy believed, probably about finding a gun and how Proctor could pawn it for twenty bucks and they'd split the loot for some booze. So Proctor walked into the trap, all juiced up with happiness."

Long felt it coming and his voice was like ice. "Don't give me any crap about Jimmie Corrigan being part of the scheme, buddy."

"He didn't know he was," Burke said quietly. "He was suckered too." He took a breath, lit up a cigarette and stared down the street again. "Just before that, Shelby got some of his supposedly clean front men to hand over their wallets. He had them planted in Proctor's room to make Proctor look like a regular heist artist. Then he roped in some hooker to do a stalling act in case the timing wasn't just right."

"What the hell are you talking about?"

"Something Corrigan remembered that wasn't in his report because it didn't seem to be part of it."

"He'll confirm it?"

"Sure, but you won't find the dame, that's for sure."

"Go ahead."

"Shelby knew Corrigan's routine and about what time he'd go by Turley's pawnshop. Corrigan was a little late, but the hooker stalled him nicely while Proctor went ahead into the pawnshop. Finally Corrigan got away from the broad and walked toward the shop where Turley was discussing buying the gun from Proctor and just as the cop came by, Turley threw up his hands like he was being robbed. Corrigan spotted him, came in with his hands up and when Proctor turned around with the gun in his mitt Corrigan thought the guy was going to let him have it and he fired first."

Bill Long stared at him in disgust. "There's one hell of a hole in the story, Gill."

"There is?" Gill was smiling now because he knew what Long was going to say.

"Yeah, a big one. It was night out. There was no way for Turley to spot the cop coming up through the window. It's completely covered with all those pawned items."

Burke nodded. "It sure is."

"Well?"

"Remember me telling you it was Helen here who put me on to it."

She looked at him strangely.

"You were waiting in the car for me outside. The windows that flank his doorway reflected you and the car perfectly when you stand in the right position, and that's exactly where Turley was . . . not behind the counter where he usually transacted business. He was able to spot Corrigan and go into his act with no trouble at all."

"Damn," Bill Long said. There was no ice in his voice this time. He could sense the logic behind, the clever reasoning, but what dug into him most of all was the way they had used the beat cop for a gun hand.

"The gun Shelby used was a hot one and it worked out

beautifully for him. We traced it to a couple of other ills and there it was, laid out perfectly, and everybody fell for it." He stopped for a minute, then looked at Long again. "Not everybody, though. Corrigan never did like the picture, but he couldn't deny it. Something had been bothering him all this time and he could never figure out what it was."

"Oh?"

"I found out what it was," Gill said.

Long waited. "The fingerprints."

A frown creased the cop's forehead. "They were all Proctor's on that gun."

"Yeah, too many of them. There was no print at all on the trigger where his forefinger should have been. That print was on the plastic butt grip. Proctor didn't even know how to handle a gun. He had his entire hand wrapped around the butt."

"How the hell did we miss. . ."

"Easy, pal. It was all too easy to look for any roadblocks."

Long shifted in his seat, his mind working. "If you're right, we still have Turley."

"They might have so much heat on him he'd never talk."

"They can't even begin to lay heat on him like we can though."

"Then let's try it."

"Okay, you smart son of a bitch. I just hope you're right."

"I am. But do me one favor."

"Name it."

"I make the initial approach on the guy. He knows me

now and I want him to know me better. I want to be the one who loosens him up for the big shove."

"Listen, Gill, your department. . ."

Burke was flat and hard when he said it. "I'm the one they did it to, pal. It's still my department."

"Your department," Long finally agreed.

Burke turned the key on and pulled away from the curb. Up ahead another car turned the corner, disgorged a passenger and drove on. Burke parked and cut his lights.

There was no spit left in Mark Shelby's mouth. The heat of violent rage and fear had dried it up and his lips were like parchment. The broken knuckles in his hand ached as he clamped them around the gun and he could feel something knotting his intestines like a tangled line.

He saw the lone figure get out of the car opposite him and go in the pawnshop and the impatience grew in him like a cancer. For a few minutes he stayed in the shadow of the old panel truck, waiting, but the guy didn't come out and he looked across the street again. He couldn't see too clearly through the rain-frosted glass door, but there was something familiar about the way the man stood, the way his shoulders were set and the motion of his hand when he pushed his hat back.

Then he knew who he was and the vomit hit his throat so fast he almost gagged and his eyes began to water as he made his last, mad dash across the empty street with the little gun ready to take out the two monstrous obstacles to all his years of planning and working and when he rammed the door open a hoarse shout grated from his mouth and he saw Turley's eyes widen with horror and he triggered the automatic into a wicked blast aimed for Burke's back.

But Burke had seen Turley's eyes too and dropped with the instinctive agility of a cat and the shot caught Turley flush in the chest and left him dead before he could hit the floor.

He almost had Burke, who was still clawing for the gun at his belt but before he could pull the trigger again he heard the roaring thunder behind him and felt the mighty hammer of a slug drive into his spine and on through his heart and a huge gout of blood spewed through his lips drenching the very spot he fell on.

Outside Helen was screaming her head off and Burke looked up into a pair of eyes so filled with hate he thought Long was going to pick him off right there.

He almost did, but the years of training took hold and he holstered the .38 and waited until Burke got to his feet. "You dirty bastard," Bill Long said. "You miserable, dirty bastard."

Burke looked at him, saying nothing.

"You made a patsy out of me. You did the same thing to me that they did to Corrigan. You set it all up and let me play gun for you."

Burke's eyes didn't falter. They were as flat and cold as the cop's were and his voice was there to match. "You said there weren't coincidences in this business, Bill. Now you just saw one."

"No, old buddy." Long's voice had a tired quality to it now. He sounded old and disappointed. "You're a bastard, Gill, a rotten, dirty bastard and I had it figured right all along and didn't know it."

"Suppose I prove it to you."

"You can make the try, Gill, but you won't prove anything to me." He glanced at him with begrudging admiration. "You're clever, man. Damn clever."

"Do I try?"

"Sure. What difference does it make now?"

"Probably none."

"Then call Lederer and the crew. Get this mess cleaned up and we'll move."

Long made a wry face. "Yeah, let's do that."

In the doorway, Helen was watching them both with unbelieving eyes, her hand clamped over her mouth to keep from getting sick.

16

Lederer got there with the medical examiner and stayed while the detectives took everything down and the morgue crew moved out the bodies. The TV crews and the reporters were covering everything and this time Lederer was glad to have them on tap, because he was able to throw them a big one for holding down the news about the murder of Richard Case. Now he could blow everything in one grand gesture and in the back of his mind he could see the upcoming election and almost see his name up there for the Big Seat.

He even had good words for Burke and his admiration for Bill Long's action was apparent to everyone. Having a witness in Helen Scanlon made it even better and when Burke said he had more to do and would finish the report in the morning, Lederer was more than happy to turn him loose.

In the car, Bill Long chewed on his lip with amazement. "He bought it," Long said. "They all bought it. They bought the biggest con I ever saw. They bought it and they have to keep it. I even have to back you up on it and I know better."

"You don't know anything, Bill."

Helen squeezed his arm. "Please, Gill."

"Want me to tell you what I know?" Long asked. There was a near-note of humor in his voice, like that of a man who has seen just too much and had to laugh at anything that was anticlimactic.

"Yeah, Bill. Tell me."

The captain leaned back in the seat, his head resting easily against the cushion. "Not too long ago, in a certain South American country—and you read about this in all the papers—mobsters were being found dead all over the place. Big hoods, little hoods . . . sometimes singly and sometimes in bunches. Occasionally they were in the open, other times they were in hiding, but they were carefully tracked down, shot to death and left lying where everybody could see them.

"For a while they thought it was another gang war, but it wasn't that at all. They finally found out that an execution squad was at work and the only pros that could handle that kind of action were part of the police force.

"Oh, the crime rate sure dropped down to zero and the mobsters got the hell out of that country in one big hurry and maybe the situation was the better off for it, but it left a funny feeling in everybody's stomach because the more you kill the easier it gets and with a force that big, powerful and deadly, it could turn its talents someplace else when it ran out of punks to gun down.

"Luckily, it didn't seem to go any further, and it was pretty damn effective, so not much more was said about it. It was practically forgotten. But let's suppose it was well remembered by somebody who saw how the pattern could be used right here in the United States. Not only used, but modified and sophisticated to such an extent the ramifications took on unbelievable proportions.

"First, it would take a pro who was familiar with as many details of the syndicate operation as anybody could be. He had to have knowledge, the time, the ability and the money to plan it out and put it into effect without ever risking exposure himself. He had to work them against themselves and when only a few were left, put the frosting on the cake with a completely legal maneuver that left him successful and satisfied."

Burke drew into the curb outside the apartment building and cut the switch. When he got out, Helen and Bill Long followed him. The captain looked at the building and Burke said, "Shelby had an apartment here."

"It's not in our files."

"It is in mine," Burke told him.

As Burke expected, there was no apartment listed under Shelby's name, but when he flashed his badge and gave his description, the doorman remembered Mark and said he visited Miss Helga Piers in 21A. In fact, he added, he was there that very evening and had left quite hurriedly a little after ten o'clock.

"You have a passkey?"

"Yes, I have."

"Then you'd better come with us."

"Sir," the doorman said, "don't you have to have. . ."

"We can get a warrant in five minutes or you can do it the easy way," Burke told him.

One look at those eyes of his and the doorman didn't hesitate. He led them to the elevator, took them up to the top floor and pointed out the door. While Helen and the doorman stayed to one side, Burke and Long flanked the door and looked at each other.

A thin line of light lined the sill and from inside a TV program rambled on. There was another sound too, an intermittent wail of hysterical laughter coupled with an overtone of anguish.

Burke pushed the doorbell and waited. Nothing happened. He tried it again and there still was no answer. He snapped his fingers and the doorman opened the lock with his passkey. Gill turned the knob, threw the door open an inch and looked back at the doorman. "Beat it," he said.

They went in together, guns ready, spreading out inside, poised like cats, taking in the entire situation in a fraction of a second.

Nobody came at them.

All they heard was the TV and that strange wail, with an odd aromatic smell permeating the air. With professional caution, they picked their way through the area to the living room until they got to the arch and saw the remains of the furniture and the nearly naked wreckage of the woman who squatted on the floor in a pool of her own blood, rocking and writhing in pain, a lit candle in front of her that she kept hacking at with a knife in ineffectual, weary motions.

Bill Long had seen a lot of things, but this one almost made him sick. The terrible beating she had taken was beyond anything he had witnessed before and whoever did it had to be so twisted he never should have lived through his own birth.

Gill yelled for Helen and this time there was no fear or disgust in her. It was a woman recognizing the emergency and becoming equal to it. She didn't even give them time to phone, making them help her get Helga on the couch, finding the towels, the compresses and the medication until the eyes that were so blanked out from shock suddenly became alive from pain and all she could say was, "No . . . no . . . please, no more."

"You're all right," Helen told her. "We're friends and we'll help you."

"Help . . . me?"

"That's right." She waved to Gill and said, "Better get the ambulance now."

He made the call, then followed Long over to the bar. The entire back section was wrecked, a large religious picture and a plaster statue lying in smashed pieces on the shelf. The cop said, "Crazy. She dragged herself all over the place in that condition. You see that blood trail?"

"I saw it."

"It doesn't seem possible."

Burke looked at the red splotches around the back of the bar and on the shelving. There were other smears on the end table and the arm of a chair where she had propped herself as she pulled her wracked body around the room. "Maybe she was motivated," Burke said.

"What . . . to get to a religious picture?" He kicked over a four-legged metal holder, looking at the wax fragments in its base. "Maybe you're right." He picked the holder up and showed it to Burke. "I guess people who got a strong religious conviction can do damn near anything. She thought she was dying and wanted to light a candle to herself."

"Then why was she chopping at it with that knife?"

"Maybe it's part of her religion," Long said sourly.

"Gill . . ." Helen was waving him over to the couch.

"She coming around?"

"He told her his name was Norris. He was keeping her, all right, but do you know she knew who he really was?" Before he could answer she held out a cheap magazine folded open to a full-page picture of recognizable faces. "She had it under the couch. She pointed him out to me."

He glanced at it, flipped the cover over and tapped his finger under the issue date at the top. "This is this month's copy."

Helen got the message and nodded. "She just found out who he really is. That poor kid."

Burke said, "Come here, old buddy." When the captain walked up Gill showed him the photo. "There's your man," he said and tapped the photo of the one in the background.

"Mark Shelby," Long said softly.

"I hope you feel better now," Burke said.

"About him," Long grated, "but not about you. You're still a bastard."

Helga's hot eyes stared at the two of them, her mouth working, trying to form words. Bill Long had to be sure. He held the picture out, his finger indicating Shelby. "That the one who did it?"

Her nod was affirmative. "He. . ."

"Don't try to talk," Helen told her.

She made a feeble motion with her hand and her mouth worked again. "He got . . . mad about . . . something. Then he . . . found out about . . . Nils."

"Nils? Your husband?"

She shook her head. "Friend. We were . . . going to . . . marry. Take his . . . money and . . . run away."

Burke said, "You want me to call this Nils for you? Look, if. . ."

The pain in her eyes washed out into one of incredible sorrow and tears flowed slowly onto her cheeks. "Nils . . . was here. He saw me . . . and he . . . ran away . . . too." She managed to force a gruesome smile to her lips. "All gone. Nothing left . . . at all. Only his . . . beautiful candle. He . . . loved the candle. Now I . . . kill that . . . damn thing."

It hit Burke first, the entire implication of the whole thing, the beauty of the way Shelby had disguised it. He walked to the middle of the floor, blew the candle out and picked up the blood-stained knife she had tried to kill the candle with. He ran the tip of it down the side of its foot-long length, rammed the blade into the crack and pried the waxen cylinder open.

The rolls of microfilm were stacked one on top of the other and when Burke held it up for Long to see he said, "The ultimate proof, friend. We just got it in time. If that candle kept burning it would have destroyed the whole bundle. Old Shelby was covering every angle, even to a built-in self-destruct. Who the hell would blow out a religious candle anyway?"

"Someone with no religion, maybe," Long said. "Or no conscience. Like you."

"Go fuck yourself," Burke said.

Bill Long gave him a tight smile. "You see I'm right. You *are* the one. A whole execution squad wrapped up in one man. There was a time when you would have jumped me for saying what I just did, but you can't now because you know I'm right and you never could fake me out."

"Don't you ever quit?" Gill asked him.

"Not on this one. I think I'm going to burn your ass on this one, Gill. I won't even have to try hard because I know what's been on your mind since the very beginning. There's only one guy you're really after, the top man of the whole schmear . . . Papa Menes. He's still alive and still holds the power and even if what's on those films can indict him he'll get away before he can be convicted. There are plenty of places he can go and still be head man in the operation. Luciano did it, a few others did it, living out their old age in lush comfort in the Old Country, still pulling the strings to stay on their ego trips.

"But you can't let that happen. You started it all rolling and now you have to finish it. Someday, when I have time, I'm going to make a project out of you. I'll backtrack every move you made. I'll dig up everybody you ever contacted or used . . . I'll have your entire operation detailed down to the last iota and perhaps the civilized world will realize what kind of a terror they harbored."

Burke gave him a flat grin. "Maybe the uncivilized world will realize it too. The joke would be on you then . . . if all the crap you're spouting was true."

"It's true enough," Long smiled back. "The past might be too difficult to prove at the moment, but the future move will be easy because I know it has to happen."

Annoyance was in Burke's voice. "What has to happen?"

"You have to kill Papa Menes."

"And if I don't?"

"Then I'd be wrong, wouldn't I?"

"You can still go fuck yourself," Burke told him.

From across the room Helen was watching them both, something in her eyes vascillating between belief and disbelief.

The big house on Long Island had been built by a New York banker during the two years he had been a multimillionaire. He was the son of a middle European immigrant and had been put to work shining shoes in downtown Manhattan, turning over his entire income to his impoverished parents so they could live in a cold water tenement, existing on day-old bread and inexpensive grocery leftovers. Once a week they had a Sunday treat of tough boiled beef or wrinkled frankfurters and he hated the tentacles of poverty that enveloped him.

But he was a good shoe shiner, with a flair and a flourish, a memory for names of the Wall Street tycoons who enjoyed his streetside show and tipped heavily from their fat wallets. He began to save, then, until he could afford a two-chair cubicle in a narrow space between buildings suitable for nothing else.

With two chairs occupied there was always an interesting conversation above his bowed head and one day he listened carefully at what was being said, took sixty dollars he had accumulated and purchased a few shares of the stock that had been under discussion. That afternoon he had a profit of two thousand seventy-four dollars.

He kept listening and within a month his bank account totaled over six figures. He kept the shop for another thirty days, sold out to his assistant and spent his time at the ticker tape.

When he had made his third million he sent his parents back to the Old Country with enough for them to live on, established himself in a fabulous office with an apartment on Riverside Drive and commissioned an architect to build him a tasteless, fortress-like mansion on six acres of waterfront footage on Long Island.

He had shined shoes for twenty-four years. He was then thirty-eight years old, a multimillionaire with a grand estate and ready to marry the most beautiful showgirl on Broadway. The year was nineteen twenty-nine.

When the stock market crash broke the backs of the paper rich, the girl laughed at him and he jumped out of his own office window. The house on Long Island went through six owners before a company that was a personal front for Papa Menes obtained it. It was an address no one knew, a fortified castle no enemy could take and a luscious retreat where Papa could operate from until the heat was off and the lawyers could bring things back together again while they snarled the workings of justice in its own red tape. All he needed was time and he had plenty of money to buy that little commodity.

And having bought it, he was going to use it well with the lovely hunk of flesh he had imported from Miami, his own three-way woman who improved with each session, always having something new and different ready for him until he began to wonder if coming so much would drain him like pulling the plug in the bathtub.

That wild Louise Belhander would tease him until he was ready to blow his mind apart and had the shakes like some palsied old man, then at the right time she would whip herself over into that delicious position on her hands and knees, offering her own lewdness to his and he'd bury himself inside her in a frenzy of passion so exhausting that he'd collapse on top of her and she'd have to roll out from under him and wipe him down with a cold wet rag to revive him.

She had already pocketed a little over five thousand bucks of Papa Menes' generosity, which was about all she needed to make sure she could get clear of the retribution that might possibly come after her final act revenging herself on Frank Verdun. Or his friends.

The nine specialists Captain Bill Long had assigned to locate the whereabouts of Papa Menes had put out feelers all over the city without being able to make contact. The legitimate enterprises owned and operated by the shattered underworld kingdom were all functioning normally so there was an active hand still behind it and that only hand had to be the old man's.

Legal advisers for the many corporate structures readily admitted having orders transmitted to them, but had no knowledge of the source except that the coded identification was authentic and all they could do was carry out instructions. Across the country, city and state attorneys were working day and night trying to break down the barriers of ownership other attorneys had set up and found themselves up against a dead wall on every occasion. The other side had bought better men, they had a longer time to prepare for the eventuality and long before any breakthrough could be made, the actual owners could liquidate their holdings and leave without having to face any criminal action.

Downstairs in the lab the microfilms had been

cleaned and put on the enlarger with a select audience of viewers from federal officers to local police personnel and within minutes after the final slide was shown, warrants were issued for various persons in thirty-two states in the union. There would have been more, but the rest were dead in the Chicago blast, or wiped out before the open war had started.

Robert Lederer sat at the head of the table opposite Bill Long and Burke looking at the check marks he had made on his list, indications of persons beyond prosecution now. "It's that damn root you have to watch out for."

Long scowled at him. "What?"

"You can kill the fruit and cut down the tree, but leave the root in the ground and it can start all over again. So we can hit all their drops and put a dent in the narco trade. We can close some bookies and lock up some prostitutes. What good does it do? With all those legitimate assets bringing in the money one big guy can finance the entire operation in a matter of months . . . just one guy big enough for the foreign operators or the big locals to fear enough to trust."

"We'll knock off Menes yet, Bob. Relax. Take your time."

"There isn't any time, damn it. You know that as well as I do."

"Something . . ." he glanced at Burke who sat there impassively, ". . . or somebody will break."

"What's that supposed to mean?"

"It means that the old man isn't long for this world. Right, Gill?"

Burke's eyes barely flicked up at him. "I wouldn't doubt it for a minute."

The tap of Lederer's pencil went on for ten seconds before he said, "You two know something I ought to know?"

"Not really, Bob. It's pure speculation."

The D.A. got up and scooped his papers into his attaché case. "You'd better hope something happens."

When he left, Bill Long leaned back in his chair, his hands folded behind his head. "When is it going to happen, Gill?"

"How many times do I have to tell you to go fuck yourself, buddy?"

"As many as you want. I'm too damn curious to see how you work it to get insulted. I really want to see how you kill the old man. I want to see how you react, how it affects you."

"You ought to know, Bill. How did Shelby's death affect you?"

"Ah, that wasn't my kill, friend. That was yours, all yours. It was my finger on the trigger, but your mind that pulled it."

Burke stood up and slipped into his coat. "Bill, I hope that brain of yours is good enough to snap back when you really know the answers."

The party on Long Island had gotten more boisterous with every network news flash. From the time of Mark Shelby's death to the daily recapitulation of events, the wine and booze had flowed freely throughout the house, celebrating the sole ownership of Papa Menes' empire. The guards outside had to wait their turn to indulge, and their replacements brought out enough refreshment to hold them over until they, too, were relieved again.

It had been a long time since Papa had been drunk. Artie Meeker had started too early and was snoring away beside the stupid redhead he picked up in Brooklyn and Remy was dragged away by the two broads who took care of the office work.

Not that Papa minded. He was alone again with Louise and the champagne had gotten to them both and Louise was giving him a rubdown with those agile fingers of hers and he could feel the sensation all the way down to his balls. The communiqués from his legal advisers assured him that all was well and as long as he wasn't available to accept a subpoena there was nothing much that could happen to him. His men on the outside had already squelched a couple of the Philadelphia outfit who were talking big and Moss Pitkin from St. Louis stopped the raid he was making on the dry cleaning joints there when he had his head banged around for him. By now everybody knew the old man meant business, knew his business and they were happy to sit back and let him run things.

Louise giggled when her fingers made Papa squirm and she got her hands under his shoulders and pushed. "Roll over, Papa."

"No . . . keep doing what you were. I like that."

"I'll make it better for you," she teased. "I can't do it while you're lying on your stomach."

Papa let out one of his chuckles, amazed at how the

blond twist could get to him. His pecker had been hard so many times it was starting to ache and here it was coming up again and he couldn't fight it back because whatever she did was new and different and worth any ache he might feel. Her naked body was slithering all over him, warm and throbbing, lubricated by the sweat of her unique exertions. Her teeth nipped at his neck and her tongue probed his ear, making his shoulder muscles twitch and gooseflesh stand out over his seamed skin.

"Come on, roll over," she said again.

This time he was fully prepared and let her flip him onto his back and was pleased when Louise let out one of the funny gasps when she saw him in the full glory of manhood. He didn't know that the gasp was really a supressed laugh and she pounced on it too quickly for him to even speculate on it.

She stopped when she felt the signs and he tried to push her back. "Keep going," he told her. Damn it to hell, don't quit now. Just . . ."

"I'm boss now," she reminded him lightly. "If you like my specialties, you let me do things my way."

He kept his eyes closed tightly. "Yeah, okay, sure. But hurry up."

"Oh, no, this is one time we don't hurry at all because it's going to be the biggest and best of all. It's something so very extraordinary I have to build up to it step by step, otherwise you'd never appreciate it."

This time his eyes opened, bright with anticipation. "What're you gonna do? You tell me."

"Lay back, relax, and I'll show you, big daddy. I just promise you one thing . . . you'll never forget it."

For the first time since he was a little kid, Papa Menes took an order from a woman and did what he was told. He lay back and relaxed, wondering what surprise she had waiting for him.

There wasn't much to see from the miniature terrace outside Burke's living room windows unless you understood the raw, primitive nature of the real New York. There was nothing aesthetic about black tarred rooftops with their ugly slanted doorwells gouged into their tops. TV antennas stood barren and angular, reminiscent of a denuded forest held together by stands of soot-dirtied clotheslines.

Here and there patches of green showed where somebody who still had a feeling for soil had tried to grow things, and empty beach chairs were bright splotches of color waiting for those who sought the sun that managed to penetrate the smog.

Even the smell was visible, rising on the heat waves from the streets below, driven upward by the artificial thermals, dancing to the heartbeat of blaring horns and heavy rumble of traffic. Darkness was coming on and when the lights winked out in the towering office buildings uptown, they blinked on again in the high rise apartments and lower silhouettes of the renovated town houses and tenements closer by.

Jet traffic made a mockery of the free sky, creating artificial clouds with their contrails and an illusion of space with their pulsating red and green false stars. Only the emerging moon was real and they had even contaminated that.

Burke said, "Let's go back inside," and closed the sliding doors behind them.

For a minute Helen looked back while he made fresh drinks for them, her mind spinning like a centrifuge, trying to throw out the fragments of unreality so there would be some core of true substance left.

How long had she known him? It seemed like a lifetime, but it had only been a little while. And how long had she known the others? She had been exposed to death and destruction since she had been born, had associated with the good and the evil from birth to maturity . . . so she should be able to make an evaluation herself.

Yet she was part of it all, was there enmeshed in the violence, and all she could hear were those deadly words of accusation that Bill Long spoke that made him, if the words were true, the most frightening human being who ever lived.

"Unless there was justification."

She spun around, her breath caught in her throat. "What?"

"I know what you were thinking," Burke told her. He handed her the glass and she took it. Her hand was trembling.

"I'm sorry."

"He made pretty good sense."

"Gill. I'm going to ask you something. Will you answer me truthfully?"

"That's a silly question if you think I've been lying to you."

"Have you?"

"No. Do you think I have?"

"No."

He sipped at his drink. "Good, then ask it."

"Did you arrange for . . . or did you even know Mark Shelby would be there?" She watched his face closely.

There was no explanation. He simply said, "Nope," and she believed him. Nothing in the world could make her disbelieve after the way he said it.

"Don't you want to ask me some other questions?" he queried.

Helen shook her head. "No, I don't think I do." She got a strange look in her eyes. "Frankly, I don't think I want to know one way or the other. Not now, anyway."

"Why?"

"Because I love you, Gill. In that street language you enjoy I'm so fucking much in love with you it comes out my ears and that's all that counts."

"Knock off that talk. You're a lady."

"Not around you, wild man."

"You know what's going to happen to you in another minute, don't you?"

Helen smiled up at him, her tongue wetting her lips. She put her drink down and reached for the zipper at the back of her dress. In one smooth motion she let everything drop to the floor and with the second she threw away the remaining pieces of sheer nylon and stood there in shimmering, naked beauty and said, "I hope so."

And while the darkness enveloped the city outside, shutting off the ugliness, leaving only the bright shining lights in the window, they exploded together in a welter

303

of spilled cushions and knocked-over ashtrays and the two drinks that drenched them in a refreshing bath that made the whole crazy orgasm better than it had a right to be.

They lay on the floor tracing wet lines on each other's bodies with ice cubes that seemed to give out more heat than they drew and as the last one melted into eternity Helen looked up at him and asked, "What's Shinola?"

"What a time to talk of shoe polish."

"No, really."

"It's a standard brand shoe polish. Why?"

"It just occurred to me."

"You're nuts, Helen. I love you and I'm going to marry you anyway. I'm just glad I found out that you're nuts first. I'm going to have you treated. What brought that on?"

"One day Mr. Verdun was mad and I heard him shouting. He said he couldn't get hold of the old fart because he was probably out at Shinola doing the aye aitch bit again."

She felt him go tight beside her and looked at his face. He wasn't Gill Burke any longer. He was a machine, a human, thinking machine that had an advantage over any computer an engineer could build because it could initiate its own program and handle the variables any way it wanted. She didn't know it, but he was reaching back into the recesses of a million cells, trying to resurrect a word he had come across in some obscure item a mechanical computer would never have processed into its tapes. She watched him search it out, locate it, then push himself erect until he found the phone and dialed a number. She couldn't hear what he said, but saw him nod once, thank the person on the other end and hang up.

He started to get dressed.

"Where are you going?"

"It doesn't matter."

She waited until he buckled on the gun, then got up and slipped back into her clothes. "You're wrong, Gill. It does matter. What did I tell you?"

He looked at her, and looked at her, and looked at her. Finally he said, "Where Papa Menes is."

"I'm going with you. You know that, don't you?"

He kept looking at her until he decided, then nodded. "If you do, you might get answers to the question you haven't asked yet."

"Do I deserve it?"

"You deserve it."

The ice in his eyes was far colder than the ice they had just made love with.

Downstairs they were about to get in the car when Bill Long came out of the shadows and said, "Looking for company?"

Gill Burke held the door open for him so he could slide in beside Helen. "Not especially, but as long as you're here you might as well enjoy the sleigh ride."

When they pulled out into traffic, Long asked, "Any special destination?"

"Yeah," Burke told him. "Shinola."

The word stirred something in the captain's memory, but he couldn't put his finger on it.

Burke said, "A nutty, extravagant mansion out on

Long Island built by a former shoeshine boy who won and lost his shirt in the stock market. His enemies called his attempt at pretentiousness Shinola."

Long remembered then and threw Burke an odd look. "What's out there?"

"Papa Menes," Burke said.

"How do you know?"

"I told him," Helen said.

He was going crazy. The damn dame was making him go crazy and if he didn't come in another minute he was going to kill the bitch for teasing him this way and tear her cunt inside out. She had his nuts hard as pebbles and he was hurting in every fucking tube and gland in his withered body and she wouldn't let it blow out of him. She was stronger than he was now, depleting him with what started out to be gentle ministrations and wound up with him a quivering mass of old flesh and even though he knew she was absolutely wild about the way he had brought her on, indulging her in the perversions he absolutely loved, she was killing him with the very things he had taught her and he was loving every minute of it. He shook and trembled violently when her mouth touched him and when her fingers located the right spot and squeezed just right, his mouth opened and he gasped like a fish out of water. All he could think of was DO IT, DO IT, DO IT, but she wouldn't let him alone. She loved him so much she was tearing him apart and he couldn't fight back any longer. He was all hers and anything she wanted to do was all right, but just for the fucking relief of it all, DO IT, DO IT, and she still kept on with those awful things he wished that fat Jew broad he had married could have done and he knew she hadn't even hardly begun. She was talking to him while her hands and her mouth and her legs worked against him. He could taste and feel every part of her, not because he wanted it, but because she put it there and she was telling him about how lovely it was when he was the first one to tumble her over in the attitude of abject humiliation and stick it up her ass and how wonderful it felt after the initial pain was over and the sensuality of it all began and how slippery it was and how it filled her up until she thought she would burst with pleasure and how each time it got better and better and reached the time when there was no pain at all and only pleasure that was better than anything she had ever experienced in her whole life and how it was a shame only a woman could enjoy it, but if she tried, how a man could enjoy it too and when she asked him if he wouldn't like it the old man screamed out YES, YES, YES and she rolled him over on his stomach again and propped him on his knees with his head down between his arms.

Louise Belhander said, "This is for what Frank Verdun did to me," and shoved four inches of the barrel of a .38 revolver up his ass and pulled the trigger.

The guard stationed outside the door heard the strangely muted sound, the horrible scream, looked inside and shrugged his shoulders. He couldn't care less. He had been paid in advance. He told the others, they shrugged too, picked up whatever they thought could be useful to them and left to go back to where they came from.

It wasn't their jurisdiction and it wasn't their right, but it was a different time, a new era, and circumstances had changed all the rules. They went past the place somebody had nicknamed Shinola after that long forgotten Wall Street genius, cruised it twice, looking at the lights in the windows, the open gates and the total absence of sound or motion. The only thing alive was the young blond girl getting on the interstate bus three blocks away and the guy in his pajamas walking his dog. The estate was there, waiting, looking vitally awake, yet having all the signs of death.

Burke drove up in front of the ornate, columned porch and cut the engine. For a few minutes they sat there, guns in their hands, then Bill Long and Burke got up, looked around and went up the steps.

They had been in places like this too many times before and nobody had to tell them it was all over, whatever they expected to happen had already happened. Out of force of habit they obeyed all the rules of entry, covering each other while protecting themselves, absorbing the details of what had gone on, cataloguing them for future reference, correlating them for immediate use. Later the experts from the lab could come in and add their findings to the computers and the files.

When there was nothing on the lower floor left to see they walked to the staircase and went up to the second floor. The first door they pushed open was Papa Menes' bedroom and he was still in that obscene position on his hands and knees with his head twisted backward trying to let out a scream that had died before it had been born because the bullet from the gun that was still shoved up his asshole had tunneled its way right through to his heart and he never really got a chance to remember that special thing Louise had saved for him.

Gill Burke had forgotten about Helen until she came up and took his hand. There was something satisfied in her expression when she turned and looked at Bill Long. "You said it was speculation . . . just a story you were going to tell."

It was done, completed, but it didn't happen right at all. Logic and truth had come apart because the fickle finger of fate goosed the wrong hind ends and there was no answer any more. None at all.

The captain made a vague gesture with his shoulders and said, "Oh, shit."

Helen didn't let him alone. "Bill, can we hear the story again . . . about the execution team . . . and Gill Burke."

The cop looked at them both, then focused on Gill for a long time, then he said, "It's strange the way things work out. I'm glad I'm retiring. I'm glad you're going back to Compat. I don't want to think about these things any more because no means justifies the ends, yet here it happened and it turns out for the best. I don't want to believe or know that any one man could be in back of all this and still walk away without a scratch on his person or his conscience. I don't want to know that, Gill, but I do. I know it was you all the way and somehow I'm happy and somehow I'm glad. I'm just happy that I don't know for sure and we can go on being friends even if I still have all those reservations in my mind that never will be resolved because I'm dropping the package right here."

"Your choice, Bill."

"Is it over?"

Burke nodded soberly. "It's over now."

The captain walked away and they could hear his feet echoing down the stairs, heard him pick up the phone and make the call to headquarters.

The obscenity on the bed didn't bother her any more at all now. She glanced up at the face of Gill Burke whom she loved so much, smiled gently and asked, "Tell me, *was* it you?"

Suddenly he was his other self again. "Would it make any difference if it had been?"

"Not a bit."

He smiled at her oddly. "Then what difference does it make at all?"

Helen nodded and smiled back. "Let's go home," she said.